Modern Persian
Short Stories

MODERN PERSIAN SHORT STORIES

Translations by
Minoo S. Southgate

© Minoo S. Southgate 1980

ISBN: 0-89410-032-7
ISBN: 0-89410-033-5 (pbk)

LC No: 79-89930

All rights reserved. Reproduction in whole or in part, except for reviews, in any form, now known or hereafter invented, is forbidden without the written permission of the publisher.

Cover Design by Tom Gladden

Three Continents Press, 1346 Connecticut Ave., NW., Washington, D.C. 20036

Acknowledgments

I wish to thank Bjorn Robinson Rye, James C. Southgate, Patrick J. Leach, and Edward M. Potoker for their Assistance.

Minoo S. Southgate

"A Joyous Celebration" (Jashn-i farkhundah) was published in *Arash*, 1:1 (Aban 1340/1961).

"The First Day in the Grave" (Ruz-i avval-i qabr) is the title story in a collection published in Tehran in 1965.

"A Land like Paradise" (Shahri chun bihisht) is the title story in a collection of stories by Danishvar, published in Tehran in 1962.

"The Carrousel" (Charkh-u-falak) was published in Gulistan's collection of short stories *Juy va divar-i tashnah*, Tehran, 1968.

"Seeking Absolution" (Talab-i amurzish) was translated from Hidayat's collection of short stories *Sih gatrah khun*, Tehran, 1932.

"Why Do They Go Back?" (Bara-yi chah bar migardand?) was translated from the text of the story published in *Payam-i Nuvin* (Azar 1346/1967).

"The Snow, the Dogs, the Crows" (Barfha, sagha, kalaghha) was first published in *Sukhan* (13 Isfand 1336/1957). The present translation was made from the text of the story in Mirsadiqi's collection *Musafirha-yi shab*, Tehran, 1971.

"The Warm South" (Junub-i qarm) was published in *Jung* (Spring 1346/1967).

"Teaching in a Pleasant Spring" (Tadris dar bahar-i dil angiz) was published in *Kayhan-i Haftah* (28 Isfand 1341/1962). It was reprinted in Sadiqi's collected stories *Sangar va qumqumah'ha-yi khali,* Tehran, 1970.

"The Game Is Up" (Bazi tamam shud) was published in *Alifba*, No. 1, 1973.

"A Historic Tower" (Burj-i tarikhi) was published in Shahani's collection of short stories *Vahshat abad*, Tehran, 1969.

"Agha Julu" was published in *Arash*, 2:1 (Tir 1343/1964).

"The End of the Passion Play" (Akhar-i ta'ziyah) appeared in Amirshahi's short story collection *Ba'd az ruz-i akhar*, Tehran, 1969.

"Of Weariness" (Az diltangi) was published in Mahmud's short story collection *Za'iri zir-i baran*, Tehran, 1968.

"Gowhartaj's Father" (Pidar-i Gowhartaj) was written in 1962 and printed in Kiyanush's short story collection *Dar anja hichkas nabud*, Tehran, 1345/1967.

Introduction

The genre of short story was introduced to Iran in Jamalzadah's *Yaki Bud Yaki Nabud* (Once upon a Time, 1921). But the short stories and novels of Sadiq Hidayat (1903-1951) had a much greater influence on the development of modern fiction in Iran. Both writers used European fiction as their model. Hidayat's language and prose, his interest in folklore, and the style of his stories and novels set the direction of Iranian fiction.

Like Jamalzadah, Hidayat tried to bridge the gap between the written and the spoken language by writing in *zaban-i amiyanah*, or "the language of the people." The prose of "Seeking Absolution," which is translated in this anthology, is characteristic of his abundant use of proverbs, formulae, slang terms, and colloquialisms. Hidayat's prose was widely imitated by later writers.

Hidayat studied Iranian folklore and used fiction to show the characteristics of various classes, their speech, and their beliefs. His interest in folklore was shared by most writers who followed him, and was also reflected in Iranian literary journals which in the sixties and seventies published studies in folklore and folk arts such as *ta'ziyah* (passion plays) and *naqqali* (story-telling), and printed examples of these plays and stories. Valuable anthropological studies have been inspired partly by a desire to preserve in writing the disappearing characteristics of a certain locale.

Interest in folklore explains the abundance of local color writing which attempts to describe a certain locale and produce the speech and mannerisms of its inhabitants. Often local color short stories fail to reach any larger truth beyond the surface verisimilitude. Most of the stories in this collection contain elements of local color. "The Warm South," "Agha Julu," and "Of Weariness" all portray life in Southern Iran. On occasion, interest in local color weakens the focus of the story. In "The End of the Passion Play," for example, the description of the neighborhood, the Muharram mourning, and the prankish children deflects attention from the central character and his initiation experience. Interest in local color is partly a result of the writer's nostalgia for the scenes of his childhood; scenes which have disappeared or are disappearing fast in the context of the rapidly changing society of contemporary Iran. A large number of pieces presented as short stories have very little plot and are no more than local color sketches.

In addition to creating an interest in folklore, Hidayat's works introduced realism and surrealism to Iranian modern literature. Realism has been the dominant school of writing since Hidayat, the majority of whose novels and short stories were realistic. Hidayat's major work, *Buf-i Kur* (The Blind Owl, 1937), although surrealistic, has a uniquely native quality resulting from its Eastern setting, symbolism, and imagery. Most surrealistic short stories lack this native quality and seem pretentious and alien to Iranian culture.

Hidayat's understanding of Asian culture enabled him to absorb European philosophy and literature and to deal with larger aspects of life and human nature. Most of his successors, however, were not adequately familiar with their own culture and consequently failed to digest Western influences and to come to terms with them. Their fiction is often limited in vision and perspective. To a degree the Iranian educational system is to blame for people's unfamiliarity with their cultural history. In schools, classical prose works are used in teaching the spelling of hard words. Long poems are learned by heart as an exercise in memorization, with little attention to their meaning. Contemporary literature is not studied in high schools and colleges.

Classical epics and romances reflected accepted beliefs and mores which provided a context where the writer would view and judge a particular incident in terms of something larger than itself. Similarly, the Sufi poets were inspired by the notion of man's divine nature and the possibility of his union with God. No such dominant belief or ideology exists in contemporary Iranian literature. Writers are generally unable to view an incident in a general context, to transcend it, and to give it universality. Contemporary fiction rarely gives a rounded view of a situation. A narrow and biased point of view mars the works of most contemporary writers.

Contemporary fiction explores and condemns some of the religious and moral values that support the traditional family and social structure. The character struggles to free himself from the past—often represented symbolically by his father. Sometimes he succeeds. But he is usually abandoned before he makes a successful transition to a new way of life and adopts new values. An understanding of the past could enhance the writer's understanding of the present, and, perhaps, show him the way toward the future.

The contemporary writer is generally familiar with the content, form, and ideology of Western literature, but his ability to draw upon it is limited since he knows little about his own culture. Western literature with the wealth of human experience it depicts cannot help the Persian author whose vision and experiences are sadly limited.

Too many Persian short stories are based on childhood memories and a great number deal with tyrannical fathers. Contemporary poet and critic Reza Baraheni sees "son killing" as characteristic of the culture and cites examples of it in literature since Firdausi's eleventh-century epic, the *Shahnamah* (Cf., the death of Suhrab at the hand of his father, Rustam). The Persian father's tyranny over his family is sanctioned by custom and tradition, and enhanced by an economic system which offers no opportunity to the young to attain a degree of independence by earning money during their school years. It is natural that the writer's traumatic childhood should be reflected in his writing, yet preoccupation with childhood is also an indication that his experiences and the subjects he can handle are limited. Tyrannical fathers and oppressed sons (and sometimes daughters) have become stock characters, and the stories are always from the child's point of view. I have not read a single author who attempts to give an insight into the father's behavior (as Joyce does, for example, in "Counterpoints," in *Dubliners*): Why does an adult, in some cases a father himself, continue to see the father as "the other"?

Small as this collection is, it offers several examples of tyrannical fathers. "The Joyous Celebration," a story about the unsettling effects of sudden social change, is told from the point of view of Abbas, a boy in the sixth grade. His father, Hadj Agha, the religious head of the quarter, regularly addresses his son as "you ass." Hadj Agha's treatment of his wife and daughter is not any better. "The minute he found one of us near—my mother, my younger sister, or myself—he'd start ordering us about," says Abbas. When Hadj Agha is ordered to take his wife to a party, without a veil (or, as he puts it, bare-headed and bare-bottomed), he takes out his anger on his family. He beats Abbas, even though his son is quick to follow orders. Abbas hates and fears his father. When a drop of water falls from his father's hands on his, he shudders; and when his father's goldfish are massacred by the cat, he rejoices.

In "Agha Julu," fathers awaken their sons "with a kick in the spine," as a matter of course. The boys in the story feel close to the Italian engineer, Agha Julu—even though he does not speak their language—and take his side in the conflict between him and the men of the town (their fathers).

The daughters do not fare much better than the sons. In "Agha Julu," Zeinab is given in marriage to the Italian when he pressures her father and threatens him with scandal. The father shows no concern for his daughter's well-being. The father in "The Warm South" buys the silence of the head of the village, who threatens to inform on him, by letting him sleep with his eldest daughter. The father of five daughters, he regrets that he has no son "to send him to Kuwait and Dubai to smuggle goods." He sends four of his daughters to Shaghu, where they become prostitutes. His younger daughter is in love with a doctor who wants to marry her and take her to Tehran. But the old man refuses to let them marry because he needs her to run the coffeehouse he plans to build. He forces her to sleep with a lecherous driver in return for a hundred tomans (roughly thirteen dollars, but with much more buying power). Thus he keeps his daughter and gets the money he needs to start his coffeehouse. "I'd never spent so much money on that," says the driver, "but when I got down to business I saw it was worth it. The old man hadn't lied. She was a virgin."

After reading numerous stories about tyrannical fathers and selecting a few for this collection, I decided not to translate any more of them. But, my moratorium was broken in favor of "The Game Is Up." In this well-written story, son-killing and son-gagging become rituals in which all the adult males of the community participate. Unlike most childhood stories "The Game Is Up" achieves universality. The author places the motif in a mythic context and sees it as a sort of reversed Oedipus complex.

The present collection presents a disturbing picture of the Iranian family. Discord results from rivalry between wives in polygamous marriages. In "Seeking Absolution," Aziz Agha, a childless wife, allows her husband to marry Khadijeh, in order to have children. But out of jealousy, she murders Khadijeh's first two babies and finally poisons Khadijeh herself. In the same story, to assuage Aziz Agha's guilt, Khanom Gelin confesses that she married her step-sister's husband, caused her step-sister to become ill, and finally killed her on the way to the shrine of the Imam. In "Gowhartaj's Father," Moluk is beaten by her husband's first wife. "Poor girl," says Moluk's mother. "She hasn't seen a happy day in her life. She hadn't been married for two days when that bitch, his other wife, beat her up for no reason . . . and on top of that complained to her husband." In "The Snow, the Dogs, the Crows" the first wife forces her husband to divorce his second wife, Turan Khanom. When Turan's baby is born, the first wife takes it by force and abandons it in the snow.

In Iran, sex outside marriage is strictly forbidden for women. The society, the woman's parents and relatives join hands to safeguard her virtue. The Iranian penal code is very lax in punishing men who commit murder in defence of their "honor." If a man finds his sister or daughter in bed with a man to whom she is not married and kills one or both of them, he is imprisoned for one to six months. (If a man kills his wife in the same circumstances, he is considered innocent by the law.) Girls are expected to remain virgins until they get married. The girl who loses her virginity loses her chance to get married. Generally she is then rejected by her family and by society. Cheap popular fiction has frequently exploited the fate of girls who are rejected by their families after losing their virginity; and who, unable to support themselves, turn to prostitution. In "First Day in the Grave," Hadji Mo'tamed reminisces on the sad fate of his ward. "I was mad with love for her. I wanted to marry her. But when her belly began to rise, she ran away, straight to the brothel, afraid of what people would do to her." By the time he finds her in the brothel, she has aborted the baby and become a prostitute. "Why the hell did you do that? he asks her. "People made me feel so ashamed; I couldn't face them any more," she replies.

In the present anthology, as in the bulk of contemporary Persian short stories, love stories are conspicuously absent. In this collection, love appears in "A Land Like Paradise" and "The Warm South"; but, the emotion of love is not of interest to the writer in itself and thus is not examined nor analysed. In "The Warm South" the love of a young doctor from Tehran for an illiterate village girl perhaps could not stand too much examination. Here the love theme is secondary to the portrayal of the harsh Southern locale and the cruel father who sells his daughters into prostitution. In "A Land Like Paradise," disappointment in love is simply one among a number of disappointments in a tale of thwarted hopes. Even in the stories of other writers not represented in this anthology, such as Amin Faqiri (see his *Dihkadah-yi purmalal)* the emotion of love is generally secondary to love's social repercussions.

The absence of love stories results from social restrictions imposed on male-female relationships. These restrictions have been somewhat relaxed, but at the time the present generation of writers was growing up they were in effect. In Iran, boys and girls attend separate schools and social contact between the sexes is limited. Dating is never allowed and premarital sex, while forbidden for girls, is available to boys only through prostitutes. This lack of contact between the sexes leads to idealized and romantic, often secret loves, in which the emotion is not dissimilar to that in courtly love. In the modern setting, this kind of love appears adolescent and absurd, and therefore cannot be treated seriously as the main theme of fiction. As adults, males choose other males for companionship, and, again, there is little communion between the sexes. Little wonder, then, that most stories about marriage show the husband and wife in a hate, rather than a love relationship, and concentrate on recording details of marital squabbles.

But these conditions have been changing rapidly. The generation gap in "Gowhartaj's Father" is a result of such change. The daughter of illiterate, old-fashioned parents, Gowhartaj has had some schooling and "won't consent to marry a plain worker." She wears her *chador* and behaves to please her parents, although, in her heart, she has rejected their way of life. Her old-fashioned parents believe that "a girl should enter her husband's house in her *chador* and leave in her shroud." The westernized Mrs. Razavi, on the other hand, thinks that in marriage "the important thing is that husband and wife be compatible. As they say, they ought to understand each other." The recent Islamic Revolution, itself in part the fruit of social and moral dislocation, aims to restore weakened traditional mores.

The husband and wife in "The Carrousel" are a new breed. They discuss their problems in a civil though distant manner. The wife seems content with her role as wife and mother, but the husband searches for something beyond his family. "I'm happy because you love me too. But is that enough?" he asks his wife. The wife wonders why he cannot be happy, since he has everything. The problem is not resolved. "Be happy. Laugh, talk," she tells him. "All right," he says, but we know better. Gulistan's modern couple have modern problems to contend with.

In addition to domestic life, contemporary Persian literature reflects Iran's social and political conditions. A sense of despair and general discontent with life is common in contemporary stories although opposition to the government is not explicit in these writings, at least not in what is allowed to be published. Politics and the confrontation between the writer and the government are not dealt with overtly in literature. Instead, to elude censorship, writers resort to allegory, symbolism, and esoteric writing.

"Why Do They Go Back," ostensibly the story of an outlaw on his way to surrender after twenty years of fighting the government, might be about radical intellectuals who felt they could no longer effectively oppose the Shah following the reforms of the sixties. The outlaw decides to surrender because he no longer has a cause. "You must learn to accept that everything has changed," he tells his servant. "They've done a lot of things. Things you and I can't judge. They've built schools and towns for you. . . . Abdollah is working on his own land. What am I supposed to fight against?"

The young men in "Of Weariness" are serving time in Langeh, a torrid Persian Gulf port. The writer is vague about what they have done, in order to elude government censorship. In an interior dialogue, the narrator reveals that he and his companions defied danger and got themselves into trouble for the sake of the people. They are therefore political prisoners, but no trace of their revolutionary ideas remains. They live from day to day, get drunk at night, and count the hours before they are set free.

Limited as the anthology is in the number of authors and works it presents, it is rich in variety. Hidayat's tightly structured story with its surprise ending contrasts with the undisciplined yet entertaining work of Amirshahi. Chubak's tale has the simplicity and force of a medieval fable, while Gulistan's subtle story reminds one of Hemingway's slice-of-life pieces. Danishvar creates a storybook land in her work.

The short stories in this collection are indeed some of the best contemporary Persian short stories. In Iran, the genre is still defined rather loosely to include sketches and vignettes. Many writers do not seem to consider the plot essential. A great deal of what has been published is unfortunately devoid of literary value, and, even in the works of good writers, there are signs of carelessness and haste.

* * *

I have arranged the stories chronologically and spelled Persian names phonetically, rather than transliterating them. Persian words which are not footnoted are explained in the Glossary following the last story.

Minoo Southgate

Note on Transliteration:

"The Persian Romanization system used throughout the Notes on Contributors and Bibliography is a modification of the Library of Congress system. For example, where diacritical markings are used only on titles of articles and works they are not used on personal names. Also, the Library of Congress capitalization system is not followed throughout the Bibliography, because of special problems.

Contents

Introduction   vii

Seeking Absolution Sadiq Hidayat   3
The Carrousel Ibrahim Gulistan   13
The Joyous Celebration Jalal Al-i Ahmad   19
A Land like Paradise Simin Danishvar   34
Teaching in a Pleasant Spring Bahram Sadiqi   53
The Snow, the Dogs, the Crows   62
    Jamal Mirsadiqi
Gowhartaj's Father Mahmud Kiyanush   75
Agha Julu Nasir Taqva'i   89
Why Do They Go Back? Nadir Ibrahimi   104
The First Day in the Grave Sadiq Chubak   114
The Warm South Shapur Qarib   134
Of Weariness Ahmad Mahmud   151
The End of the Passion Play   161
    Mahshid Amirshahi
The Historic Tower Khusraw Shahani   173
The Game Is Up Ghulamhusayn Sa'idi   180

Glossary of Persian Terms   203
Notes on the Contributors   205
A Selected Bibliography of Works in Persian and English   209

Seeking Absolution

SADIQ HIDAYAT

The scorching wind whipped up the earth and sand, blowing it into the pilgrims' faces. The sun burned and shrivelled everything. The camels stepped to the monotonous clang of iron and brass bells, their necks swaying rhythmically, their frowning snouts and drooping muzzles revealing their dissatisfaction with their lot.

Through the dust, the caravan moved slowly down the middle of the gray dirt road. The ash-colored, dry, sandy desert stretched as far as an eye could see, shimmering in the heat and at times forming a series of low mounds at the side of the road. For miles not even a date palm relieved the monotony. Wherever there was a handful of stagnant water in a ditch, a family had pitched a shelter. The air burned everything, taking one's breath. It was like stepping into the corridors of hell.

The caravan had been on the road for thirty-six days. Their mouths dry, their bodies weak, their pockets empty, the pilgrims had watched their money-supply diminish like snow under the hot Arabian sun. But today the chief of the camel-drivers formally announced that they had reached their destination and received tips from the pilgrims. They saw the top of the minarets in the distance and uttered the *salavat*. It was as if new life had revived their tired bodies.

Khanom Gelin and Aziz Agha, in dusty black *chadors*, had been tossed up and down in the camel litter from the time they had joined the caravan in Ghazvin. Each day had seemed like a year to them. There wasn't a sound bone in Aziz Agha's body, but she reminded herself that the more one suffers on a pilgrimage the greater one's reward.

A barefoot Arab, dark-skinned, with glaring eyes and a thin beard, whipped the mule's bleeding thighs with a thick iron chain. From time to time, he would turn and stare at each of the women. Mashdi Ramazan, the man in their party, and Hosein Agha, Azis Agha's stepson, occupied the other two camel litters. Mashdi Ramazan was carefully counting his money. Khanom Gelin looked pale. She pulled aside the curtain between the two camel-litters and addressed Aziz Agha.

"When I saw the top of the minarets, my soul flew to them. Poor Shabaji! It wasn't her fate."

Aziz Agha, cooling herself with a fan in her tattooed hand, replied:

"May God absolve her! She was a charitable woman. But how did she become paralyzed?"

"She quarrelled with her husband, which led to divorce. Then she ate pickled onions. The next morning half her body was paralyzed. We tried everything, but she didn't get well. I was bringing her to the Holy Imam to cure her."

"Maybe the camel ride and all that rocking wasn't good for her."

"But her soul is in heaven. The minute you decide to go on pilgrimage and set out on your way, all your sins are forgiven; and if you die, you'll go straight to heaven."

"No. Every time I set eyes on these coffins, I tremble. I want to go into the shrine, open my heart to the Imam, buy myself a shroud, then die."

"I had a dream about Shabaji last night. God bless you, you were in it too. We were walking in a big, green garden. A descendant of the Prophet, surrounded by light and dressed all in green, wearing a green tunic, green turban, green sash, and green sandals welcomed us. He pointed to a green mansion and said, 'Go there and rest.' Then I woke up."

"Good for her!"

The caravan moved along noisily. The caravan leader in front sang:

"Whoever longs for Karbala, welcome!
Whoever wishes to go with us, welcome!"

Another caravan leader answered:

"Whoever longs for Karbala will thrive!
Whoever wishes to go with us will thrive!"

The former sang again:

"In Karbala your spirit comes to life;
Zaynab's laments pierce your ear like a knife."

And the latter answered:

"May God grant that you visit Karbala!
I sacrifice my worthless life to Allah!"

The first caravan leader waved his flag and sang again:

"Damned be the tongue that would not say,
To God's beloved Mohammad we pray!
To Imam Ali, his eleven sons,
We send our greetings each and everyone."

At the end of each verse, the pilgrims repeated the *salavat* aloud.

The splendid golden dome with beautiful minarets was soon matched by a blue dome which looked out of place among mudbrick huts. The sun was almost set when the caravan entered the streets lined with broken walls and small shops. The caravan was greeted by a strange motley crowd. Ragged Arabs; men with dull faces, wearing fezes; turbaned men with shrewd faces, shaved heads, henna colored beards and nails, telling their beads, walking around in sandals, loose cotton pants and long tunics. Persian, Turkish, and guttural Arabic spoken from the depth of the throat and entrails deafened the ear. The Arab women had dirty tattooed faces and inflamed eyes, and wore rings in their noses. A mother had forced half her black breast into the mouth of the dirty baby in her arms.

The crowd sought customers in various ways: one sang lamentations, another beat his breast; the next sold prayer-stones, beads, and sacred shrouds; another caught jinns; the next wrote prayers and sold amulets for protection; and another rented rooms. Jews in long caftans bought gold and jewelry from the pilgrims.

In front of the coffee-house an Arab was picking his nose and rubbing the dirt out from between his toes. His face was covered with flies, and lice crawled all over his head.

When the caravan came to a stop, Mashdi Ramazan and Hosein Agha ran to help Khanom Gelin and Aziz Agha down from the camel-litter. The pilgrims were assailed by a great crowd. Every piece of their belongings was grabbed by someone who hoped to rent his lodgings to them. In the midst of all this, Aziz Agha disappeared. They looked for her and asked around, but couldn't find her.

Khanom Gelin, Hosein Agha, and Mashdi Ramazan rented a dirty mudbrick room for seven rupees a day, and then resumed their search. They looked everywhere in town. They questioned all the shrine attendants one by one, gave them Aziz Agha's name and description, but found no sign of her. Sometime later, when the courtyard around the shrine was less crowded, Khanom Gelin entered the shrine for the ninth time and found a crowd of women and priests surrounding a woman who was grasping the grating around the sepulchre, kissing it and crying out, "Oh Imam Hosein! Help me! The Day of Judgment, when graves give up their dead, the day when eyes roll up to the tops of our skulls. What am I to do? Oh help me! Help me! I am penitent. I have done an awful thing. Forgive me! Forgive me!"

After they had pleaded with her for a long time, she turned, tears flooding her face, and wailed, "I've done something Imam Hosein won't forgive." Khanom Gelin recognized Aziz Agha's voice. She went forward, took her hand and dragged her into the courtyard, Hosein Agha went to her assistance and they took Aziz Agha home. There they gathered around her, gave her tea, and fixed the water pipe for her. She promised to tell them her life story, but asked her stepson, Hosein Agha, to leave the room before she began.

"My dear Khanom Gelin, after I married Geda Ali, God bless his soul, for three years we lived so happily that I was the envy of all women. Geda Ali worshipped me. He kissed the ground I walked on. But all that time I didn't get pregnant. He kept after me that he wanted a child and wouldn't take no for an answer. Every night he would sit by my side and say, 'How can I endure this misery? I'm childless.' I went to every doctor in town. I got amulets, but to no avail. One night, he wept and said to me, 'If you consent, I'll take a *sigheh*.* She'll help you around the house. I'll divorce her after she bears a child, and you can bring up the child as your own.' Bless his soul, he fooled me, and I said, 'Fine, I'll take care of the whole business myself.'

"The next day I put on my *chador*, went to Hasan, the yogurt-maker, and asked his daughter, Khadijeh, in marriage for my husband. Khadijeh was ugly and dark-skinned, her face ravaged by smallpox. She was so feeble, if you pinched her nose she would give up the ghost. Well, I was the mistress of the house. She did the chores, cooked and cleaned. But barely a month had passed when she began to fill out. She put on weight, then got pregnant, just like that. Well, it was obvious she had gotten herself established. My husband gave her all his attention. If in the middle of winter she craved cherries, he would leave no stone unturned until he got them for her. I was the lowest of the low. At night, when he came home, he would go straight to her room to empty out his bundle, and I had to live on whatever she gave me out of charity. The daughter of Hasan the yogurt-maker, who came to my house barefoot and in rags, now put on airs with me.

"I could kick myself. I realized what a mistake I'd made. Khanom Gelin, for nine months I kept it all in and maintained appearances in front of the neighbors. But during the day, when my husband wasn't home, I'd give her hell—may he never know of this in his grave! In front of my husband I'd slander her. I'd say to him, 'In your old age you've fallen in love with a chimp? You can't have children. This isn't your child. Mashdi Taghi, the smith, got her pregnant.' And Khadijeh would slander me behind my back, trying to turn Geda Ali against me.

*A woman married by way of a temporary marriage.

"To make a long story short, you can't imagine what went on in our house every day. Such a to do! The neighbors were fed up with our constant yelling and screaming. I was scared to death she was going to have a son. I had a fortune-teller divine by means of a book, I resorted to witchcraft, but to no avail. It was as though she had eaten pork and had become immune to witchcraft. She just got bigger and bigger, and at the end of the nine months she had the baby, and despite all my pains, it was a boy!

"Gelin Khahom, in my own house now I didn't count for anything. I don't know whether she had a charm or had given Geda Ali some potion. This beggar, this woman that I'd gone and brought to my own house, had me in her power. Right in front of my husband she'd say to me, 'Aziz Agha, I'm busy. Will you wash the diapers?' I'd fire up and in front of Geda Ali call her and her son whatever came to my mouth. I told Geda Ali to give me a divorce. But he, bless his soul, kissed my hand and said, 'Why are you acting like this? She'll get angry and her milk will make the baby ill. Wait till he starts to walk, then I'll divorce her.'

"But I couldn't eat or sleep, I was so worried. Until, may God forgive me, in order to break her heart, one day as soon as she went to the public bath and I was left alone in the house, I went to the baby's cradle, took the safety pin I used to pin my headkerchief with, turned my face, and thrust the pin into the top of the baby's head. Then I hurried out of the room. Khanom Gelin, the baby didn't take breast for two days and two nights. Every time it cried, my heart sank. The amulets, the doctors, and the medicine did no good. On the second day, it died in the afternoon.

"Well, as might be expected, my husband and Khadijeh cried and mourned. But I was relieved. It was like someone had poured water on fire. I said to myself, at least now they have no son. Let them eat their hearts out. But barely two months had passed before she got pregnant again. I didn't know what to do this time. I swear to Imam Hosein I got ill and remained half conscious and bed-ridden for two months. At the end of the nine months, Khadijeh whelped another son, and she became the favorite once more. Geda Ali would give his life for the child. God gave the Israelites the promised land and Geda Ali a son! For two whole days he stayed home and just sat there with the baby wrapped up in diapers in front of him, looking at it.

"It was the same story all over again. Khanom Gelin, I couldn't help it. I couldn't stand the sight of a rival wife and her child. One day Khadijeh was occupied, I used the opportunity, took the safety pin again, and thrust it into the top of the baby's head. It died the next day. As you'd expect, there was moaning and groaning. This time, you can't imagine the state I was in. On the one hand, I was pleased as pie to have deprived Khadijeh of her son, on the other hand I was worried about the blood I'd shed twice. I mourned for the child. I cried so hard, Geda Ali and Khadijeh were sorry for me and wondered how I could love the offspring of a rival wife so much. But I wasn't crying for the baby. I was crying for myself, for the Day of Judgment, the darkness of the tomb. That night my husband told me, 'I guess it wasn't in my star to have children. They die before they can walk.'

"But it wasn't yet forty days, when Khadijeh got pregnant again. There wasn't an offering my husband didn't make so the child would live. He vowed to marry it to a descendant of the Prophet if it were a girl, and to call it Hosein if it were a boy and let his hair grow for seven years, then weigh its equal in gold and take the boy on the pilgrimage to Karbala. After about eight months and ten days, Khadijeh bore a third son. But this time it seemed like she'd gotten onto something. She wouldn't leave the baby alone for one second, and I wasn't able to make up my mind between killing the child or doing something so Geda Ali would divorce Khadijeh. But all this was idle dreaming. Khadijeh was on top of the world. She was the mistress of the house, she bossed me around, and her word was law. Meanwhile, the baby grew to be four months.

"I looked for a good augury day and night, wondering whether to kill the baby, until one night after a big fight with Khadijeh, I decided to do the baby in. I bided my time for two days. On the second day, Khadijeh went to the corner grocery to buy some figwort camphor. I ran into the room and took the baby out of the hammock. It was asleep. But as I pulled the pin and was about to thrust it in, the baby woke up and instead of crying, smiled at me. Khanom Gelin, I don't know what came over me. My hand dropped. I couldn't bring myself to do it. Well, no matter what I'd done, it wasn't like my heart was made of stone. I put the baby back and ran out of the room. Then I said to myself, 'Well, it isn't the kid's fault. The smoke rises from the firewood. I've got to do the mother in and end the trouble.'

"Khanom Gelin, now as I tell you this I tremble, but what could I do then? It was my wretched husband who chained me to the daughter of a yogurt maker—may he never hear this in his grave!

"I took some of her hair to Mullah Ebrahim the Jew, who was famous in the Rahchaman district, to put a curse on her. I put a horse-shoe in fire. Mullah Ebrahim charged me three tomans, and promised she would die before the week was up. But a month went by and she just got bigger and bigger, like Mount Ohod. My faith in witchcraft and such things was shaken.

"A month later, the winter had just begun when Geda Ali got sick—so sick that he made his will twice, and we poured holy water down his throat three times. One night, when he was very sick, I went to the market place and bought some rat poison. I brought the stuff home, poured it into the stew and after stirring it in thoroughly I put the stew back on the stove. I'd bought some food for myself. I ate it secretly, and after I was full, went to Geda Ali's room. Twice Khadijeh said, 'It's late; let's have supper.' But I told her I had a headache and didn't feel like eating. I'd feel better with an empty stomach, I said.

"Khanom Gelin, Khadijeh ate her last meal and went to bed. I went to her door and listened. I could hear her moan. But it was cold and the doors were all shut. No one else could hear her. I spent the whole night in Geda Ali's room, pretending I was watching after him. When it was nearly morning, I went to her room again, trembling and fearful, and listened behind the door. I heard the baby cry, but didn't dare open the door. You can't imagine what I went through.

"In the morning, after everybody got up, I opened Khadijeh's room. She was dead, and had turned black as coal. She had struggled so much that her mattress and her covers were all over the room. I dragged her over to the mattress and covered her with the bedspread. The baby was crying and sobbing. I left the room, went to the pond, and washed my hands. Then weeping and beating myself, I took the news of Khadijeh's death to Geda Ali.

"When people asked me what she died of, I said she'd been taking medicine to become pregnant and that she'd been overweight and maybe died of apoplexy. No one suspected me, but my conscience gave me no peace. Was it I who had shed blood three times? My face in the mirror scared me. My life was poisoned. I'd go to hear professional mourners tell the story of the Imam's death in the tragedy of Karbala. I'd weep, give money to the needy, but I could find no peace. The thought of the Day of Judgment, of Gog and Magog, and the darkness of the tomb—God knows what I went through. Then I decided to go to Karbala and live near the holy shrine in penitence. Since Geda Ali had made a vow to take us to Karbala, he wasn't unwilling to go. But he kept finding excuses and procrastinating, saying, 'We'll go to Mashhad next year. There is a plague in Karbala this year.' And so on and so forth, he put if off till he died.

"This year, I made up my mind to go. I sold all the property and turned it into cash, as he had decreed in his will. And when I heard about you and Mashdi Ramazan leaving for Karbala, I joined you at Ghazvin. The young man who is with me and thinks I am his mother is the same Hosein Agha, Khadijeh's third son. I told him to leave the room so he wouldn't hear my story."

Mashdi Ramazan and Gelin Khanom heard the story in amazement. Aziz Agha's eyes filled with tears.

"I don't know whether God will forgive me, or whether on the Day of Judgment the Imam will intercede for me. Khanom Gelin, I've been waiting to tell somebody what troubles me. Now that I have, it's like someone poured water on fire. But I worry about the Day of Judgment. . . ."

Mashdi Ramazan tapped the ashes out of his pipe:

"Come, come! Why do you think we're here? Three years ago I was a coachman on the road to Khorasan. I had two rich passengers. On the way, the coach overturned and one of them died. I strangled the other myself and took 1,500 tomans out of his pocket. Now that I'm growing old, I got to thinking the money was gained unlawfully, so I decided to come to Karbala to make it lawful. Today I gave the money to a religious authority. He took 500 for himself and gave me the rest, cleansed and purified. It only took two hours. Now the money is as much mine by right as was my mother's milk."

Khanom Gelin took the water pipe from Aziz Agha, exhaled a thick smoke, and after a short silence said:

"You remember Shabaji who was with us. I knew the camel ride would do her no good, but I brought her along anyway. You see, she was my stepsister. Her husband fell in love with me and married me. I tormented her so much that she became paralyzed. And on the way, I killed her so she wouldn't get any of our father's inheritance."

Aziz Agha was weeping for joy. "You? You too?" she said.

Khanom Gelin took a smoke and said:

"Haven't you heard the preacher? Even if your sins are as numerous as the leaves on a tree, the moment you take a vow and set out on your pilgrimage, you're as pure as a new-born babe."

1932

THE CARROUSEL

By Ibrahim Gulistan

"Let's go out, Daddy," his daughter had asked, her hair down. He knew she was not acting on her own. But, she was his daughter, with a sparkle in her eyes; and her wish, even if originally her mother's, was now her wish. Outside the window, a bamboo curtain blocked out the light, leaving the room in soothing darkness. "All right, dear," he had said. "Go ask Mommy to braid your hair."

He was now in the foyer, standing near the door. He knew that his wife was taking her time in order to hide her interest in the outing. He leaned against the door. Then he heard his daughter approaching with the footsteps of a four-year-old. Small fingers pulled at his fingers, which were linked behind him. He took his daughter's hand. Then his wife came. He turned and looked at her, but she was not looking at him. She busied herself with the girl's hair, pretending to adjust it.

The man said nothing. He was about to turn his eyes away as she raised her head, but he decided not to.

The woman understood. She realized that he was not being contrary. She knew that he could be contrary, but did not wish to be. He always pretended to be unwilling to give in. But his wife knew that his unwillingness was only a pretense. The woman was at peace. Once more she could pretend to have triumphed, although she was aware that her husband knew that only his own magnanimity had made her triumph possible. Still, she liked to continue to pretend, to look at him coldly. Only after she had done so would she look at him warmly and become herself. Just then, she became herself—took her husband's arm, nudging the girl to go before them. They crossed the courtyard together. The man looked at the unripe apricots in the tree. The girl ran to the outside door, pulled the latch, and opened it.

In the street the sun was fading. The shadows of the trees lining the street crisscrossed the sidewalk.

"Run ahead, dear!" the woman said to the girl, who was walking between them, holding their hands. The woman wanted to free her hand. "Do run ahead, dear! You were the one who wanted to go out," she said, aware that her husband knew the falsehood of that claim. "I want to walk between you," the girl said. The man looked at the woman. He had noticed that his daughter was slowly understanding the world of the grown-ups.

"Why didn't you go?" the woman asked the man.

The man made no answer.

"I don't understand," the woman said.

The man made no answer.

"I don't understand at all," the woman said.

"What am I supposed to do about that?" the man said.

"Swing me! Swing me!" the girl said, pulling their hands. Neither had been giving her any attention.

"You're right, of course!" the woman said.

"You know damned well I'm right," the man said.

The girl pulled their hands again. "Swing me! Swing me!" she said.

"Did I say anything wrong?" the woman asked.

"You sounded sarcastic," the man said.

"Sarcastic, ah!" the woman said.

"Don't quarrel!" the girl pleaded.

The man glanced at his daughter with affection. Her hair was parted in the middle. Her braids were tied with silk ribbons made into a bow. The street was alive with the sounds of early summer afternoons. The setting sun sprinkled gold dust between the shadow of trees and turned the leaves light green.

"Do you remember the night when we were just married and I had company? You went to the movies and when you came back you said it felt strange to be alone."

Their hands, which were almost touching, were pulled again. "Don't Minoo, dear," the man said.

"Swing me!" the girl said, hanging from their arms.

"Stop it," the man said.

"But now you enjoy being alone," the woman said.

"Will you stop it!" the man said.

"Isn't that the truth?" the woman said.

"Zari, don't pick on me so much," the man said.

The girl pulled her hands out of theirs and began to walk away slowly.

"Do you see what you've done? Go on, keep harping," the man said.

The woman made no answer. Sadness numbed her. The man took the girl's hand.

"Let's ride the carrousel," the girl said.

The father took her in his arms and kissed her. "All right, dear. My own pretty daughter. Give me a kiss." He was suffused with a feeling of warmth at the touch of her skin. He kissed the little girl again. He felt the woman's arm touching his. He took her arm with his free hand.

They crossed the street and entered the amusement park. The unpaved path was dry. The box branches were untrimmed, their leaves dusty.

"Daddy, go and do some target shooting," the girl said.

"All right, after your ride," the man said.

"No, Daddy, dear, you'll get bored. Do it while I'm riding the carrousel."

The woman smiled.

"All right, dear. You can ride as many times as you want. Did I say you couldn't?" the man said to the girl, rubbing his nose against hers. The girl squeezed her tender cheeks against his face, then kissed him.

"Nice Daddy!" she said.

They reached the carrousel. A shabby elderly woman sitting on a wobbly chair sold tickets. She wore her grey hair in a bun. Her skin was dull, her voice listless. The man bought a ticket. The children were riding the ugly swans and dwarf horses, or sitting in the small wooden seats of the carrousel, waiting for it to begin turning. The man kissed his daughter and tried to put her on a long-necked swan. But the girl wanted to get on the swan's back by herself. The man put her down. She held onto the swan's neck and got on its back with some effort. The children were talking and laughing, watching and waiting. The girl smiled at her father. He watched her eyes, her face and hair, and her simple happiness. "I'll sit here and watch you," he said.

"Then I'll have more than one ride," the girl said.

"All right, two," the father said.

"No, three."

"All right, three."

"No, four."

"Now, look . . ."

"Didn't I tell you to do some target shooting, Daddy?"

He laughed. The woman sat down on a bench. The girl caressed the swan's neck. "Ready, children!" an unshaven man cried from the axis of the carrousel. The children's happy cry rolled into a wave of laughter. A shabby boy circled the carrousel, which was not in motion yet. He made a little boy hold tightly to his wooden horse, then stepped aside and waved his hand. The carrousel began to move. The children cheered again. The man and the woman were now sitting side by side on a bench. The carrousel was turning. The man glanced at the children, the carrousel, the garden.

"I want to talk to you," the woman said.

"Not again!" the man said.

"Yes. When I talk to you . . . Why have you changed?"

"Can't you find something else to talk about?"

"I want to understand."

The carrousel was turning.

"You weren't like this," the woman said.

"Leave me alone."

"I don't understand. What is it you want?"

The man looked at her. Everything faded from his view. He could only see his wife. He looked into the woman's shining eyes. His heart warmed. He turned his head and scraped his foot on the gravel.

The carrousel stopped, but the children remained in their

seats. "Everybody down!" the unshaven man cried. A woman wanted to get her child down, but the child resisted. The children were holding onto their seats tightly. A girl riding a swan changed places with a girl riding a horse. The man and the woman watched the children. Their daughter gazed at them, expectant. The man noticed and nudged the woman. She rose, bought another ticket and gave it to the girl. She returned to the bench and sat down. The shabby boy collected the tickets and waved his hand. "Ready, children!" the unshaven man shouted. The children's happy cry rolled into a wave of laughter. The man waited for the carrousel to turn. He was impatient. The carrousel began to move. The man glanced at the children, whirling with the carrousel in silent pleasure.

"I don't want to go anywhere without you," the woman said.
"I know," the man said.

The carrousel hummed softly. Then it slowed down. The woman bought another ticket and gave it to the girl. She came back to the bench and snuggled close to the man. The man stretched his arm along the back of the bench; he put his finger on her shoulder, as if embracing her.

"Listen Zari, you know how much I love you," he said.
"And you know how much I love you."
"Be serious."

The woman looked at him loving and demure.

"My love," the man said, pressing her shoulder with his finger. The woman smiled.

"I really love you," the man said.
"And I love you."
"I know. If nothing else, I'm happy because you love me too. But is that enough?"

"Why do you talk like this? You always want to show that you're not happy. Why? I can't find anything wrong with us, except that you want to be a recluse."

The man pressed his eyeballs with his palms, then rubbed his palms down his face. He watched the carrousel, his chin in his hand. Their daughter passed them by on a painted, long-necked swan, disappeared behind the axis, and came to view again. She whirled round and round and, as she passed them by, the sun shed gold dust on her chestnut hair; her eyes, mouth, and face all laughing.

"Do you see that?" the woman asked.

The man said nothing.

"Smile!" the woman said.

"All right," the man said.

"Be happy. Laugh, talk."

"All right."

"One must laugh, talk, have fun. Sadness, my dear, comes from within. You create sadness for yourself. You find things to feel sad about."

"I said all right."

"All right what?"

"All right. I said all right," the man said.

His daughter appeared from behind the axis, riding a wooden swan. She passed them by, then turned and threw them a kiss. When she reappeared she was clapping her hands and laughing. As the man watched, the shabby boy jumped to his feet and shouted at her. He ran until he reached her. Still running, he put her hands around the swan's neck. The girl disappeared behind the axis, the boy still running by her side. When they both came into view, she was holding unto the swan's neck, her chestnut hair dusted with gold. But there was no laughter in her eyes, face, and mouth.

The man rose. The swan whirled past him and disappeared behind the axis.

"What did you do that for?" he shouted at the boy.

"She almost fell," the boy said, glancing at him.

The carrousel brought the girl back. The man rushed to her. She was going to jump off the swan before the carrousel had slowed down. The man caught her. The swan disappeared, empty. The children were laughing and the unshaven man was turning the carrousel.

The father kissed the girl. "That's enough, dear," he said.

1950

The Joyous Celebration
BY JALAL AL-I AHMAD

When I came home from school at noon, my father was doing his ablutions at the pond for the noon prayer. Before I could say hello, he started ordering me around:

"Come! Wash your hands, then run up to the roof and bring my towel."

This is how he was. The minute he found one of us near—my mother, my younger sister, or myself—he'd start ordering us around. I put my hands in the pond; the goldfish were scared away. Father yelled:

"Gently, you ass."

I ran up the stairs that led to the roof. He liked his goldfish a lot. They were red and gold. They wouldn't budge when he did his ablutions. But the minute I'd approach the pond, they'd wiggle their tails and dive to the bottom. I hated them for that.

I cursed the fish on the way to the roof. It was freezing even though the sun was out. Our neighbor was feeding his pigeons. They weren't afraid of me any more. I said hello to our neighbor. He had recently married off his daughter and lived in the house all by himself. One of the pigeons had feathers around its legs down to its ankles. It stepped gracefully, cooing. The feathers curled over the ankles, all the same length. I said:

"Asghar Agha, how come its legs are like that?"

"It's one of a kind. I stole it yesterday."

"Stole it?"

"Yes, someone did me a bad turn, so I sent some pigeons over and lured his."

My father disliked Asghar Agha and had forbidden me to talk to him, but I couldn't obey father's every command. A couple of times the pebbles Asghar Agha tossed at his pigeons to make them fly dropped into our courtyard and my father made a fuss. Once when my father was at the pond doing his ablutions, a stone fell right into the water and scared away the fish. You should have seen him rant and rave. His position as the religious head of the district did not stop him from cursing Asghar Agha. His curses made our hair stand on end. But Asghar Agha didn't so much as open his mouth. I got to like him from then on and would greet him and talk to him about his pigeons every chance I'd get even though father had told me not to. I was asking him what kind of pigeon he had stolen, when I heard father yell:

"Where are you, you ass?"

I'd forgotten the towel I'd gone to fetch for father. I rushed down the steps; I almost fell. I handed him the towel, trembling with fear. A drop of water from his hand fell over mine. I shuddered as though he'd slapped me. As I was going inside the house, there was a knock at the door that led from the courtyard into the street.

"See who it is," father called after me. "If it's Mashd Hasan, tell him I'm on my way."

Every time father was late Mashd Hasan would come from the mosque to fetch him. I opened the door. It was the mailman. He gave me an envelope and left without a word. He didn't like us because father never tipped him, not even on New Year's Day. I wondered why he bothered to bring father's mail at all. I was afraid he would stop some day, so I'd planned to save something out of my pocket money and give it to him, pretending that it was from father—Hadj Agha, as he was called by the people in the district.

"Who was it, you ass?"

Father was calling from his room. I stood in the doorway, stretched out my hand with the letter. "The mailman."

"Open it and read it. Let's see if they teach you anything in these schools."

My father was sitting on the *korsi*, combing his beard. I opened the envelope and was relieved to find a printed invitation. If it had been handwritten, especially in one of those fancy handwritings, I wouldn't be able to read it and he would start criticizing me again. The only handwritten word was father's name in the middle of the printed line. The invitation was signed by one of the priests in the district. He had recently turned to wearing a hat instead of the traditional turban.* He used to visit father once in a while until a year ago.

"Go on, what are you waiting for?"

"You are cordially invited to attend a reception in my house, celebrating the joyous anniversary of Jan. 7th, the Day of Women's Liberation. . . ."

"Let me see, you ass."

Father snatched the letter from my hand. I ran away. You had to get out of his way when he was angry. In the courtyard, I could hear him repeat, "That son-of-a-bitch, that atheist, that apostate!" I knew what an atheist was, but what was an apostate? I didn't know that one. What could be in the letter, I wondered. I gathered from the first glance that it was an invitation, but my father's titles, "The Proof of God," and "The Light of Islam," which I was accustomed to find after his name in all the letters he received, were missing. Just his first and his last name. And before his name, there was the word Mrs., which I couldn't understand. Of course I knew what it meant; after all, I was in the sixth grade and due to receive my diploma that year, but what did it mean before my father's name? I'd never seen anything like that before.

As I passed by the pond, I made faces at the fish, which thrust their round heads half way out of the water and opened their mouths rhythmically. But that didn't satisfy me, so I threw a handful of water over them and ran to the kitchen.

---

*Reza Shah Pahlavi banned Iranian native attire in an effort "to modernize" the country. Women were forced to appear in public without their veils (*chador*), and men were required to wear suits. As the story demonstrates, some Iranians had difficulty adapting to the change.

Mother was frying eggplant. The kitchen was full of smoke and her eyes were red, like the times she came from religious gatherings commemorating the martyrdom of the Imams.

"Hi. What's for lunch?"

"Hello. You can see for yourself. Has father left yet?"

"No, not yet."

She had piled the fried eggplant halves in the dish, with fried onions around them. I picked a few pieces of onion and sucked them. Mother knew I was hungry.

"Go spread the cloth with your sister and set the dishes. I'll be right up."

I took some more fried onions, which melted in my mouth before I left the kitchen. My sister was sitting in my mother's place, making a rag-doll with mother's torn stockings. It was a fat, ugly doll.

"You dog-shit, sitting in mother's place again," I said, kicking her stuff.

"Oh God! Here comes this wretched Abbas again. You son-of-a-bitch," she wailed.

I wasn't in a mood to beat her. I was hungry and the fried eggplant halves were so nicely browned. I didn't want mother to get mad and make me go without lunch, so I paid no attention to her and went to the niche where I kept my things. I put my books on one side. I picked up my stamp book and made sure my sister hadn't been fooling around with it again. I was tired of stamps from Iraq and Syria, but what could I do? These were the only places father received letters from. My favorite stamp in the collection was from Iraq. It had a spiral tower which got thinner as it neared the top. At the foot of the tower, there was a man on a horse, the size of a fly. I wished I could be that rider, or even his horse. . . .

"Abbas!"

It was father, shouting again. God, what does he want now? He was yelling the way he did when he wanted to beat me. I ran down.

"Come, you ass. Go to the mosque and tell them I'm not feeling well. Then run to uncle's office and tell him to stop whatever it is he's doing and come over for a minute.

"Let the boy eat something," mother pleaded. I didn't know

when she had left the kitchen, but I knew they were going to fight again and spoil our lunch.

"You loudmouth. Are you interfering with my affairs again? Now I've got to take you to a reception, bare-headed and bare-bottomed."

Father was so red in the face, it scared me. I had seen him angry often—with myself, with my mother, with his disciples and the shopkeepers in the district. But I'd never seen him like that—Mother was dumbfounded. She didn't know what was going on. The veins in father's neck bulged like ropes. I was putting my shoes on when mother came with a big sandwich for me and told me to run off before he got nasty.

I jumped out the door with half the sandwich still in my hand. There was an icy wind, and no trace of the sun. I swallowed the rest of the sandwich in the street in two bites. By the time I reached the mosque, I'd even wiped my mouth. At the entrance, old shoes were arranged in rows. Inside, people had gathered for prayer, standing in lines more crooked than those of school children. My father's disciples were talking among themselves, two or three together telling their beads. When they saw me, they knew that father wasn't coming. I didn't have to say anything. They rose one by one to say their prayers. They were used to father's absence.

I ran towards the bazaar. My mouth watered as I passed the kebab shop. The kebab-smoke filled the air. I glanced at the burning charcoal and the skewers Mashdi Ali was turning. On the counter, there was a large tray with alternating rows of scallions and radishes. The rice place next door never whetted my appetite. Its closed door and curtained windows gave the impression that the customers did immoral things inside instead of eating. The soup shop was deserted and there was no soup pot boiling and bubbling over the fire. Already it was the season for *halim* and the soup shop did its best business in the morning, especially cold freezing mornings. In front of the shop, a whole skinned sheep crouched in the center of a large tray, its neck resembling a tree trunk. A big tray full of wheat and a giant bowl sat on top of the other counter. But I had to run and fetch uncle, or else I would get no lunch.

At the end of this section of the bazaar, a vendor gripped a pot of thick noodle soup between his legs while his customers slurped their soup. Most of them were workers, with their hats under their arms. In the shoe market, the smell of leather turned my stomach. I walked faster into the inner area of the bazaar, where the cold could not penetrate. Shavings covered the ground and boards were scattered around. They smelled good. I wished I had three boards to build shelves in my niche. One for my books, one for odds and ends, and the highest one for things I didn't want my sister to touch.

I finally reached my uncle's office. He was sitting in front of the charcoal-burner in the back room, his tunic over his shoulders, eating rice and *fesenjan*. I said hello and told him all about the letter and what father had said to mother. "Really? Really?" he said a few times, as he continued eating noisily. He made me sit down and gave me a spoonful of *fesenjan* on some bread. I swallowed the food, and we got to our feet. Uncle removed his long tunic, folded it and tucked it under his arm. As we left the office he thrust his skullcap into his pocket.

I knew why. The year before, in the same section of the bazaar, a policeman had stopped him in front of everybody, because he wasn't wearing a bowler hat. He wouldn't leave Uncle alone before he had torn his tunic to shreds. I'll never forget that day. Uncle had turned as white as chalk. He kept talking about honor and calling upon God and the Prophet to intercede for him. But the policeman thrust his hand into the sleeve-holes of Uncle's tunic and ripped it from end to end, then crumpled it up, threw it into the street, and left. Something had come up that day, just like today. Father had sent me to fetch Uncle and we were on our way when that incident took place.

On the way, Uncle asked me whether father had renewed his travel permit. I did not know. Every time father wanted to go to Ghom or Ghazvin we had this headache. I would take his permit to Uncle, who would go to the police station and renew it. That's why Uncle inquired whether the head of the police station had been to our house. I said no. I knew the man. I had met him a few times at our door when leaving for school. He was probably one of father's disciples. When he visited father he wouldn't wait at the door but go straight to his room.

When we reached home, Uncle went to see father and I rushed upstairs to eat. Mother had set aside my lunch. From the amount of eggplant left in the dish I could tell that she hadn't eaten anything herself. She did that whenever she and father had an argument. I gulped down my lunch and rushed to school.

When I passed father's room, I heard him yell "apostate" and "atheist" again, probably cursing the mullah who had sent him the invitation. I wished I could go to the roof and watch Asghar Agha's pigeons for a minute, but it was cloudy and the pigeons had probably gone in. Besides, I was late for school. I wasn't late really. But because of a special problem, I had to get to school before everybody else. We were forced to wear shorts to school. But being the son of the religious head of the district, how could I walk around in shorts? What if father saw me? I didn't like the idea one bit myself, I despised the foppish boys who had become boy scouts and wore whistles round their necks and ran around in shorts and berets. But when I refused to wear shorts to school, the Dean kicked me out and told me either to cut the legs of my trousers, or go to the mosque school.

It was in the beginning of the term, around the end of September, when mother thought of a solution. She cut button-holes in my trouser legs on the inside and sewed buttons inside the legs above the knee. She showed me how to roll the legs up from the inside. I'd roll up my trousers when I got to school. When school was over, I would undo the buttons and pull the legs down.

It worked, except that my pants got too cumbersome and I couldn't run easily. Once, when I jumped into a pool over a bet with Fatso, water got into my trouser legs and they welled up. The boys made fun of me. But whatever the drawbacks of mother's invention, the Dean left me alone.

Because of my trousers, I tried to get to school before everybody else and leave after everybody had left. When the day was done, I'd linger at the boys' room long enough for everybody to leave so no one would discover the secret of my shorts. I guess the boys knew about it but didn't care. They'd nicknamed me "the Sheik" from the start. At first it really bothered me, but then I thought it over and decided it wasn't so bad. It was a title, at least. Not like "Softy," which was our monitor's nickname.

When I got to school I was dripping in sweat from running so hard. The school was crowded and the Dean was on the veranda, slapping his whip against his trouser legs. I couldn't roll up my trousers in the corridor, so I started to do so in the street. A large woman who was standing by watched me. She was wearing a wide-brimmed hat over a big kerchief which covered her head and neck and disappeared inside the collar of her loose, long overcoat.

"God curse them!" she said. "See what they're putting these poor kids through!"

"What's it to her?" I thought, and ran inside.

I returned home in the afternoon. My elder sister had come over with her baby. She lived in a street close to ours, so she could come and go even during the day. She would look out and dash to our house if there were no policemen around. She was wearing a red kerchief and had probably come over for her bath. The baby was sick. It wore out my patience with its incessant crying. Mashdi Hosein, the muezzin of the mosque, was taking the water pipe to father's room. Father had company. As mother poured my tea, she said to my sister:

"You know, dear, it's the evil eye. Too bad they did away with the Morvarid Cannon. Otherwise, you could take the baby and walk under the Cannon twice. It would be like pouring water on fire."

* * *

I remembered the times I had climbed the Cannon when I was in the first grade. I used to ride the lions that flanked it. We played hide and seek between its wheels, and skipped stones in the pond which was surrounded by the tall pine trees of Ark Square. On the green water, the stone would jump seven or eight times, sometimes ten times. It was such fun! I slurped my tea and swallowed a piece of bread. Mother went on:

"You can do something else, though. Take the baby to the police station and walk under a rifle."

"Heaven forbid, mother. You can't go near the police station these days."

"Well, why don't you tell your husband to take the baby, walk under a rifle with it two or three times, then give something to the rifle's owner."

Mother and sister were trying to decide whether the policeman or the government was the rifle's owner, when I finished my second glass of tea and went to get my stamp book. I hadn't yet reached the page with the spiral tower when mother called.

"Dear, will you take two or three armfuls of firewood to the bath. Come, be a good boy."

Annoyed, I went on turning the pages, as if I hadn't heard anything. Then my sister started:

"Shame on you. You're a big boy. Do you want her to carry the firewood herself? You need a bath too. Dirt is crawling all over you. You used to be a good boy. What happened?"

The bath was a nuisance. When the police started pulling the women's *chadors* off their heads,[*] father built the bath so mother wouldn't have to leave the house to go to the public bath. But the bath turned into a seven-day-a-week operation. The firewood filled the house with smoke. All the female relatives came for their bath, and, what's worse, I was in charge of taking the firewood to the furnace. At least twice a day, I had to carry ten armfuls of firewood from the basement, which was at the other end of the courtyard, to the furnace which was in the kitchen. It's true washing at home saved me from the torture of having to accompany father to the public bath, where he would have the barber give me a haircut like his own, practically shaving my skin off. But this one advantage wasn't worth all that trouble. Every time I carried

---

[*]Women who refused to remove their veils were harassed by the police in the 1930's by order of Reza Shah Pahlavi.

the firewood I'd cut my hands in two or three places. The branches were crooked and full of splinters. I had to climb the heap of branches and take the bundles down from the top; otherwise father would make a fuss.

As I entered the basement, the hens cackled furiously and ran away. It was dark and cloudy, so they'd gone in earlier than usual, thinking it was evening. I was getting the second bundle together, when a mouse ran by my feet into the pile. It was tiny. I guess it was a baby. I tried to catch it with the tongs but failed. I gave up and went to the pile. I was taking the fourth bundle to the kitchen, when someone knocked at the door. I thought Mashd Hasan would open the door, so I paid no attention. My sister was giving sweetened hot water to the baby, and mother was filling the lamps with kerosene. When she saw me, she said:

"Can't you hear the door, dear? Go open it. Mashdi Hasan has gone back to the mosque."

So father had decided to stay home again. It was getting dark. I opened the door to a military man. Behind him stood a woman without a *chador*. She had a small kerchief on, and was about my sister's age. No woman had ever stepped into our house without a *chador*. She carried a handbag, and walked on her toes. The officer wore decorations. I didn't know him. I wondered what he wanted so late in the day and with that woman dressed as she was. Curious things had been happening in our house that day. I suddenly felt scared. But the corridor was dark and they couldn't see that. I wondered if father's travel permit had run into complications. Maybe he had missed the mid-day and evening prayers at the mosque because of that. I left the door open and ran to mother to tell her who it was. Mother put on her *chador* and came to the corridor. She greeted the man, who talked to her for a while. I realized that he was not a stranger and I was relieved.

"I'll leave my daughter with you and go to see Hadj Agha," the man said.

Mother took the woman inside and I led the man to father's room. Then I took him tea, before father told me to. My uncle, the head of the police station, and another man were sitting around the *korsi*, my uncle next to my father. As I put the tea down, I heard the officer talk in a fancy style:

"Yes, Hadj Agha. She will be your spouse. You can make whatever arrangement you please."

I left, wondering what "spouse" was. I'd heard too many new words in one day. Mother couldn't read or write, so I wasn't able to ask her. When father was in a good mood he enjoyed being asked questions like that, and he liked to cut my reed into a pen for my calligraphy class. Whenever I needed money or wanted him to do something for me, I'd go to him with a couple of questions like that, or a reed with a broken tip. I decided to find out who the woman was.

My mother was sitting near the door under the *korsi* and had given her own place at the head of the room to the woman. At the door, her high heeled shoes towered over the rest, like a tall person standing in a line of people kneeling in prayer. There was a peculiar smell in the room which I couldn't identify at first. But then it occurred to me that it was like the smell of our physical education teacher, especially in the morning. It was perfume. The woman's lips were red. She was sitting near the *korsi*, covering her legs with the large counterpane. As I entered the room, I heard her ask, "Did the baby have a bowel movement today?"

"No ma'am; that's why he has a stomach ache. I gave him some sweetened hot water, thinking it would help. But it had no effect at all."

"How many children do you have?" mother asked. The woman lowered her head. "None," she said. "I'm still studying."

"What subject?"

"I'm studying to be a midwife."

Mother turned to my sister, "What are you waiting for? Bring the baby and let the lady take a look at him. I'll go bring some tea."

She got up and left. I took my stamp book from the corner and began to turn the pages. My sister undressed the baby on the *korsi*. The woman touched the baby's belly, which was white like the belly of my father's fish. Before she'd said anything, I heard father shouting from his room, calling me. I

29

threw the stamp book onto the niche and ran to his room. Mother was eavesdropping behind his door.

"You said you were going to get tea," I said to her.

"Mind your own business, you wretch."

Father told me to bring them more tea and fix the water pipe, which had burned up all the charcoal. I collected the tea glasses. Father was relating the history of Amr-u As's battle against the Romans. I knew the story. Whenever father had someone from the civil service, he'd talk about his journey to India; if his guest was a merchant, he'd talk about his pilgrimages to Mecca and Karbala. Now he had two army officers in the room. I left, went back with the tea and returned to the kitchen to fetch the water pipe which mother had fixed. When I took it to father's room, he had reached the point where Amr-u As, all by himself, was taken captive by the Romans, and made a speech in the presence of Caesar. I wasn't in a mood for that, and I didn't feel like going upstairs and watching the baby's wet bottom and smelling the woman's perfume, so I went into the street. But there was no trace of the kids. Apparently they had left without waiting for me. We used to get together in the evening and do something. Sometimes we would go into the street and imitate the policemen, snatching the workers' hats. Sometimes we played leap frog, or swapped odds and ends. I wanted to show the kids the Tarzan I had gotten for a pencil, but no one was there. He had a dagger at his waist and a noose over one arm. He was holding one hand in front of his mouth and imitating a lion's roar. But that evening there was nothing to do. I sat at the door, watching the people. From the end of the alley I could hear the beggar who passed by every evening, stepping slowly as his walking stick slipped on the ground, and fixing his eyes on the sky. Instead of praying or pleading, he only repeated "Oh, God Himself." The vendor who sold baked beets passed by. I couldn't see anything on his tray, but he cried out the praises of his beets all the same. A woman wearing a *chador* stuck her head out of the door opposite ours, checked her right and left carefully, then dashed for a door a few yards away. She pushed the door, but it was locked. She knocked furiously, looking to left and right.

Finally the door opened and she went in. Then I heard Abolfazl:

"Oops! I got you!"

He was catching flies. It was dark and the street light was dim. I wondered how he could see the flies in the dark, especially in that freezing weather. It was probably his imagination. He lived two doors from us and had gone insane long ago. He'd sit at the door of his house and catch flies. People said he ate them, but I hadn't seen him do so. I think he only pretended to. "I'll make a delicious *fesenjan* with you," or, "You don't know how good the legs taste," he would say. In the beginning he was good entertainment. Teasing Abolfazl was one of our evening pastimes. But now his wife came to our house every ten days to do the wash and it wasn't right to tease him. He beat her all the time and kicked her out of the house. But she felt sorry for him and went on taking care of him. I decided to talk to him.

"Abolfazl, what did it taste like?"

"Like popcorn. Imagine, big as a sparrow!"

"Maybe it's your imagination. Whoever heard of flies in weather like this?"

"What do you know about it? I put a spell on them and they come on their own. Wait."

He searched the pocket of his torn jacket for the matchbox in which he kept his flies. I was bored, and I'd nothing else to say to him. I got up to go home when our door opened. From where I was I saw the officer and his daughter leaving our house. I was ashamed to be seen with Abolfazl. I sneaked behind him so they wouldn't see me. Then I realized that they didn't know Abolfazl, so I didn't have to hide from them. But it was too late; if they saw me now, it would be even worse. As they passed by, I heard the girl say to her father:

"You want me to become his *sigheh**, father?"

"Only for two hours, dear. Just long enough so he can go to the reception with you. . . ."

"Oops! I got it. See how big it is."

---

*A woman married by way of a temporary marriage.

Abolfazl didn't let me hear the rest of the man's words. I wondered what they were talking about. Was father going to marry that girl? What for? And then I understood!

I looked at the matchbox. It was empty. I didn't feel like fooling around with Abolfazl. I went back inside. The door was open. In the dark corridor I heard uncle say:

"Good heavens! It's really something. The precious daughter of the Major. . . ."

My footsteps cut him short. When I went closer I saw the head of the police station and stupidly said hello. I went straight into the living room. My elder sister wasn't there. Mother was running around in the kitchen. The bath furnace smoked like a volcano. I didn't feel like waiting for dinner. I took my clothes off and sneaked under the *korsi*. My nostrils itched from the smoke. I was thinking about Abolfazl and his empty matchbox and about what I had discovered. Then I heard uncle chuckle:

"Sister, you barely missed it! You almost lost your husband!"

Uncle called mother, who was his sister-in-law, *sister*, just as his wife did. I heard mother say:

"You mean that girl? God forbid! Her toes were on the earth and her heels up in the sky!"

"Aren't you going to cover the pond with boards? It's going to freeze soon."

Doing my ablutions at the pond the next morning, I discovered that father's room was locked. He had gone away again. Every time he went to Ghom or Ghazvin, he'd lock his room. The goldfish were at the bottom of the pond, asleep, but red scales were scattered near the pond and there was blood at one spot. As always, the cats had taken advantage of father's absence and feasted on his fish. I felt great. Back in the living room I asked mother:

"Where's Hadj Agha gone?"

"I don't know, dear. He left at dawn. Your uncle said he was going to Ghom."

At breakfast mother told my sister and me that Asghar Agha's pigeons were all stolen the night before. I ran up to the roof. Now that father was away there was nothing to stop me from talking to Asghar Agha. I was upset about the pigeons. It was cloudy and there was a chilly wind. I saw the empty dovecot. The roof was quiet, with white patches of pigeon droppings here and there.

1962

A Land like Paradise
BY SIMIN DANISHVAR*

Mehrangiz, the Negro girl, slept in the same room with the children. They would spread the beds side by side in the large room; the oldest bed belonged to Mehrangiz. After Ali and his two sisters had filled the room with their play until they were tired they would lie down in their beds, the eldest sister would lower the lamp, and they would wait for Mehrangiz, who would still be washing dishes in the kitchen opposite. Ali could hear the sound of dishes and the splashing of water. Then when Mehrangiz put out the kitchen light he would curl up happily in his bed and squeeze his face against the pillow.

Mehrangiz would tip-toe into the room, blow out the lamp and lie down in bed so quietly that if Ali didn't stay awake waiting for her he would never hear a sound. Then, in the darkness, Ali would begin to plead with her to tell him stories.

These stories were always the same: tales of Mehrangiz, her mother, and of other Negro nurses.

"Mehrangiz's mother, as a child, is playing naked by the river with other Negro children when a big man in an Arabic headdress gets off the camel-litter and cries out to them, '*Taal! Taal!*' 'Come! Come!' Only Mehrangiz's mother, who is the youngest of all the children, runs toward him. The big man gives her a few sweets, sweeps her into his arms, and puts her into the camel-litter. She begins to cry and struggle.

*Translated by Minoo S. Southgate and Bjorn Robinson Rye.

A hand holds her mouth firmly. She bites the hand. The man hits her on the mouth and she begins to bleed. Then, exhausted from crying, she falls asleep. When she awakes, she finds herself in a boat, and although the boat is full of Negroes—men, women, and children—her father and mother are not among them. She cries and cries. A Negro woman gives her a red apple. "Are we going to my mother?" she asks, but the woman just shakes her head and repeats "Alas, alas," in her own language.

Mehrangiz's mother learned this language and can still remember it, but Mehrangiz never learned it at all.

Then the little Negro girl, Mehrangiz's mother, is sold to Ali's Grandfather, who calls her Baji Delnavaz.

Ali has heard the story many times, but every time he hears it he promises Mehrangiz that if he ever lays hands on the big man he will cut him to pieces with the kitchen knife.

"Fine. Now go to sleep," Mehrangiz would always say.

The next night she would tell him another story: "Nurolsaba, Navab's Negro nurse, was above all nurses. She wasn't as dark as Delnavaz and Mehrangiz. Her nose wasn't flat. Her eyes were almond-shaped instead of round and her hair wasn't kinky. She was as beautiful as the two statues of Negro girls in the living room. She wasn't like me, Ali, with no eyebrows, and eyes the size of a split pea.

"Anyhow . . . I was still at your grandfather's when one day Nurolsaba came to the house from Navab's. She had come over to invite the mistress to the funeral of Master Navab, who had been shot in front of the consulate. She wore a black silk chador, and when she entered the room she was so tall that she had to bend her head to avoid hitting the lintel of the door. She didn't kiss your grandmother on the shoulder, she only said "hello." That's all. Then she took a saucer of roasted coffee beans from a black silk handkerchief and put it in front of grandmother.

"Not long after that all Shiraz learned who she really was and what she did. One day, my dear Ali, three new, shiny carriages stop in front of Navab's house. A nigger dressed up in a suit and sheepskin hat gets off the first carriage, and he is followed by other niggers, all wearing suits and sheepskin hats and ties and shirts. Behind them all, another nigger gets off carrying a chest covered in red velvet. They are all ministers of Nurolsaba's land. They knock at Navab's door. Navab's wife sends for Nurolsaba. When she comes they bow down to her. They all bow down to her. In the chest, my dear, there are gowns from India, and jewels. They give them to Nurolsaba to put on. When she walks past them to climb into the carriage the niggers bow to her again, so low their heads knock against their knees. She climbs into the fine carriage in her gowns and her jewels and they drive her away. She never comes back; she is a queen, at last, in her own land.

"From that day on, my dear, it has become the dream of every nigger nurse to be taken away like that by someone."

"Maybe they'll come for you, too. If they come, will you leave me and go?" Ali would ask. And Mehrangiz would always answer, "Now go to sleep—we'll see about that in the morning."

Ali knew that Baji Delnavaz was Mehrangiz's mother. But who was her father? Ali's mother always talked about the old days when more than twenty slave girls would sit down to each meal in her father's house, about her mother's pilgrimage to Mecca and her father's joking with the ship-captain. This last she hadn't witnessed, but had heard about.

Ali's mother always said that Baji Delnavaz had been dearer and more respected than the other slaves. They had even taken her on the famous trip to Mecca. But after the journey she became homesick and carried on terribly for a while.

Mehrangiz had been the playmate of the young masters and mistresses, and when Ali's mother had married she took Mehrangiz to her husband's house as part of her dowry. She was sad about having had to put her to work. "It isn't proper to put a person whom one takes as part of one's dowry to work as a domestic; she should attend instead to her mistress's wardrobe. But there was no wardrobe to need an attendant. What else was I to do?"

Ali himself remembered one day when Baji Delnavaz came to their house. She was so old she had to walk with the help of a stick, and she wore torn, worn-out clothing. His mother was at the pond, doing ablutions to prepare for her prayer when she saw Baji Delnavaz arrive. "Mehrangiz," she cried, washing her feet, "Come—your mother is here."

Mehrangiz brought Baji Delnavaz into the living room, where Ali and his sisters stayed out of the way and unusually quiet. Ali's mother stood at her prayers.

Baji Delnavaz sat near the door and wept as she told Mehrangiz how her master had turned her out with no place to go now that she was old. Ali and his younger sister began to cry. The younger sister brought her old jacket and gave it to Delnavaz. Ali was pleased. He brought all the raisins and nuts he had saved and poured them into the old woman's lap. His mother was still praying, and Ali could tell by the tone of her whispering that she was angry with them. They were all waiting now for her to finish, but she lingered so long over the supplication that it was obvious she was deliberately prolonging the prayer.

When she finally finished, Ali breathed a sigh of relief. Delnavaz went at once and kissed the mistress's shoulder. Awkwardly, she began her story over, but Ali's mother stopped her.

"I heard every word. It's enough."

"Only let me sleep in your basement tonight," Baji Delnavaz pleaded. "I've no place to go. . ."

"No. How many mouths must we feed? Even Mehrangiz is one too many."

"Mistress . . . I'm old and an invalid; I'll have to beg in the streets."

"Beg, then. What do I care?"

Ali's mother turned back into the house; Ali and his younger sister followed, crying and pleading with her to help Delnavaz. She only glared at them.

They could hear the slow tapping of Delnavaz's cane as she left the house. Still pleading, Ali ran to open one of the living room windows so that he could shout to Delnavaz in the street, but his mother pushed him away and leaned out herself. "Go to Monavar Khanom," she cried out when the old woman came into view. "Is it a sin to be the elder sister?"

Ali went into the kitchen to be with Mehrangiz. She was putting wood into the stove, tears running down her cheeks as she worked. One drop glided over her chin and down her neck.

Ali sat beside her. "Don't cry," he said. "If my aunt doesn't keep you when you get old, then when I grow up . . ."

"I'm not crying," Mehrangiz said. "It's the smoke."

"What smoke?"

Mehrangiz put a finger to her lips. "Don't tell the mistress I cried," she whispered.

A month passed, or a little less. One day, around evening, Monavar Khanom's husband came for Mehrangiz, who had gone to the baths. He whispered something to Ali's mother. "My poor sister, what a bother," she said, shaking her head. The uncle nodded solemnly.

"Run to the baths and tell Mehrangiz to come home immediately," his mother shouted to Ali. He was putting his shoes on when he heard her tell his uncle, "Why don't you go too and pick her up on the way? I don't want her to be making scenes here."

When Ali and his uncle reached the baths they waited outside, behind the thick cotton curtain of the entrance. The uncle called the bath-keeper and whispered something in her ear. Then they waited. Ali heard Mehrangiz's voice from inside: "Let me just wash my hair, then I'll come."

"No, you must hurry. It's urgent!"

"Has someone come to ask me in marriage?" Mehrangiz asked, and Ali heard her snap her fingers playfully.

"Your mother's dying and you snap your fingers?" shouted the old bath-keeper.

Ali heard Mehrangiz's cry and he burst into tears.

Mehrangiz fell three times before they reached Monavar Khanom's house.

"Why on earth did you bring the child?" his aunt asked her husband at the door.

"He came on his own."

"Come Nayer," his aunt called out. "Ali is here." Then she turned to her husband. "May God forgive her. She died at a bad time. It's evening."

Nayer and Ali went outside to play. "Let's play dying," Nayer said.

"Is Baji Delnavaz dead?" Ali asked.
"Yes. Just before Mehrangiz came."

On the fortieth day of Delnavaz's death, Ali and Mehrangiz went to Sofeh Torbat Cemetery to visit her grave. They searched for a long time and asked many people before they finally found it. There was nothing but a mound marked by a brick. Mehrangiz embraced the mound and cried so wildly that Ali was frightened.

That night Ali waited for Mehrangiz to blow out the lamp in the kitchen and come to tell him stories. One story had been added to her tales: the story of her mother's death. But the kitchen turned dark and still Mehrangiz did not come. Ali was worried and couldn't sleep. Finally, late at night, he heard her whispering in another part of the house. Later still his father's shadow crossed the doorway.

The next morning Ali's father couldn't find his glasses. They looked everywhere; even the children helped. But Ali's mother didn't lift a finger, as if it were none of her concern. She sat and watched the search and from time to time smiled mockingly to herself. Ali didn't like her mocking smile.

Ali went to search her folded prayer rug, thinking the glasses might be there, but he hadn't yet touched it when his mother was at his side. She pushed him into the middle of the room, screaming. "Leave it alone! Your hands are unclean."

Finally his father went to work without his glasses. He had to buy a new pair, and from that night on he slept with them on.

Ali hadn't started school yet, although both his sisters went. One morning soon afterwards, Mehrangiz had taken them to school and had just returned. Ali's mother was in the kitchen. Ali was sitting at the doorway of the big room where he could see everything that went on in the house. When Mehrangiz entered the kitchen Ali's mother began to hit her over the head with a piece of firewood. Ali jumped from the doorway and ran through the courtyard into the kitchen. He tried to hold his mother's hand back. His mother wore a strange mocking smile. Mehrangiz's head was bleeding.

"Please don't. I'm scared, I'm scared," Ali begged his

mother. He was crying, but Mehrangiz wasn't crying.

"The nigger is bleeding, why are *you* crying?" his mother demanded, suddenly turning to him.

Mehrangiz went to the pond and washed her head. The blood didn't stop, and Ali was surprised that Mehrangiz wasn't crying. His mother picked some burned tobacco from the water pipe, which was by the pond, and put it on the wound. "You'll end up a whore," she said.

"What's a whore?" asked Ali.

"I'm going to have you examined by a midwife," his mother continued.

Then Mehrangiz burst into tears.

*

What was wrong with summer was that it would separate Ali and Mehrangiz. In summer, the pond was covered with a platform; Ali would sleep there with his parents and sisters while Mehrangiz slept in the yard on a mattress.

One evening, Monavar Khanom and her daughter, Nayer, came to visit. Monavar sat crosslegged beside Ali's mother, smoking a water pipe. The two women talked in low voices and Monavar cried, wiping away the tears with the corner of her *chador*. The children were playing fortress on the steps that led to the big room. Nayer and Ali were on one side and the other kids on the other side. Once, when Nayer and Ali captured the fortress they embraced and kissed.

"Shame on you, Ali" shouted Ali's mother, who had been keeping an eye on the children as she talked to Monavar Khanom.

"There's nothing wrong with that, sister," said Monavar Khanom, putting the pipe aside. "Didn't we intend them for each other from the beginning?"

"It will be as God wills," sighed Ali's mother.

Monavar Khanom and her daughter stayed over that night, and slept in the bed usually occupied by Ali's father. Then Mehrangiz brought out the bed from the kitchen and made it up for Ali's father. Ali's mother insisted that Mehrangiz sleep indoors, but Monavar Khanom interceded, saying, "She'll die of heat, sister," so that Ali's mother surrendered. Mehrangiz slept on her mattress in the yard.

The moonlight kept Ali awake that night—that and the fear

that he would wet his bed, and that the wet mattress would be spread out the next day to dry where his cousin could see it. His mother was asleep. Monavar Khanom was snoring. Then, as he lay sleepless, he thought he heard Mehrangiz's whisper and was glad. He sat up in bed and called softly to her, but there was no answer.

Then, in the moonlight, he noted something strange about his father's bed—the blankets looked swollen and misshapen. He thought *bakhtak* was sitting on his father's chest, and held his breath, straining to see. Mehrangiz had told him about *bakhtak*. He waited for his father to grab its mud nose and make it reveal the hiding place of its treasures. He couldn't see *bakhtak's* nose, yet he could tell that there was a struggle going on. He was frightened, but hopeful. Then the struggle subsided, and *bakhtak* got up. Ali screamed, "Catch it! Grab its nose!" to his father. His mother, lying beside him, cried, "Go to sleep," in a hoarse whisper, and in his excitement he realized he had wet the bed.

The next morning Mehrangiz was once again hit with a piece of firewood and got a broken head, and Ali's mattress was left out to dry where everyone could see. Mehrangiz looked at him despondently and said, "You shouldn't have done that."

Monavar Khanom and Nayer stayed for a few days, until Ali's uncle came to the house. When Monavar Khanom heard his voice she locked herself in the closet in the living room. Then she came out and cried and they all went home. As they were leaving, Ali heard his mother say, "Don't forget to send her over, sister."

A few days later a big red-headed woman, her hands and feet colored with henna, came to the house. Ali's mother treated her with respect, rose to meet her, and called to Mehrangiz to bring in tea. But no matter how many times she called to Mehrangiz for the tea, there was no answer. Finally she sent Ali in to fetch her. He found her sitting on the bed in the kitchen, trembling like a willow.

"What's wrong? Are you cold?" Ali asked. "Go out into the sun."

But Mehrangiz didn't budge, and wouldn't answer although

they could both hear Ali's mother calling her. The big woman came into the kitchen, put her hands on her waist, and bawled at Mehrangiz to do as she was told.

Mehrangiz shook so hard her teeth chattered, but still she wouldn't move. She sat with her eyes on the tile of the floor and didn't look up. Ali was frightened.

At last Ali's mother and the big woman dragged Mehrangiz into the living room and locked the door behind them. Ali and his sisters listened behind the door. The elder sister whispered something to the younger and they burst out laughing. But they wouldn't tell Ali why.

Then they heard Mehrangiz screaming, and Ali began to tremble himself and cry.

*

Ali was fifteen and preparing for his finals, when his father became ill. His father had had many dreams, but none of them had materialized. He hadn't even succeeded in wiring the house for electricity, whereas Monavar Khanom's home had had electricity for a year. His illness became worse and worse. During this time a suitor came for the younger sister, but Ali's father did not encourage him because the elder daughter was yet unmarried.

The night Ali was studying for his physics exam, Mehrangiz ran into his room, her eyes round with terror.

"Mehrangiz! What is it?" asked Ali, putting down his book.

"There's an owl on the roof, laughing!" she whispered, "Owls know everything; the owl is a prophet among birds. I'm scared!"

"Of what?"

"It's an omen. The master's sickness . . ."

"Well? What if it is?"

"We must make the owl promise . . ."

Ali and Mehrangiz climbed the stairs that led to the roof. At the top Ali had to wait for her, for she was getting older, and was worn from work. She was carrying a tray which held a Koran, a green leaf, bread and salt. On the roof she tip-toed to the owl and sat behind it. She lifted the Koran, whispering "By this Koran, by this bread and salt . . ." Ali smiled to himself. Then, suddenly, the owl spread its wings and flew away. Mehrangiz was overjoyed. "It flew to the ruins, where it belongs. It doesn't build nests, it just lives in ruins. We've done a good thing to make it go . . ."

Ali's father died the next week and Ali failed his finals.

He was the family's breadwinner now, and stopped going to school. Instead he was given a job in the office where his father had been an accountant. When he came home from work the first day he did imitations of his boss for Mehrangiz and his sisters; he pretended to be sitting at a desk where, frowning and spitting, he opened the top drawer and measured out some tea in an imaginary matchbox, sputtered, poured a little back, counted out exactly six sugar cubes, looked stealthily over his shoulder, put one back . . . Mehrangiz and the girls laughed so hard that Ali's mother heard them from the courtyard. "How can you laugh with your father's shroud not yet dry?" she shouted angrily.

At the words "father" and "shroud," all the grief came back to Mehrangiz. She ran into the kitchen where she sat with her hands covering her face and cried. Ali's mother was furious that Mehrangiz so openly mourned the master. "Mehrangiz," she shouted from the doorway. "Collect your junk and get out of this house. I can't feed a single extra mouth." Mehrangiz cried more wildly. She beat herself over the head and pulled at her hair. But Ali put his arm around her until she was quiet and then led her to the pond. "Come . . . wash your face . . . Would I let you leave the house?"

At the end of the summer, Monavar Khanom persuaded Ali's family to remove their mourning clothes, but Mehrangiz continued even so to wear a black headkerchief. Ali's mother had not succeeded in throwing her out, but she kept threatening to do so, and struggled with Ali over her. In September, the suitor who had been turned down by Ali's father married the younger sister. Monavar Khanom and Nayer stayed at the house for a week.

In the evening, the cousins and Mehrangiz would gather in the big room. The elder sister was quiet and glum, but the younger sister, with her rosy cheeks, made-up face and plucked eyebrows, had been transformed into another being. A smile never left her lips. As for Nayer, although she wore her *chador* in Ali's presence, she would sometimes allow it to slip off her head when she laughed hard. She had grown into an easy-going, handsome, flirtatious young girl.

Ali began his imitations, but even when the others were rocking with laughter, the elder sister didn't smile. Ali did imitations of everybody except her. Then, pointing at an imaginary map on the wall with a long stick, he imitated, first, the history teacher, and then the geography teacher. Finally he mingled the two. "This long, thin strip is Egypt. This is the Nile, home of Egyptologists. The Egyptian religion believes that the world rests on the back of a hippo and that each evening the sun is eaten by a pig. This is called the wisdom of the ancients."

Ali's elder sister frowned and interrupted him. "This is blasphemy. Ask God to forgive you."

"Ezat, dear, we're just playing," Nayer said. There's no harm done."

"Playing? Are you children? If he'd gotten married, his kids would be nearly my age!"

"He'll marry, God willing," said Mehrangiz. "And I'll take care of his children myself. And you, Ezat Khanom, you'll get married as well."

Ezat said no more.

"Tell us about the pyramids," Nayer said to Ali.

"The religion insisted that kings be buried inside of man-made mountains, but it's not easy to build mountains, and man isn't like God to make mountains in the blinking of an eye. To say, 'Let there be,' and get it done. These mountains were built by slaves. They put stone on top of stone and climbed and climbed. But the pharaohs not only didn't reach the sky, they died on this very earth. Then they had themselves bandaged like a sore thumb and buried in their mountains."

Mehrangiz's eyes were wide with amazement. "Are Egyptians niggers?" she asked.

"No. They aren't niggers, but the niggers aren't the only ones oppressed," answered Ali, suddenly serious.

Ali's mother sold the large clock with the statues of Negro girls which had always sat on the mantle in the living room and the money went to the younger sister's dowry. But even with the one less mouth to feed, and even after Ali's boss made him secretary, the family could never make ends meet. Mehrangiz was constantly reminded that she was an added expense.

Whenever she had a chance now she would question Ali about Egypt. "Were they nigger slaves that built the mountains? And did they bring the niggers here from Egypt? And I've heard that Nurolsaba's land was below Egypt. A land like paradise. Nurolsaba was its princess..."

Ali's mother sold the great copper pot in which, once a year on the day of Imam Hasan's martyrdom, they had prepared *sholezard* to give to the poor. She gave half the money to a fortune-teller to help the elder sister marry; the other half she spent on a party for the new bride.

On the day of the party Ali didn't go to work, but stayed at home to act as host. Nayer and Monavar Khanom were buttering up the bridegroom and his parents. Ali's mother was in full control and, as usual, loaded Mehrangiz with more work than any four women could do. Mehrangiz rushed about like a top, offering refreshments to everyone, cleaning, preparing food. The guests left before sundown—all except Monavar Khanom and Nayer, who stayed on.

Early that evening Ali and Nayer had the big room to themselves. Nayer was saying her prayers, but her eyes were on Ali, who lay resting in such a way that he could watch her. Each time their eyes met, Nayer's cheeks blossomed like cherries. It was a pleasant, quiet time and Ali was happy. He didn't notice that Mehrangiz had entered the room until he felt her hand on his arm. She leaned and whispered in his ear to follow her. Ali didn't want to leave Nayer. Her blushing cheeks and laughing eyes were a delight to him, but he could not hurt Mehrangiz's feelings. She had taken care of him like her own son, and he felt closer to her than to his own mother. With a sigh, he rose and followed her out into the hall. She led him to the closed door of the living room, and there they stood and listened. Monavar's voice could be heard from inside. "He's a good suitor, but we haven't yet talked of . . ." The bubbles of the water pipe drowned the rest of the sentence. His mother was smoking the water pipe. "God's will

45

be done," she answered then.

Monavar Khanom spoke again, but Ali heard only one word: "engaged." His mother's answer clarified the rest. "I don't expect you to wait for us, sister. You know how small Ali's wages are, we could never afford to bring a bride into the house."

"They may be in love. It's a sin to separate them."

"Ali's still a child, what does he know of love?"

"I said all this only so there would be no blame later."

Ali was furious. "I'm going in," he whispered to Mehrangiz, but she held his arm tightly. "I'm going to tell them Nayer is mine. That they have no right to marry her to someone else. That she's been mine since we were children. That she's always been with me . . ."

He tried to pull away, but Mehrangiz stopped him. "That will only make things worse," she whispered. "Your mother will start screaming, everything will be upset. If I had a silk chador I would put it on and go to Monavar Khanom's house, and I would say . . . What would I say, master?"

Ali turned without answering and went to his room. He dressed quickly and went out without saying goodbye to his mother or to Nayer. Mehrangiz followed him to the door. "Don't worry. Worrying dries up man's root," she told him as she let him out.

One day when he came home from work no one answered his knock at the door. He could hear crying from within. He knocked harder. When his sister finally let him in, he found Mehrangiz stretched out in the flowerbed with a bloody face. The big kitchen knife was shining at the edge of the pond. His mother stood beside it trembling. Ali felt suddenly nauseated.

"My God, what's happened?" he whispered.

"Either she goes, or I go," answered his mother in a loud, firm voice. "The whole lot of you prefer her to me. Your sisters, your father, yourself. I know you're sleeping with her too."

Ali looked at her, amazed. "What are you talking about? For God's sake, what's happened?"

"What did you expect would happen? Look! She placed two little pieces of wax in his hand. He looked at them with incomprehension, and then up at his mother and sister with a blank, questioning face. Mehrangiz had begun to moan where she lay.

"Now she engages in witchcraft," he heard his mother say. "I found these two dolls in the kitchen, stuck together. I asked her what they were. 'This is for master Ali and Nayer Khanom, so they'll marry,' she says—but I wasn't born yesterday, I've dealt with these niggers all my life. 'If you know witchcraft, why don't you do something for my daughter so *she* can marry?' I ask her. 'You got to leave right now. Before Ali comes home,' I tell her. And then, the bitch, she picks up the knife to kill me."

Mehrangiz suddenly sat up, the blood dripping down over her muddy dress. "Master, it's not true," she wailed. "She drove me mad! I picked up the knife to kill myself, to free myself—would I dare kill the mistress? I've grown old in this house, and now . . ."

"Liar," shouted his mother. "You'd murder me in my sleep!"

Ali helped Mehrangiz to her feet and took her into the kitchen, where he helped her wash the wound.

That night when he came home he found her sitting on the doorstep, a bundle by her side. When she saw Ali she burst into tears. "I've got to go. Mistress says things that make my head smoke. You can't expect a woman who slanders her own child to do any better by a poor nigger."

"Mehrangiz, I . . ."

"Take these wax dolls," she told him, pulling the two figures from a fold in her *chador*. "Tie something heavy to them and drop them in the pond. Before the fortnight is over, Nayer will be yours." She forced the figures into his hand, they were warm from her body. "Now I have to go, to say good bye," Mehrangiz said, trying to hold back her tears. "I took care of you, my dear, like my own child."

"Where will you go? You have no place to go."

She dried her tears. Don't worry about me, I'll go to Monavar Khanom's. Maybe Nayer will take me as her dowry and we'll both come to your house."

"But if Monavar Khanom doesn't take you . . ."

"If Monavar Khanom doesn't take me in, I'll go to the bazaar and beg. Come and see me there from time to time, won't you."

Monavar Khanom did take Mehrangiz in, and a few months later when Nayer married, Mehrangiz did accompany her to her new husband's—but the husband was not Ali.

Ali didn't go to the wedding, even though his mother insisted that he go. That night was the first of the nights he could not sleep. He imagined there was something in his bed, but whenever he got up to look he found nothing there.

The next day there was a knock at the door. He was alone in the empty house. When he opened the door, Mehrangiz stood smiling sadly on the doorstep in a silk but worn, black *chador*.

He took her into the room. When she had sat down, she handed him something tied up in a nylon handkerchief.

"What's this?"

"Sweets from the wedding. You were on my mind."

"You shouldn't have left the bride and groom just to make conversation," he said. The sweets depressed him.

"I got permission."

They sat facing each other, saying nothing. The house was silent.

"The bridegroom is bald, but we didn't find out until last night. In the morning, when I went to make the bed, I saw him. He's bald. He's a police detective, but he looks like a wrestler. Your little finger is worth a hundred like him."

"How is Nayer? Was she happy?" Ali tried hard not to disgrace himself by beginning to cry.

Mehrangiz shook her head, lowered her eyes. "No."

"Tell me."

"Last night in the bedroom she sat on the bed. When the women wanted to put her hand in the bridegroom's she refused. She was beautiful, Ali. She wore red geraniums in her hair, and in the center of the flowers was a tiny electric bulb which she could turn on at will. I don't know how—praised be the Lord."

She looked at Ali, waiting for him to comment on the wonderful headdress, but when he didn't she went on. "Finally the bridegroom took her hand by force. A red geranium fell on the bed."

Sometimes, after that, Nayer and her son came to visit Ali with Mehrangiz. Her husband, in all the years he had been in the family, had never said two words to Ali. He never visited them except on New Year's Day.

Nayer made a military uniform for her son. The boy looked uncomfortable in it, but he sauntered around proudly, his little wooden sword hitting his leg as he walked.

"Why do you dress your son like a killer?" Ali asked Nayer once.

"He looks cute in the uniform, doesn't he?" Nayer answered—but the boy was never again dressed as a soldier when they visited.

Once when her husband was away on a case, Nayer, her son and Mehrangiz came to Ali's for lunch. Nayer had gained weight, but when she looked at Ali her eyes were sad and reproachful.

After lunch, Mehrangiz brought the boy to the big room to sleep. Ali was lying down reading the paper when they came in. Mehrangiz looked so old now that even Ali's mother no longer suspected him of sleeping with her. He put the paper aside to watch the child, who reminded him of Nayer. The boy didn't want to sleep, he asked Ali for colored pencils, but Ali had none.

"You must sleep, my dear," Mehrangiz coaxed. "Go and kiss master then come back and lie down and I'll tell you a story."

Ali closed his eyes in anticipation of the kiss, but none came.

As he lay back with his eyes closed, he could hear Mehrangiz's low voice. "They bowed to Nurolsaba. They bowed and bowed. Then they dressed her up in Indian gowns and adorned her with jewels, and took her to their own land. In their land was a king who had the niggers build him a mountain by the river. They had everything in their land except mountain and the king longed for a mountain. The niggers carried one-ton rocks on their backs and built the mountain. Now Nurolsaba can see the mountain, but no trees grow there . . ."

Ali opened his eyes. He saw Mehrangiz sitting beside the boy, rubbing his back.

"Why don't they?" Ali asked.

"I'm sorry, did I wake you?" Mehrangiz said. "The child doesn't sleep, unless I tell him stories—just like you," she said.

"I asked why trees don't grow there," demanded Ali.

"Because they shed so much blood for those mountains. To shed a black cat's blood or a nigger's blood comes to no good."

Ali closed his eyes again in the hot midday. He heard the boy ask for more. Mehrangiz told the story of the children and the man in the Arabic head-gear; then she told another story which he'd never heard before:

"My mother knew the niggers' language, but no one taught it to me. One day a nigger comes to grandfather's house and speaks to my mother in their own language. The master and mistress don't understand a word of it. The next day, my mother packs her things in a bundle and says she's going to the baths. They don't hear from her for a whole year, and although they look everywhere, it's as though she were a drop of water sunk into the ground. They all think she has run away for good—but then one day she comes back. It is in the evening, and she isn't alone, for she has me hidden under her *chador*. Well, she cries and cries until the mistress finally forgives her and she lives again in the house. But after that, once every year, she takes me and disappears for a few days . . ."

"Do you remember where she went?" asked Ali suddenly, sitting up. "Do you remember who she went to?"

I remember things like in a dream. There was a place with a well. A nigger would come and take me in his arms, kiss me, give me fresh fruit. Then I would stay with the cows—it was a farm. I was afraid of the cows, but I loved it when the buckets came up from the well and the water gushed out. The wheel sang and sang, and the water poured down. My mother and the nigger would go inside and shut the door.

The last time we went there the nigger was gone. A man told my mother that they came for him, chained him, and took him to Bushehr. My mother cried."

One evening shortly after that there was a quick knock at the door. There stood Nayer's husband, back from his assignment. He was in uniform, and his epaulets glittered with stars. Ali had a sudden impulse to pluck those stars from the uniform . . . but sometimes, too, he felt a strange affection for him, because the man was closer to Nayer than anyone else.

"Come with me," said Nayer's husband softly. Ali was frightened. "Nayer or Mehrangiz," he wondered, but did not ask. He dressed, his heart pounding.

"My servant didn't know the way, I had to come myself," Nayer's husband explained as they left the house.

"Is it Nayer or Mehrangiz?" asked Ali at last.

"Mehrangiz. She's asked for you."

"What's wrong?"

"The old woman's turned senile. She pumped the primus stove until it exploded and burned her all over. That was yesterday."

"You took her to the hospital?"

"It wasn't worth the bother."

Ali was silent. They didn't speak until they reached the house. Nayer opened the door. She held her son by the hand, and Ali saw that she was pregnant again.

"She's upstairs," said Nayer immediately. "I was afraid to sit with her longer." Her eyes were red.

Ali climbed the stairs. The door was open. He hesitated, then walked in. Mehrangiz lay on a mattress, but he barely recognized her. She looked like a charred piece of meat. Her face was so swollen with blisters that she could barely open her eyes. When she saw Ali, she tried weakly to smile. "I was waiting for you, my own master," she whispered.

"Why didn't you call me sooner so I could bring a doctor?" demanded Ali, kneeling beside the bed. "I would have taken you to hospital."

"What's the use?"

She tried suddenly to drag herself out of the bed, toward a southern window. Ali stopped her. "Do you want the window open?" he asked.

"No, I want to face the *ghebleh*, to die facing Mecca."

Ali took the mattress and, as she lay on it, carefully dragged it to the side so that Mehrangiz would be facing the *ghebleh*.

Nayer came in, a white handkerchief in her hand. She stood quietly just inside the doorway, as though she didn't want to be in the way.

Mehrangiz was calm. "The prayer stone is on the mantle. Please put it on my eyes," she asked.

Nayer took the stone and blew the dust from it. "It's broken," she said. "Let me get you a good one."

"No, let it be broken . . . it's good enough for an old nigger like me."

Ali sat on the floor then, in the silent room. Nayer continued to stand just inside the door. He could feel her eyes on him, but his thoughts were elsewhere. She asked him if he could bring up a chair, but he refused. Then the room was silent again. He could hear Mehrangiz straining for breath, could hear Nayer quietly crying. It was nearly completely dark before Nayer turned the light on: it was a naked, fly-spotted bulb which hung from the ceiling.

When Mehrangiz spoke again her voice was small and far away—as far as another world. "They put henna on my feet . . . it felt cool . . . I got into the carriage with Nurolsaba," she whispered. "The men wore sheepskin hats. At the well, he gave me fresh fruit. Cool . . . so cool . . . it made me cool inside . . . She tidied the place, she said she was going to the baths. She's at the baths. The niggers built the mountains. Below the mountains there was a land like paradise, waiting. And the water was so cool . . . so cool . . ."

Ali sat beside Mehrangiz's body. Nayer's shadow, with her prominent belly, was like a pyramid standing on one corner.

1962

Teaching in a Pleasant Spring
BY BAHRAM SADIQI

Let's imagine, if you will, that we're both sitting in a classroom. If this sounds absurd to you, or you're afraid of being alone, or you want the situation to be more official and closer to reality, we can, without any problem, assume that all of us are sitting in a classroom. All of us. All right. This way, we'll have a respectable classroom before the students learn about one another or become acquainted. Furthermore, we will hold this class in a clean, spacious room with adequate light and air, and simple comfortable benches. We will probably hang a large blackboard on the wall with an eraser and a supply of colored chalk at hand. Luckily, the idea of forming this class has come to us in a favorable season—in this pleasant spring—so we won't need a fan or a heater. A map, some pictures of historic sites, and portraits of a few great men complete the picture. Let's assume that our friends, acquaintances, and families will consider us lucky, congratulate us for being part of such a class, and foresee or wish a bright future for us. . . .

True, we are grateful to them, but at this point we are still where we were when we began: we're still imagining. And yet, gradually the situation becomes serious for us. All of us—it is not clear who we are and where we come from—see one another in the respectable, well-equipped classroom, sitting on simple, comfortable benches, our notebooks and pencils before us. We observe the rules of conduct and conditions conducive to learning. We look at one another carefully, hoping to become acquainted and to prepare the way for future friendships. But the basic problem is that there is no sign of any teacher yet. . . .

It's a quarter of an hour since the bell rang and we all rushed to class. But, there is no sign of a teacher or of the principal yet. Moreover, there is no roll book around, and no one has been appointed to act as monitor. . . .

Yes, obviously the blackboard is clean and unused. But outside the school, some people might be engaged in fanciful and ludicrously far-fetched thoughts, thinking, for example, that this class is symbolic of a riddle or a mysterious philosophical concept, and its students are representatives of various human types and their different beliefs and ways of life. What nonsense! You yourselves are witness that we conjured up this class and we imagined its benches and maps were such and such, and we pretended, too, that none of us knew the others, and we are also pretending that the teacher hasn't arrived yet and time is passing. All of this is a game, a simple diversion, designed for our leisure time, and, as you know, when things are based on assumption, anything can be said and done without any definite purpose in mind. You, too, of course, can pretend that the idea of this class is nothing but the wild dream of a mad man, or of mad men, who enjoy kidding people. However, if this is what you think, you can and you must keep away from our school and refrain from peeking through the window and disturbing us. Now, go and mind your own affairs.

In the front row, you see a very beautiful girl with blue eyes and blond hair. Apparently she knows that her entrancing beauty owes much to her eyes, for she constantly turns back and glances at the others. The beauty of her small nose and sensual lips, so dissimilar to the reality and the ugliness around us, has captured all the students, including the few females. For a little while the students imagine that this is not a classroom, nor are they indoors. Rather, it is night, the moon is shining, the angels have come to rest on the soft, green grass, and the mysterious girl is dancing in a long white dress, and if she is not dancing she seems to be about to dance. . . .

Shall we let her continue her dance? The old, the young, and the females, who have come to this class of their own will, can grant or refuse such a permission. But it is in their interest to stand up now, because footsteps can be heard, the door is opened, and apparently someone wants to enter the room.

"Thank you. Please be seated."

Silence . . . silence. The teacher paces back and forth, his head bent down. None of the students can see him clearly, not even those in the front rows. What a tragedy! They can't distinguish the different parts of his body or his face. Please be so kind as not to assume that I am lying when I say that they could see only a hazy, formless outline moving before their eyes, and they could hear a voice.... Yes, they can only hear his voice. This time, be so kind as to imagine that his voice is loud and quite clear.

The teacher suddenly stops pacing. (The students think so because they cannot hear his footsteps any more.)

"Before I take attendance, I'd like to know what you'd like to read today, what you'd like me to discuss, etc. Please raise your hands and get permission before you speak.

"May I?" a gruff voice is heard from the back of the room.

The teacher looks in the direction of the voice but, strangely enough, he too can't see anyone clearly. Dark, indistinct masses of similar size and shape have lined up side by side before his eyes. He cannot tell them apart.

"Please," the teacher says.

"Would you explain why you were late?"

In the large classroom between the teacher and the sixty to seventy students only words are exchanged. The students see one another. The teacher sees himself. But teacher and student can't see each other. Neither knows who the other is and what he looks like. The students grow impatient. They look at each other with worried and questioning eyes. 'Why can't we see the teacher clearly?' they wonder. 'Is something wrong with our eyes? Is the situation the principal's fault?' The teacher wonders whether high blood pressure, mental disorder, or some other ailment has caused him not to see his students and made him assume that they were mysterious, formless shadows.

"Why was I late? Oh yes. I'm very sorry. The principal's invitation was very vague. I spent some time thinking about it. The creation of this class in such haste, with unfamiliar students and without any specific purpose, was very strange and very interesting."

The gruff voice answers in the back of the room. The students turn their faces to this classmate, who has become their spokesman, perhaps because they can see him clearly. But the beautiful girl in the front row prefers not to turn back anymore, because her neck muscles have grown sore. She looks at the blackboard.

"But, Sir, please consider the fact that we all agreed to form this class in order to increase our knowledge and possibly to make new friends. We have even agreed to ask the principal to choose a capable teacher. We do not, therefore, see the need for so much thinking and deliberation."

"Oh, yes. I see. I fully understand. But I needed more time before I could muster enough energy to imagine that one can accept such an invitation from the principal and teach a class such as yours. This, perhaps, caused me to be late."

The teacher opens his roll book and calls. "Mr. . . . Miss. . . ." What difference does it make to him whether he calls out the names or not? He can't see any of the students clearly enough to be able to tell them apart. He closes the book.

Suddenly the beautiful girl rises. (Has everything become ugly and worthless to her?) She glances at her watch, quietly excuses herself to the two students sitting next to her, and walks to the door. 'I'm sure he's going to lecture for an hour.' she muses. 'I would've stayed, if he hadn't been late. But now I can't keep *him* waiting any more....'

Him.... It seems as if emotions have come into play. The girl walks past the benches. 'It's true the teacher can see me leave without permission,' she thinks. 'But I don't think I'm doing something wrong. According to the rules, students are free to attend classes or not.' Her blue eyes bid the class good-bye.

"Well ladies and gentlemen," the teacher begins. "You haven't yet told me what you would like us to discuss today."

There is a commotion. Many of the students glance at their watches and quietly follow the blue-eyed girl out. Has the magic of her eyes entranced them, or have the class and the teacher become worthless in their eyes too? They leave while I can neither imagine nor guess where they will go. You had better follow them yourselves, instead of peeking through the classroom windows stealthily. Who knows, you might pick up the blue-eyed girl or succeed in making friends with the truant students and find out why they ran away.

"All right," the teacher begins. "I see that you can't reach a decision. I must begin, although this is our first meeting and I'm ignorant of the actual level of your knowledge and the degree of the similarity of your ideas. You would agree that the basis of success in each subject. . . ."

One by one the students rise and leave the room. The teacher sees nothing except shadows changing place and leaving the dim disorderly space in front of him empty. But the students look at one another apologetically, as if excusing themselves for behaving so rudely and promising to be more industrious and determined next time. Some even suggest that they visit the principal and ask for another teacher. Others say that they had better see an eye doctor or a specialist in nervous and mental disorders. Each expresses his views with enthusiasm, and they all consider themselves lucky to have found an opportunity to get acquainted. Those who are more realistic assure their new friends that it is foolish and useless to visit a doctor because there is neither a class nor a teacher to be seen. The eyes, the minds, and the nerves are sound.

For didn't we imagine all these things? But those who are eager to get results insist that they ought to go to the principal and demand a more regular program and a punctual teacher. After that they leave—those who have become friends, together; and the rest individually, following, they think, the route taken by the blond, blue-eyed girl. The few old, worn-out women who were in the class start for home in order to attend to their cooking and cleaning and, if possible, rest a bit.

In the classroom, the teacher paces back and forth,

speaking clearly and firmly. ". . . Even when we connect the current, the light could remain off, because—it's very simple—because quite possibly there may be no electricity. That's why you are alerted to be always aware of the possibility of a black-out. But if the light is on, one must naturally compute the amount of electricity it uses and that can be done very simply, through formulae that you know better than I do. You know them by heart. After the electricity used is computed, we must pay for it. . . . You see, this is the basic problem: money. If it is not paid every month, they will disconnect your electricity. However, disconnecting is as absurd as connecting, because the light could stay on after the current is disconnected. Yes, this sometimes happens, when there's a short somewhere. All right, in that case, do you still have to compute the electricity used? Yes, you must, always. Now, a question comes up: what happens if we put both hands on a bare wire conducting a strong current? In my opinion something splendid will happen. This is the ideal situation, for it is in this case that no matter how much electricity is used, no matter how many times it is computed and with which formulae, they won't be able to collect a penny from you. You see, money isn't always necessary. . . . But let's not burden ourselves. I'll stop boring you. Let's assume, if you will, that the bell is ringing. . . ."

The bell was so sudden and loud that it startled the teacher and the scales fell from his eyes. Everything changed. Now he could see clearly. There was no one in the room, except for an old man dozing in the last row. The old man had experienced the same change. He watched the teacher, who was approaching him, with terror and astonishment. He could see the teacher very well—a young, strong man, his nose and ears cut off, his disorderly hair surrounding his head and neck. His large and crooked upper teeth protruded from his mouth. His small, gleaming eyes were cold and penetrating. The old man's heart was pierced with his sharp look. He trembled.

"Did everybody leave? I am so sorry. Did you find the lecture at all useful?" the teacher asked. He regarded his only student: a filthy, bearded old man, with rheumy eyes, false teeth, shabby clothes, and a shameless countenance.

"Why . . . why you . . .? Why are you . . . like this?" the old man stammered.

"Don't cross examine me. You had better answer my question."

Amazement and disgust conquered fear in the old man. "No, not a word of it was of any use," he said. The teacher stared at him. "I wish I'd left, too," the old man added. "After all these years, I imagined that I was finally attending this class. I had such high hopes. But I can see that the principal is making fun of us."

The teacher slapped him in the face. "So much for being rude! I will also tell the principal," he said, taking a small notebook from his pocket. "Give me your name."

The old man was crying from pain. One side of his face was red and his nose was bleeding. "Forgive me please! Forgive me. I was wrong," he pleaded.

"Impossible. I must have your name. I will certainly fail you this term, and if you're inattentive and rude again, I'll fail you for the whole year!"

The old man rose and began to cry again. "Please, Sir, I have a wife, children, grandchildren, great-grandchildren. God knows I didn't mean to be rude. I promise I'll always be on time and prepare my lessons. The lecture was very useful."

"After I slapped you? Did pain remind you that it was useful?"

"But, Sir, can't you see that they have all left? I'm the only one who had respect for you. . . ."

"You're very kind indeed! You stayed, so you could sit there and doze off. What good would it have done you to leave?"

"Didn't you see how they kept staring at the blue-eyed girl? They wanted to eat her up with their eyes. . . ."

"Did they leave because of her?"

"More or less. Don't let them know where you heard this. But believe me, I kept my eyes away the entire time."

"Are you trying to impress me with your good conduct? Good behavior and discipline won't make up for your academic subjects. There's no telling what you would've done if you were young."

"I am willing to take what's coming to me."

"So is everybody, especially for having run away from a class you registered for on your own. What for? What did they come here for? Didn't they say they wanted to increase their knowledge and become greater and greater men?"

"But you. . . . How can I say it, so you won't laugh? No, this is absurd. You won't believe me. . . ."

"What about me? Speak! Did they make fun of me?"

"They couldn't see you."

"So you were lying. They didn't run away out of fear."

"Whatever it was, I'm too old to understand. I'm senile."

"Or did they think I'd nothing else to do? Had they come for girl-watching? Did you say she was very beautiful?"

"Who? The girl with blue eyes?"

"Blue eyes?"

"Why, didn't you see her? She was in the front row. Strange!"

"You fool! Keep in mind to whom you're speaking. Did you expect me to stare at her too?"

"In any case, your conduct is admirable. She was very beautiful, Sir."

"Too bad . . . too bad that she. . . . Old man, don't misunderstand me. Do you see what I mean? I regret that I've been forced to punish a student on the first day. That's what I meant. I wasn't talking about seeing or not seeing her."

"So you won't forgive me?"

"No. This will be a lesson to the rest. They'll all get poor marks, even the. . . . Yes. They had no reason to run away."

The teacher wrote down the old man's name and gave him an F. The old man collapsed on the bench, put his head on his book, and continued crying. Fear and wonder were reawakened in his heart.

The bell rang. The old man began to plead. "Couldn't you forgive me this time? I have a wife, children, grandchildren, great-grandchildren. . . . I assure you nothing will happen if you do."

The teacher left the class.

"Where are you going with that hideous face? You

wretched fool. Go and do your worst," the old man shouted after him.

* * * * * * * *

We do not know what became of the beautiful girl and the rest of the students, or what grades they received. But since we have agreed to pretend, there is no reason why we could not pretend that the teacher met the principal in the corridor, exchanged pleasantries with him, complained about his new students, and went to his next class, as scheduled.

1963

The Snow, the Dogs, the Crows

JAMAL MIRSADIQI

The snow began again this morning, small flakes like white butterflies, silent and mysterious, settling on the roofs, the branches, and the ground. The men regularly shovel the snow from their roofs. But the roof of the corner room is still covered, unlike the days when Agha Mahmud would rush to the roof and shovel the snow even as it still fell. There it will last until it melts in the sun and drips down the drain pipe, making sad music.

Agha Mahmud would set the ladder against the wall and run up the rungs as if he were climbing stairs. Turan Khanom would watch him anxiously at the foot of the ladder. "Be careful not to catch cold. Mahmud, dear. It's very cold."

They lived in our house. Whenever I went to their room, which was at the opposite corner of the courtyard, Agha Mahmud would lift me over his head, throw me up and catch me. "Here's my boy! My own handsome boy!" he would say. He drove a bus. Sometimes, when he went on long trips, he wouldn't come home for a few nights. Then Turan Khanom would take me to their room, make me sit on her knees, and tell me stories. Now their room is used as a storage place for all kinds of odds and ends, large sacks of charcoal, and a few chairs and tables which broke in my brother's wedding.

On my brother's wedding night, I was sitting with Turan

Khanom at the window, watching the men who were decorating the courtyard. It had been three or four months since news had arrived that Agha Mahmud would never come back from his trip. Turan Khanom had worn black since, but on my brother's wedding day mother had forced her to take off her mourning dress. She looked pretty as a bride in her pink dress. I was sitting next to her, and she was cracking roasted watermelon seeds and putting the kernels in my mouth. When she had learned that Agha Mahmud would not return from his trip, she had asked mother to let me sleep in her room. She would take me in her arms at night and go to sleep. When she came home from the factory in the evening she would take me to her room and give me fruits and nuts. She had been working at the factory since she started to wear black. My father, Hadj Agha, had tried to stop her but she had continued working. She would get up early in the morning and light up our samovar, but leave without having tea herself.

Turan Khanom was watching the men in the courtyard as she cracked watermelon seeds for me. She was watching them like a dancer watching a full glass on her forehead. Then she rose and closed the window. "It's very cold," she said. But it wasn't that cold.

"Turi, are you cold?" I asked.

She took my head in her hands, playing with my hair. "No, dear, I'm not cold," she said.

I remembered that the night before, when she had played with my hair, she was going to tell me a story. "You were going to tell me a story last night," I said.

"All right. Let's move next to the lamp and I'll tell you a story."

We sat next to the gasoline lantern, which made a noise like a big bird. Inside the glass, the incandescent filament glowed like a golden egg. "It's so cold," Turan Khanom said again, moving closer to the lamp. But she didn't seem to be talking to me.

"Why don't you start? Tell me a story," I said. She held her hand over the lamp and began. Her eyes were fixed on the lamp. Her eyes spoke to the lamp, while her lips spoke to me, her words flowing slow and continuous, threaded together like beads. Her voice was quiet and mournful like an engine going uphill. "This time, when the prince was on a journey, he fell out of his car and down off a cliff. The prince fell off a cliff and died."

"He fell off a cliff? How?" I asked.

"His car skidded toward the cliff. . . . The prince fell off the cliff and died."

"Why did his car skid toward the cliff? Why did the prince die?"

"Why did he die?" She looked at me and fell silent. Her hands were touching the lamp, her eyes fixed on it. She looked like the Turan Khanom who would wrap her *chador* around her and watch Agha Mahmud anxiously from the foot of the ladder, saying: "Mahmud, dear, it's cold. Be careful not to catch cold."

Then, as she looked at the lamp, her irises disappeared under her eyelids. The white eyeballs looked like sparrow eggs. Then tears swelled in her eyes and rolled down her cheeks. I held her tightly. "Turi, dear, don't cry. Don't cry!" I pleaded.

"I'm not crying, dear. I'm not crying." She wiped her face with her hands.

Then Father, Hadj Agha, came into the room without any warning. Turan Khanom pulled her *chador* over her head and lowered her eyes, as if staring at something hanging from her forehead. I thought she was going to cry again and held her tightly. Father came to us smiling. "How nice Turan Khanom. I'm so glad you stopped wearing your mourning dress. God bless you, you're still young. Just look at you, you're skin and bones. And when I tell you to stay home like a lady instead of working at the factory like a nobody, you don't listen."

Turan Khanom turned pale. She bent her head. My hands, held in hers, suddenly turned cold, as if I had dipped them in ice water. I looked at her. Her eyes were shut, and her hands, which held my fingers, beat like the heart of a sparrow. I moved closer to her. Her body was cold. Hadj Agha pulled out a bill from his pocket. "Come, Ja'far, run to the store, get two packs of cigarettes. Hurry up," he said. I rose to go. Turan Khanom was holding my hands tightly. She was staring at the wall, her back to the lamp.

Turan Khanom went to the factory the next day. She went to the factory eight more days. Then she stopped and stayed home with us. Mother was very pleased because she could now leave the house in Turan Khanom's hands and go anywhere she wanted without having to worry about anything. When she came back at noon or in the evening, everything was shipshape. Turan Khanom had cooked the meal, washed the dishes, and swept and dusted the house. That was why mother was so fond of her and spoke highly of her competence and ability. Sometimes mother would take little Ahmad along to Shemiran and stay with my elder brother for two or three weeks without a care. Or, she would pack and go to Taleghan to visit my aunt, leaving the household in Turan Khanom's charge. Then Turan Khanom, Hadj Agha, and I would be alone in the house.

One afternoon when I came home from school Turan Khanom was in the courtyard, naked under her *chador*, ready to jump into the pool. Mother had been away for a few days, visiting Aunt Esmat.

"Go inside, dear. I'll just take a dip. I'll be with you in no time," Turan Khanom said to me.

"Me too, Turi dear. I want to take a dip, too." I said, undressing happily. Turan Khanom laughed. She threw her *chador* over the hedge. She was completely naked, like mother in the bath. Her skin was white as milk. Her body shone like new china; it glittered, mirroring the afternoon sun. 'If I toss a stone at her, she'll crack like glass and fall to pieces,' I thought. She saw me staring at her and laughed. "Shame on you, boy! Don't look at me like that. Shame!" she said. Then she took my head in her hands, bent over and kissed my eyes, laughing. I looked at her belly, which was round as a ball. Ahmad's belly swelled like that after lunch. I touched her belly. It was hard like stone. "You glutton! You've

65

eaten so much your belly has swollen up," I said.

"Do you want me to make you a little sister?" she asked.

"Yes, dear Turi, make me a little sister. I don't have a sister."

Then she embraced me and, laughing, pulled me with her into the pool. I held onto her, my arms around her neck, my head against her breasts. "Let me out! I don't want to go in. Let me out!" I pleaded.

"You naughty boy! Remember the way you were staring at me?" she said, her face wrinkled with laughter.

I pressed against her, panting. "I want to get out. I wasn't looking at you," I said.

She dipped me into the water a few times. The water was ice cold. I was about to cry. Then she put me out. "Run, dear. Wrap yourself in my *chador* and stand in the sun, so you won't catch cold."

I wrapped the *chador* around myself and went to the pool again. She was sitting in the water like a duck, her legs moving from side to side. She would fill her mouth with water and blow it into the pool. "Aaaaah, Aaaaah God! It feels so good. Aaaaah! It feels so good."

"I want to go in. I want to go into the pool," I said, shivering.

*   *   *   *   *   *   *   *   *   *   *

It wasn't morning yet when mother called me. I didn't want to leave my bed. "I want to sleep. I want to sleep some more," I said.

"Don't you want to be our man? Get up, then!"

I was about eight or nine but considered myself a grown man. I got up, rubbing my eyes. "Do you want to be our man, when we go to Shabdol'azim tomorrow morning?" mother had asked the night before. Our house was close to the railroad station. My parents would usually go to Shabdol'azim early in the morning, visit the shrine, and return home soon after.

"I want to be your man. I'll take you to Sabdol'azim," I'd said.

"Then you'll have to get up right away when I call you in the morning," mother had said.

I sat on the mattress, looking for an excuse to go back to bed. I was still sleepy. "Don't you want to be our man? Come on, get up," mother said.

"If we aren't going, I'll go back to sleep," I said.

Then my younger brother, Ahmad, opened his eyes and stared at us, his eyes full of sleep. Mother tried to put him back to bed, but he got up. "I want to go, too. I want to go, too," he said.

"Go to sleep, you wretch. We aren't going anywhere," mother said.

"I want to go, too," Ahmad said, louder.

"We're going to the bath. Go to sleep, and I'll give you a nickel."

"I want to go to the bath, too. I don't want to sleep," Ahmad said, beginning to cry.

"We'll go to the doctor's after that. He'll give you a shot if you come."

"I want to go, too," Ahmad cried louder.

"Be quiet, you wretch. I hope you die! You're going to wake him up."

Hadj Agha was soundly asleep, snoring. We dressed, put on our overcoats, and went to the door. In his thick overcoat, Ahmad looked like a big ball.

Naneh Sakineh was waiting for us at the door. The street was covered with snow. Naneh Sakineh was a thin, sickly old woman. She often washed our clothes on Friday nights. The neighborhood women would gather in our home and consult her on matters of religion. She was short, and she bent double when she walked, swinging both arms simultaneously, and waddling as she watched the ground before her, as if afraid of falling. Since the time Turan Khanom had gone away on a journey, she had been coming to our house to help my mother.

One afternoon, when I went home from school, Turan Khanom's room was empty. I was very sad. I didn't go to school the next day; I had a fever. They told me Turan Khanom had gone on a trip and would come back soon. But she never came back to our house. There was a lot of fighting and talk about divorce, and no one paid any attention to me. My mother quarrelled with Hadj Agha all day long. Only Naneh Sakineh looked after me and told me stories, but her stories weren't like Turan Khanom's; they were lifeless.

One morning Hadj Agha and my mother left together. When they returned at noon, mother looked very happy. "He divorced her," she told Naneh Sakineh, who had opened the door. "Poor woman! Poor woman!" Naneh Sakineh said when mother had gone to her room. Hadj Agha was perspiring and his eyes were very red. He went straight to the guest room, shut the door behind him, and didn't come out for a few days. Inside, he read the Koran and wept. From that day on, mother started to go out again. She would take little Ahmad and go to visit Aunt Esmat or my elder brother and stay for two or three weeks. Then Naneh Sakineh would see to everything.

With her black *chador* wrapped around her, Naneh Sakineh looked like a big crow as she walked through the snow. It had been snowing on and off for two days, as if someone in the sky was unravelling the skeins of snow one after the other, then taking a rest, then starting again. "Why did you bring him along?" Naneh Sakineh grumbled, pointing at Ahmad. "He'll catch cold and get you into trouble. Anyhow, it wouldn't do him any good to see. . . ."

"I couldn't help it. The miserable wretch woke up and began to cry. I was afraid Hadji would wake up."

"If Hadji wakes up and finds all of us missing, won't he get suspicious?

"It's Friday. He'll sleep till noon."

The streets were empty. Soft white snow carpeted the ground. Under my shoes, the snow crackled like dry twigs catching fire. The field on the other side of the street was dotted with clusters of crows. They pecked at the snow, looking happy. "This is the crows' snow," mother said. "Are you sure she has had the you-know-what? she asked Naneh Sakineh.

"She's had what?" Ahmad asked.

"None of your business," I said.

"Yes. Last night Bagum came over and told me," Naneh Sakineh said.

"Did she say anything else?" mother asked.

"She said she'll wait behind the door until we knock. Then she'll let us in," Naneh Sakineh said.

"Who'll wait behind the door?" Ahmad asked.

"None of your business," I said.

"Did you ask what it was?" mother asked.

"The same thing Hadj Agha wanted. A girl," Naneh Sakineh said.

"I hope he'll rot in his grave. The way he's made me suffer!" mother said.

"Shhhhh! Shhhhh! Naneh Sakineh said, as if she was saying a prayer.

"Hurry up! It's getting light," mother said.

"It's so cold," Naneh Sakineh said, bending forward as she walked.

"I'm not cold," Ahmad said.

"You're shivering," I said.

"No, I'm not."

"Stop it!" mother said.

Ahmad and I went ahead, Naneh Sakineh and mother followed. The snow sank under our feet like cotton. Every few steps Ahmad would look back at his footprints and laugh happily. In his white overcoat he looked like a fat puppy jumping around. He was panting; his face and hands were red.

"Mother, Ahmad is cold," I said.

"Serves him right; no one asked him to come," mother said.

"I'm not cold. Not cold," Ahmad said.

"Do we have long to go?" mother asked.

"No. We're almost there. It's at the end of this street."

"What's at the end of this street? I won't go to the doctor's," Ahmad said.

"Aren't we going to Shabdol'azim, mother?" I asked.

"Yes, we are. But first we'll stop by at Naneh Sakineh's, so she can pick up her things."

"Why are we going to Naneh Sakineh's? I don't want to go

there. I want to go to Shabdol'azim," Ahmad said.

"Serves you right. You should've stayed home," I said.

"Hurry up, it's getting light," mother said.

"She said she'll be waiting behind the door until we knock," Naneh Sakineh said.

"Who'll be waiting for us?" Ahmad asked.

"It all has to go smoothly," mother said.

"I know. I told her to keep things quiet," Naneh Sakineh said.

"To keep what quiet?" Ahmad asked.

"None of your business." I said.

"It'll only take a minute. Then I won't have a care in the world," mother said.

"What if she doesn't give it to us?" Naneh Sakineh asked.

"Not give it to us! How can she? We'll get it by force. We decided to, didn't we?" mother said.

"Are we going to do the thing you said last night?" Naneh Sakineh asked.

"Yes. Why do you keep asking?" mother said.

"What will you tell Hadji?" Naneh Sakineh asked.

"Hadji? He'll be glad when he finds out. One less mouth to feed," mother said.

"But ma'am! But . . ." Naneh Sakineh began.

"But what?" mother said.

"It's so cold ma'am. And the dogs. . . . It's a sin."

"What sin? It's only a bastard," mother said.

"Who's only a bastard?" Ahmad asked.

"But ma'am . . . But ma'am . . ." Naneh Sakineh said.

"Stop it! Stop it!" mother shouted.

"It's so cold . . ." Naneh Sakineh bent double.

"I'm not cold," Ahmad said.

"You're shivering like a wet dog," I said.

"I'm not shivering. I'm not," he said.

"Stop it!" mother said.

At the end of the street we turned into an alley, then into more alleys, one after the other, narrow and dark. The mudbrick cottages were strung along a curved line, like beads in a rosary. Naneh Sakineh was a few steps ahead of us. I had spread out my arms and would not let Ahmad pass me. Finally, Naneh Sakineh stopped in front of a low, wide door and knocked quietly. A fat, short woman opened the door. Her eyes glittered like a cat's eyes. Her chin moved as if she were chewing something. She motioned to mother and Naneh Sakineh to go in.

"Ja'far, dear, will you keep an eye on Ahmad, so I can go in for a minute? I'll buy you a big bag for school," mother whispered in my ear.

"You won't. You're only fooling me," I said.

"I swear I will. Just keep an eye on him for a minute. Do you understand?"

"What are you going to do in there?" I asked.

"Nothing. We're just going to pick up Naneh Sakineh's things," she said. Then she said something in Ahmad's ear and he grinned.

"All right, I won't tell anyone, but you must buy it for me," he said.

They went inside. Ahmad and I sat on the doorstep of the opposite cottage. Ahmad grinned. "Mother promised to buy me a train. She said not to tell anyone," he said, smiling. I was getting bored.

"Do you want to play hide and seek?" I asked.

"How?"

"You stay on the doorstep and close your eyes. I'll go and hide."

"No, I won't. You want to leave me here and go away yourself."

"You can hide, if you want to, and I'll close my eyes. But you don't have to play if you don't want to."

"All right, I'll go and hide."

"Tiptoe away, because
Go where you may,
The wolf is hiding on the way," I said the rime, giving him time to hide.

He ran to find a place to hide. I went down the steps quietly, and followed my mother into the courtyard. A stench hit me as I went in. The courtyard was empty, large, and run-down, bordered by small rooms, some dimly lit. Mother and Naneh Sakineh had disappeared into one of these rooms. I couldn't tell which one. I was afraid to go farther. I stopped at the door and watched the rooms. Suddenly I noticed the entrance to a basement room on the other end of the courtyard. My mother, Naneh Sakineh, and behind them the old woman, came up the stairs into the courtyard, hurriedly. Naneh Sakineh's *chador*. was swelling with something she carried under it. When they were in the middle of the courtyard two white arms, like pigeon wings, thrust out from the basement, clawing at the snow on the ground. Then the head and face of a woman emerged. Her face was white, like the snow in the courtyard. Her eyes were like two dark holes in the white of her face. Her mouth was wide open, as if she wanted to say "Ahhhhhh." She clawed at the snow and pushed herself up to her breast. She raised her head and followed mother and Naneh Sakineh with her eyes. She stretched her white, thin arms toward them, as if pleading, as if expecting someone to give her something. Her mouth remained open, as if she wanted to say "Ahhhhh." Her breath smoked in the air.

For a second I thought she was Turan Khanom. But Turan Khanom hadn't been that thin. I wanted to go closer and look at the woman. Her arms were still moving, her large, white breasts had slipped out of her dress, touching the snow. Her abundant black hair was spread on the white ground. Suddenly she fell back, slid toward the basement and fell in, head first, her arms still sawing the air, her open mouth still saying "Ahhhhh," her breath visible.

* * * * * * * *

When we had gone some distance from the house, Naneh Sakineh stopped. "What're we going to do with it?" she asked, looking at the bundle under her chador.

"You keep asking. Didn't I tell you we were going to . . ." mother said. She sounded as if she had something in her mouth.

"I can't. I swear to God, I can't. The dogs . . . the crows . . ." Naneh Sakineh said, her voice like a horn.

In the field next to the road the dogs ran here and there, sniffing at the snow and chasing the crows. On the walls and on the ground, the crows were sticking their beaks into the snow and watching us with their small, black eyes. "Mother, why is this the crows' snow?" I asked.

"Are you going to do it or not?" mother asked Naneh Sakineh.

"I'm afraid, ma'am. I'm afraid," she said, her voice like a horn.

"I'm not afraid," Ahmad said.

"You're afraid of the bogeyman," I said.

"Hurry up, woman! If the sun comes up everyone will see . . ." mother said.

"I'm not afraid of the bogeyman," Ahmad said.

"I can't ma'am. I can't . . ." Naneh Sakineh said.

"Come on! Get it over with," mother shouted.

"I can't . . . I can't, ma'am. It's an evil thing."

"What can't you?" Ahmad asked.

"I can do anything. I'm a man. A big man," I said.

"So am I. I'm a man, too," Ahmad said.

"Are you! You a man!" I said.

"Are you going to?" mother asked Naneh Sakineh.

"I'm a man. I'm a man," Ahmad said.

"I won't do it, ma'am. I'm afraid," Naneh Sakineh said, her voice sharp as a whistle.

"I'm not afraid. I'm a man," Ahmad said.

"You're afraid to go to the bathroom at night. Someone has to go with you," I said.

"So are you," Ahmad said.

"Are you going to, or not? The sun is coming up," mother said.

"Ohhhhh God! Ohhhhh," Naneh Sakineh said, her trembling hands shaking her *chador*.

"Where do you want her to go, mother?" I asked.

"Damn you! Give it to me. I knew you didn't have enough guts," mother said.

Naneh Sakineh opened her *chador* and offered a white, long bundle to mother. As mother stretched her arms to take the bundle, the white cloth slipped aside, revealing two shiny black circles that moved rapidly. Mother quickly hid the bundle under her *chador*. "Wait here till I come back," she said.

"Where are you going? I want to go, too," I said.

"Me too. I'll cry if you don't take me," Ahmad said.

"I won't be a minute. Wait here. I won't buy you anything, if you don't," mother said.

*   *   *   *   *   *   *   *

It had grown light, but the streets were still empty. The dogs ran around in the snow and from the top of the walls the crows alighted on the ground. The dogs sniffed at the snow. The crows pecked at the snow, as if snatching away bits of earth's flesh. Two dogs followed Mother, sniffing the snow. The sky was like a bowl of blood.

When mother came back, it became cloudy again and snow began to fall. We walked on in silence. Mother was staring at the snow, her head bent down. "It's so cold," she said.

"I'm not cold," Ahmad said. Naneh Sakineh was carrying him on her back.

"You're shivering like a wet dog," I said.

"No I'm not. You're shivering like a billow," he said.

"Say, 'you're shivering like a *willow*,'" I said.

"You're shivering. You're shivering," Ahmad said.

"I'm not shivering. I'm not cold at all," I said.

Mother stared at the snow.

"It's so cold," she said. She sounded like a horn.

Then we all went to visit the shrine at Shabdol'azim.

1963

Gowhartaj's Father

BY MAHMUD KIYANUSH

The slim girl pulled down her white, dotted *chador* to the middle of her forehead, unwilling to hide her corn-silk blond tresses, but fearful to leave them exposed, for she had heard the sound of gruff coughing from the courtyard.

"It's father," she said softly.

Her large hazel eyes shone with joy, excitement, restlessness; she blushed to the ears and her oval face grew more innocent and more beautiful. In her eyes and movement there was both love and hope, both anxiety and sadness. She took two hesitant steps to the door of the room.

"Mother, what are we going to do? Are we going to tell him?" she asked, lowering her voice.

The woman was sitting under the mantlepiece, near the samovar. She was thin and her face was wrinkled. She moved a little, her voice calm yet authoritative and bearing a touch of reproach.

"I said I was going to tell him. Stop nagging."

"If they find out . . ." the girl began, worried.

She did not finish. The short, old man entered the room, coughing.

"A girl ought to be modest," the woman said under her breath, as the man continued coughing. "Good heavens! What's the world coming to!"

The old man took a dirty handkerchief out of his tunic

pocket and wiped his mouth.

"What? What did you say?" he asked in a low, authoritative voice.

The woman put the tea-glass under the samovar, filling it with the bubbling hot water.

"Nothing. Sit down and drink some *ghandagh**" she said with feigned indifference. "It will soothe your chest."

The old man sat on the small floor mattress and leaned against the beddings which were wrapped in large bedspreads. He coughed again. The woman put the tea-glass and the sugar before him.

"Have you heard that Mashdi Gholam's son has become a *Karbalayi*?"** she asked in a mocking tone as the old man continued coughing. "Yesterday their house was mobbed. The whole town had come to get dates, prayer-stones and beads. They had slaughtered a sheep. What pomp and circumstance! May God send them luck! The year we came to this neighborhood, Mashdi Gholam wore an old shoe on one foot and a torn slipper on the other! The way they rob people!"

The old man dropped a few sugar cubes into the tea-glass, and assumed an air of importance, paying no attention to his wife.

"Why are you standing there like a lamp post?" he said to the girl. "Either sit down, or go do something."

The woman felt a smile coming to her lips, but hid it before it spread to her face.

"He's right. Go get your embroidery and sit down here and finish it. What's become of the kind of diligence my generation had? I'd cut a garment in the morning and finish sewing it before sundown."

The girl tried to catch her mother's eyes. Succeeding, she winked at her knowingly and left the room. The old man took a sip from the *ghandagh* and put the glass down.

"Smells like dishwater," he said with a frown.

---

*Sweetened hot water.
**Title given to a person who has performed the pilgrimage to Karbala.

"Come! Come! Dishwater! What an idea," the woman cut him short. "Are you trying to find something to complain about? I rinsed the glass twice myself, and Gowhar washed the samovar clean as a whistle."

The old man made no answer. He smoothed his short, gray beard. His sad eyes lighted with pride. He shook his head slowly, musing.

"At the time I set out on the pilgrimage to Karbala, if you so much as heard the word "travel" your hair would stand on end. Blood-thirsty highwaymen plundered caravans, terrifying the travellers. They robbed, decapitated, and cut people open. The journey took months. We went day and night, in heat and cold. It was a struggle to get from one village to the next. That was pilgrimage for you! When you saw the dome and the shrine of Hosein you couldn't help weeping for joy."

The woman drank up her tea out of the saucer, then blew at the burning charcoal in the samovar.

"Today, they get to Karbala fast and easy," she said. "And they don't have to spend a fortune. They act like they're vacationing rather than performing a pilgrimage!"

"On my first pilgrimage two men and one woman in our caravan died," the old man continued, as if he had not heard the woman. "We never found out what they died of."

"The pilgrim needs a pure heart and lawfully earned money," said the woman.

Reluctantly, but as if trying to hide his reluctance from the woman, the man took another sip from his glass. He wiped his tear-filled eyes.

"When the Imam calls you, even if you are in your death bed facing *Mecca*, you'll get up and go," he said with feeling.

The girl, excited as before but now also worried, entered the room, squeezing a big, white bundle against her chest. She sat close to her mother, sheltered from her father's eyes. She opened the bundle in her lap and searched through it with nervous fingers until she found the unfinished embroidery and pretended to get busy. But after a few moments she nudged her mother impatiently.

Did you tell him? she questioned with her eyes. Tell him at once, her eyes ordered.

"When it gets close to their arrival," the woman said to the girl, "straighten yourself up and go sit in the parlor. Then bring the tea."

"Fine," the girl said, nudging her mother again, not realizing what she planned to do. But the old man's curiosity was aroused. He turned to the woman, fixed his eyes on her, yet tried to hide his curiosity. The woman assumed an air of importance.

"In half an hour, they're coming to speak about Gowhar," she explained.

The old man pretended that he knew nothing about the matter.

"Who's coming?" he asked in an authoritative voice.

"I told you last night."

The old man said nothing. Uneasy and a bit annoyed, the woman continued.

"Didn't I tell you Manuchehr Khan's mother, Mrs. Razavi, would be coming over to speak about Gowhar? She sent word the day before yesterday that she'd be coming over today to see Gowhar and to speak to us, maybe with her son . . ." She stopped herself and pushed the girl away.

"Get up, girl. Go to the other room," she said nervously. "What's the sense of sitting here and listening to us? By heaven, today's girls are so immodest! In my day, if someone so much as mentioned the word "suitor" we would die of shame. Girls hid their faces from the sun and the moon, let alone people."

The girl hurriedly collected the bundle and left the room. For a while only the boiling samovar could be heard. Finally, the old man resigned himself to the worst.

"Why do they want to talk to me?" he ventured to say. "You, the girl, and the suitor can do what you want."

"For heaven's sake! Aren't you the girl's father? At the ceremonies if you don't give your consent the priest won't marry them. And you say we can do what we want?"

The old man tried hard and finally managed a frown.

"You never worried about having my consent before."

"Good heavens! Are you going to start complaining again? What do you want to do with the girl? Do you want her to become an old maid? Her breasts have grown like two watermelons. Soon enough no one will marry her at all."

The man kept his frown, but tempered it with resignation. "Woman! How can you give your daughter to someone you know nothing about? These days you can't even trust your own eyes. Besides, they are too high class for us."

"It's true I don't know them," the woman said with convincing assurance. "But you should've heard Fatemeh, the bath-attendant, rave about them. She's known the family for many years. She washes their clothes, works for them, knows everything about them. She says such good things about Manuchehr Khan, and what a gentleman he is."

"Did you say he is a teacher?" the old man asked.

"High school teacher. He's a perfect gentleman — modest, decent, intelligent. His little finger is worth a hundred like Gowhar's cousins."

The man jerked suddenly. "So now my nephews aren't good enough for you? You'd sell them for an effeminate fop?" he said hotly.

The woman could no longer contain her anger. With a fierce, abrupt movement she removed the teapot from the samovar and placed it under its tap, too angry to turn the tap on, her eyes blazing with hatred and scorn. Her wrinkled face contracted as if she had sipped vinegar.

"If you are planning to disgrace us, say so. You're killing the children and me. Do you want to ruin them all? Your poor sons work their asses off but can't make ends meet. You gave your elder daughter to that good-for-nothing idler. When I see her kids my heart breaks. Poor girl, she hasn't seen a happy day in her life. She hadn't been married for two days when that bitch, his other wife, beat her up for no reason, pulled out her hair in handfuls, and on top of that complained to her husband."

The old man's temper rose. He shut the door, and sat before her, mad as a wounded tiger. He coughed a few times, then put his forefinger to his lower lip.

"Did *I* tell Moluk to marry that stupid fool?" he asked. "Or was it you who asked him to stay for lunch or supper every time he came over, buttered him up and sang his praises to me day and night? Every evening I came home he was sitting there surrounded by the whole lot of you, tittering and flirting."

As if she was going to attack him, she stretched up, bent forward, made a fist and put it at her lower lip: the image of wonder, denial, and hatred.

"I can't believe it! You talk like he was a stranger. Isn't he your own nephew? Wasn't it you who said, 'Let's give Moluk to Hasan and get rid of her?' The liar will die dumb. A lot of good your pilgrimage has done you!"

The man writhed with anger. He looked as if he was going to hit her on the head with his fist and break every bone in her body.

"Keep your trap shut," he said commandingly and with finality. "Don't force me into an ugly mood or you'll live to regret it till the day you die."

The woman was taken aback. She remained silent and seemed to be deeply in thought, but hatred cried out of her face. She trembled, gnashing her teeth.

The old man's dry, rough coughs were followed by a few forced ones. His face assumed a sickly, weak look. His anger subsided. Her hands trembling, the woman filled the teapot with hot water and set it on the samovar. Then she took the old man's tea-glass, rinsed it with water from the samovar, and poured him another glass of hot water. She placed the glass before him, trying to hide the kindness she felt for him.

"Well, stop getting excited and let's keep calm," she said. "I know whatever I do, I'm in the wrong. It's my luck. I've spent thirty-five years of my life with you and this is what I get from you. What can I expect from a stranger?"

The old man remained silent, trying to regain his calm. His eyes were fixed at a point in the corner of the room without seeing anything. His face mirrored the confused thoughts that crowded his head, thoughts he was going to keep private.

"Well, anyhow, the boy's mother is coming to see Gowhar," the woman said in a mild yet anxious tone. "They want to speak to you. Fortune only knocks once. Of all your children, give her a chance for happiness. She has some schooling;

she won't consent to marrying a plain worker."

She realized that she had gone too far and hastily modified her last statement.

"Today's girl knows nothing about life," she said. "All she sees in a man is his suit and tie. She wants a husband who works in an office. She doesn't care if he can make ends meet. She prides herself that her husband works in an office. What can you do? Do in Rome as the Romans do."

There was no conviction in her voice. She was bribing the old man to bring him round. The old man coughed. He took a reluctant sip from the *ghandagh* and was about to speak when the woman cut him short.

"As they say, tie the donkey where the owner wants. The girl is dying to marry him. I didn't let you notice, but you've no idea how she's been nagging and insisting for the past few days that she wants no one but him. I think he also has seen Gowhar somewhere — they live nearby — and she's caught his eye. Well, the rest is up to you. They'll be here. Talk to them. See what's on their minds. Ask about him and his job. Then do what you please."

There was a long silence.

"Well, when are they coming?" the old man finally asked.

"I told you. Any minute now."

She sounded as if she wanted to continue but could not, or did not think it wise to do so. The man rose to his feet weakly, walking like a sick man, his hand on his waist, seeking her sympathy and affection. He sat down again on the floor-mattress, leaning against the beddings. Silence built a wall between them, each inwardly debating, planning, choosing the right words, the woman more intently than the man.

"What can I possibly say to them? I don't even know them." The old man said at last.

"Well, neither do I. You're a lamb with everybody, but a lion with me. Just say something. Make conversation. If the boy comes, fine. If not, you can find out through the mother what they're like, to make sure they're all right. Only . . . Only . . ." she did not finish and remained quiet and anxious.

"Only what? What were you going to say?" asked the old man.

"Nothing."

"Say what's on your mind. Don't beat about the bush."

"I'm afraid you'll take offense and lose your temper again."

The old man was hurt, but he said nothing.

"You see, Gowhar has been nagging . . ." the woman began.

"Nagging about what? What does she want?" asked the old man with indifference.

"You see, she doesn't want them to find out that . . ." she stopped, hesitant and unsure.

The old man was curious, and his curiosity was changing into irritation. The woman suddenly opened her heart.

"What I mean is, don't say things that will disgrace us. Watch your tongue. We're old fashioned. We don't know what the modern folk like, so we're better off if we keep our mouths shut, or at least if we think twice before saying something."

"I don't understand," said the old man angrily. "First you say they're coming over to speak to me. Then you say I'm better off if I keep my mouth shut. The modern folks! Why are *you* saying these things? Have you too become westernized? What do you want me to do, sit politely before a penniless fop and his mother, keep my mouth shut, awaiting the pleasure of modern folks?"

The woman was about to say something to pacify him.

"The hell with anyone who is ashamed of me," he shouted, forcing her into silence. "Anyone, even you, who are my wife."

She leaned close to him and placed her hand on his knees.

"What do you mean ashamed?" she said quietly. "What are you talking about? All I'm saying is tie the donkey where the owner wants. Just this once control yourself and do as the poor thing wants."

"What the hell do you want me to do?" shouted the man impatiently. "Eat rat-poison? Hang myself? Take a needle and sew up my mouth?"

The woman pretended to sympathize, her voice sad and remorseful.

"What an age! Your own children, who've sucked the sap of your life, can't stand you." She slowly moved her head from side to side as she talked. "They'd rather you disappeared from the face of the earth." Sensing that she had gone too far, she hastily changed the subject.

"You see Fatemeh, the bath attendant, has told them some things on her own. They asked her what you did for a living and she told her you were a merchant in the bazaar. How dishonest people are!"

The old man's face froze with hatred and astonishment. He tried to ignore the pain her words had caused him and to salvage the remainder of his self-respect.

"The hell with what she said. You can't keep people from talking. Anyway, does a merchant put his business on his daughter's back to take to her husband as a dowry?"

"No. No. Actually, the rich are less generous than we are. They send off their daughters with no more than the dress on their backs. And the husband is happy he's married the daughter of so-and-so, the merchant."

The old man agreed. "Like they say, they don't care if their bellies are empty, as long as they can keep a servant for show."

The woman laughed for the first time. Her laughter was empty and cold. The old man remained distant and depressed. There was a knock at the door. The woman jumped nervously to her feet and hurriedly wrapped herself in her *chador*.

"Here they are. Here they are," she said. "Remember, don't say anything about what you do for a living. That's all. Please, just control yourself."

The old man too had suddenly grown nervous. He turned pale and weak, like the accused facing the prosecutor.

"All right. All right. A curse upon the Devil," he stammered weakly.

The woman left the room. In the middle of the courtyard she saw the girl going to the door.

"Not you. Get back. Go inside," she shouted.

The girl froze in her place, then returned hesitantly to the parlor.

II

The parlor was smaller than the living room. It had a double door and a window. The floor was covered by three rugs that didn't match. Red satin drapes covered the windows and hung over the fireplace beneath the mantlepiece. A portrait of Imam Ali in a gilded frame and a prayer printed inside a decorative border were hung on the wall. On the mantlepiece was a round mirror. The room was dark.

Blushing and trembling, the girl held the tea-tray before the guest, who was sitting near a small footstool at the head of the room. She was middle-aged, had make up on, and did not wear a *chador*. The girl's weak smile expressed servile obedience. She wanted to offer that smile to Manuchehr Khan's mother when her parents were not looking. Her heart fluttered like a captive bird's. Manuchehr Khan's mother looked at her carefully and took a glass of tea from the tray.

"Thank you."

The girl said nothing, but smiled more bravely, her excited glowing eyes betraying anxious desires and longings. She left the room, relieved that she hadn't spilled the tea, or made any mistake. She hesitated at the door, wanted to turn her head but decided not to and disappeared in a hurry.

"Well, do they teach the Koran where your son teaches?" the old man asked after clearing his throat.

"My son teaches high school," the woman said, smiling. "The Koran is taught only at elementary school."

"Well, what does your son teach?"

"Mathematics."

"Mathematics," the old man repeated under his breath, not knowing the word. "Times have changed," he sighed. "People have lost their faith because of these satanic sciences."

"Come, come! Children don't go to school just to learn the Koran," Gowhar's mother said.

The woman smiled with approval. She was about forty-five and swarthy, with dyed black hair and dark brown eyes. She was wearing a thin woolen dress; her legs were fleshly, smooth and shiny.

The old man was sitting at the edge of the chair, fidgeting, and trying to keep his eyes away from the woman's bare legs. A vague sadness lingered at the bottom of his eyes.

"Please have your tea. It'll get cold," Gowhar's mother said, rising. "Would you excuse me? I have to check the dinner."

The woman smiled and was about to rise, but stopped herself. Gowhar's mother rushed to the living room. The girl was watching herself in the mirror and smiling. Hearing her mother's footsteps she turned and sat near the samovar.

"Girl . . ." said the mother, bending and speaking in her ear.

"Did you tell him?" the girl asked.

"Yes. I told him," the woman said, impatiently. "I came to tell you to be more lady-like. You shouldn't laugh, but don't frown either. Just behave like she's an ordinary guest. If she thinks you're immodest, she'll have nothing to do with us."

The girl blew at the charcoal in the samovar. "What did I do? Did I dance in front of her? If her son had been there you'd have a point," she said.

The woman paid no attention to her. "By the way, remember the chairs aren't ours," she said. "You were the one who begged Mahin Khanom to lend them to us. Be careful not to spill tea over them; that would be the end of us."

"All right," said the girl impatiently. "Why do you keep nagging? Would I spill tea over the chairs on purpose? You keep criticizing me."

The mother left the room, assumed a happy calm look, and returned to the parlor without going to the kitchen. This time, Manuchehr Khan's mother automatically half rose in her seat.

"Please do sit down," Gowhar's mother said hurriedly.

The old man took the opportunity, hesitantly rose from the chair and sat on the floor, leaning against the chair. His wife gave him a harsh look, but said nothing and smiled at the woman awkwardly. The old man became nervous and coughed a few times.

"I'm more comfortable on the floor. Well, it depends on what you're used to. In the old days, they sat on cushions—simple and comfortable. We didn't have all this paraphernalia. People have forgotten their bellies; luxury is all they think about."

"Come, this is no time for such talk," Gowhar's mother interrupted him reproachfully.

The woman fidgeted in her seat and looked at them, then glanced at the door.

"He's right," she said. "It depends on what you're used to. But today you can't live like the old days. Times have changed. But let's talk about what concerns us." She smiled nervously and turned to the old man. "My son wanted to come today," she continued. "But I came alone, so we could talk. Of course, after we come to an agreement he would like to speak to your daughter, and to you too."

The old man grinned, showing his teeth. "Of course. Haste makes waste," he said, smoothing his beard. "Like when you unravel a skein. If you rush, you mess up the whole thing."

"Enough. Lay off your proverbs and your anecdotes," Gowhar's mother shouted. She turned to the guest, smiling apologetically, trying to win her sympathy.

"Khanom, Karbalayi and I—that is all our family—believe that a girl should enter her husband's house in her *chador* and leave in her shroud," she said.

Manuchehr Khan's mother grew uneasy at the word "shroud." She placed the empty tea-glass gently on the table and glanced at the door again.

"Yes, everybody feels that way," she said. "Every parent wants his child to be happy. The important thing is that husband and wife be compatible. As they say, they ought to understand each other. And the girl, of course, should know how life is lived today."

Gowhar's mother was about to respond, when she saw that the woman was looking at the door. Gowhar was listening at the door. Her mother looked at the floor, embarrassed.

"Gowhar, where are you? Bring some tea," she called out, smiling awkwardly.

The girl appeared at the threshold in no time, and was greeted by the woman's pitying smile, her mother's angry look, and her father's indifference. Pretending to adjust her *chador*, she exposed her face and her figure, then wrapped the *chador* around herself. Still wearing her guilty and hesitant smile, she took the tea tray from the table.

"No, no, thanks. I don't want any more tea," the woman said. "Come young lady, come and sit down."

As if her prayers had been answered, the girl put the tray down and sat next to her mother, who gave her a reproachful look.

"You don't have to hide yourself in your *chador* like that. There's no man here who shouldn't see you," the mother said. "But you should've brought the lady more tea anyway. Don't you know any better?"

"Please have another glass," she said to Manuchehr Khan's mother. "It's freshly brewed. It's good."

"No thanks. I don't usually drink tea this time of day."

The girl listened to them for a minute, then sat at ease. The old man had been quiet for some time. He shifted his legs and took a deep breath.

"We weavers have a saying that goes like this . . ." he began.

Gowhar's mother angrily cut him short. "Are you going to get to the point, or do you want to give us anecdotes and proverbs? The lady has no time for these things, and you have to be at your off . . . office in an hour."

There was a commotion. The girl looked at her father bitterly and rushed out of the room. The guest frowned uneasily. The old man pulled himself together, but his face hardened with anger. Gowhar's mother was all confusion and didn't know what to say. She expected the woman to rise any moment, curse, and leave. The old man could no longer bear the insults he had suffered.

"What is it? What is the matter with you? What did I say?" he exploded.

The woman fidgeted in her seat and Gowhar's mother blushed with embarrassment.

"No, you didn't say anything wrong," she said to him with feigned calm. "But what's the use of all this talk? Say something to the point rather than . . ."

"Woman, what is it?" he sat on his knees, his anger beyond control. "Do we want to marry our daughter or tell a lot of lies?"

Gowhar's mother was too upset and confused to respond.

She looked spellbound. The old man rose, coughed a few times, took his dirty handkerchief from his pocket and walked towards the door. He stopped near the threshold, giving rein to his anger. "I knew from the first this was no use. Let them say what they want. Honesty is the best policy. I am a weaver. A weaver. I don't have an office, and I'm proud of it. I've lived with honesty for sixty years. I didn't cheat anyone, or ask anyone for a handout. And I'll give my daughter to someone who'll worship the ground she walks on."

He left the room, coughing. The woman rose. She stood, amazed and confused, her swarthy face flushed, her eyes full of contempt and regret. Gowhar's mother struggled to her feet.

"I'm really sorry. Forgive me. I'm so ashamed. I wish the earth would open up and swallow me. He is a bit irritable. I don't know what came over him."

"It's all right," the woman said. "It's not important. You must be upset. I'd better go. We can't discuss the matter now. Sorry to have bothered you."

Gowhar's mother followed her into the courtyard.

"I'm really sorry. Don't pay any attention to him," she said at the door. "He's old and senile. Well, when will you come again?"

"I don't know," the woman said. "We'll see. Maybe I'll come with Manuchehr. Good-bye. Please say good-bye for me to Karbalayi."

"I will. Thanks for coming. Please give our regards to Manuchehr Khan and Mr. Razavi."

The door closed behind the woman. Gowhar's mother went to the living room, where the girl had curled up in a corner, crying. The old man could be heard coughing. The girl saw her mother and cried harder. She began beating herself on the head, sobbing wildly and shaking. "I'm ruined. Damn you, you fools! You idiots! They won't come back. They won't."

The woman tried to calm her. "Come, come. Let them go. Husbands aren't in short supply. Stop blubbering. Go check the food. Get up! Up!" she said and left the room.

1963

Agha Julu

BY NASIR TAQVA'I

The sea, which is neither blue nor green, has pushed the town back, halfway up the mountains. At high tide the waves' white froth sinks in the sand at the threshold of the first houses. The waves beat against the dykes between the stone wall that circles the low land and the dock. Behind the wall built along the dock are a few shops and a shellfish cleaning factory, and the shade cast by the wall is the porters' hangout.

Dark, patternless brown mountains hump behind the town, curl around the bare sandy hill, and disappear into the sea, except for a few scattered rocks jutting out of the water here and there. The beacon blinks a bit farther away in the sea. At night, the moon shines into the rooms through open windows. On the water, the beacon fuses its red beams with the moonlight each time it flashes. At dawn, when the moon grows pale on the mountains, the long distant line between the sea and the sky casts a white gleam. You can hear the fishermen's voices and the sound of their oars as their boats approach the horizon, black against the silvery glitter of the water. When the white line in the horizon turns yellow and the sun reaches the high ventilation towers of the houses and the dome-like covers of the tanks, the fishermen return. The sun looks from above. On the sandy beach, old men shade their eyes from the sun, watching the boats anxiously. Once fishermen, they now weave fishing nets and wait for the boats, hoping to make a few pennies by repairing the nets torn by sharks. The women wear loose gowns with embroidered skirts. They watch the boats through the two holes of their black veils, anxious to get the fish in time for their husbands' meals. Naked children stand beside a mound of colorful loincloths, ready to jump into the water when the boats get nearer. Farther away, the porters sit in the shade, leaning against the wall, waiting for a boat—or a ship, if it has been a few months since the last one's arrival.

From the tops of the ventilation towers, the sun penetrates the rooms through the colored glass windows, painting rainbows on the plaster walls. The large house facing the children's playground never catches the sun in its windows. The townspeople have broken the glass with stones.

I

It was in this house that Engineer Agha Julio almost settled down. While he lived there, the light went on at night in the room at the right side of the house, and sometimes a woman's cries broke the cemetery-silence of the large house. Engineer Agha Julio was a big, ruddy Italian. Children loved the two lines in the corners of his always laughing mouth. The photograph he gave Dolu before he left is still in the box under the bed. Dolu hasn't looked at it again since he found it. However, for him the memory of Engineer Agha Julio is something more than a photograph in a box, something he has hidden in a secret corner in his mind.

The day Engineer Agha Julio arrived at Langeh, the children were sitting on the dyke, their fishing lines in the water, watching a ship that had anchored where the water was darker. The water was shallow near the shore, so the cargo had to be brought in by rowboats. He came in the second rowboat, wearing a black beret. Four porters went to the boat with a chair and held it by its legs while he climbed onto it. Then they carried him toward the shore, the water up to their knees. Suddenly the porter in front tripped over a rock and let go of the chair. Engineer Agha Julio fell into the water and his shorts, socks, and shoes were soaked. The porters were frightened, but he smiled at them. Still, they were afraid and did not charge him for the lift. He walked past the children in his black beret, khaki shirt and shorts, a camera hanging at his side and water squishing in his shoes. But the children did not laugh at him; they said hello.

As long as the ship was in the harbor, no one thought that he would stay in Langeh. But he stayed for a year, or maybe a bit longer. He seemed to be up to something, or maybe he had conceived some wild scheme on his way back from the Bostaneh mountains. He rented a house facing that of Mirza Hasan, the owner of the shellfish cleaning factory. The engineer had proposed a joint stock company to him. Mirza Hasan had not understood the details of the deal. "If I'm going to get hoodwinked," he had said, "it won't be by that Italian." The engineer had not repeated his offer. That year Mirza Hasan suffered a loss. The shellfish were carried off to the sea by an unseasonable storm.

Then the Engineer Agha Julio struck a deal with a truck driver who used to bring fruit from orchards on the other side of the mountains. On every trip the truck had broken down and the fruit had spoiled, but the driver continued the enterprise, hoping for better luck. The last time the truck had broken down, its main spring was bent so badly that it could not be straightened. The Engineer Agha Julio was good at making a bargain, and was an expert mechanic as well. He examined the engine and the four tires like a man checking a donkey's snout and knees. The truck was back on the road in no time. When it passed through the streets, the children would push their loincloths under the strings they tied around their waists and chase it in the dust, barefoot. One day the truck went by loaded with workers. Engineer Agha Julio was driving toward the mountains. The workers were mostly fishermen and porters. He had told them that there was sulphur in Bostaneh Mountains, and they had been carried away with the dream of success. Only Mirza Hasan was skeptical and had no faith in the enterprise. He didn't know why, but his pessimism proved justified. The mine collapsed and crippled three workers. Two of them were porters at the dock. The fishermen and porters returned to their former callings. The latter were angry at the engineer. The people divested the ruddy Italian of the title 'Engineer' and reduced his name to Agha Julio.

The truck, which was falling apart, was put to work at the dock. The porters would glare at it angrily when it was loaded, but the head of the town, Kadkhoda, was happy. One night, in the Jame' Mosque, he registered the first freight company for the port of Langeh and vicinity in the name of Agha Julio in the Koran. The Shiites' objection to having a heathen's name in the Koran was overruled by the Sunnite majority. In protest, the Shiites stopped attending the Jame' Mosque. They did not remain idle, however. Covert activities began at Mirza Hasan's instigation. The porters, who were mostly Shiites, congregated in the shade behind the wall and talked for a few days and nights. They argued, cursed, and gave one another the finger, until those in favor of smashing the truck were dissuaded by fellow workers who were afraid of having to pay damages to the red-faced Italian. In the end they voted for passive resistance and decided to fight the Italian by charging less. Soon after, scarcity of business forced Agha Julio's freight company to close down. Agha Julio complained about the porters' syndicate to the Kadkhoda. Kadkhoda was scared. He had heard the word 'syndicate' on his battery operated radio. He intervened, the Shiites and the Sunnites were united, and the Shiites began to attend the Jame' Mosque again. When their religious leader, Mirza Hasan, resigned, the Shiites thought nothing of his resignation. And when Kadkhoda made it up to Julio by registering his new occupation in the Koran, no one left the Jame' Mosque.

The run-down truck was bartered for Abdollah Patar's old convertable Ford (which Sheikh Jaber's son had brought from Adan years ago) and Langeh's first cab company was established. The cab would go to the countryside also—if it could find a passenger. The Ford was old and had spoked wheels. The horn, which Agha Julio himself could not stand, stampeded the donkeys, so Kadkhoda forbade honking in the town.

Whenever Agha Julio had no passenger—which was always the case—he would take the children for a ride and sing for them. This was the beginning of their friendship with him. He wanted to learn their language and he had picked up a few words, although he and the children understood each other perfectly without words. He hadn't had much success in learning their songs, however, and generally sang Italian songs. The children could not judge his performance. Some made fun of him; others nodded with approval. Agha Julio's behavior cost him the grownups' respect. They dropped 'Agha' from his name and called him simply Julio. But the children continued to call him Agha Julu.

II

Agha Julu's ruddy face turned brown in the summer and his black beret gave place to a straw hat. The less people respected him, the more he enjoyed himself. He was that kind of man. He consumed more arrack as his taxi consumed more gasoline. But business was dull because everybody in Langeh had his own private donkey. Agha Julu was forced to sell the car back to Abdollah Patar, who was now proud to have two cars in his garage.

Agha Julu was idle for a while, then disappeared for about ten days. The children went back to playing on the beach and fishing in the deep waters between the rocks. After all those rides, they found the walk to the rocks exhausting. One evening, when the children were playing in the square, Agha Julu returned. They gathered around him and he had them clean up one of the lighter rooms in his house. He hung a black curtain on the wall facing the window, and put up a big sign at the door. Mirza Hasan saw the sign when he left this house early in the morning. He cursed for a while, then called the townspeople. But Kadkhoda was pleased. Agha Julu had opened Langeh's first photo studio. The children were in clover. With the long red strips of film paper, which had a nice smell, they made hats, belts, and swords, and invented new games to play. Instead of thread spools, they now used empty film reels in their toy carts. The townspeople were curious and only the fear of Mirza Hasan prevented them from having their pictures taken right away. But it wasn't long before they all did so, when they caught him looking the other way.

The daughter of the progressive Kadkhoda was the first

female to go to Agha Julu's studio for her picture. Zeinab followed suit, out of rivalry with Kadkhoda's daughter. She even took off her veil, so her picture would be prettier than Kadkhoda's daughter's. After a few weeks, Agha Julu told the children to take the sign down. The town had a small population and everybody had his picture taken during Agha Julu's short career as photographer.

Once more Agha Julu was between jobs. The children would gather around him after play and teach him their songs. They would ask him to tell them about his town. He would unbutton his shirt pocket, pull out and unfold a piece of paper crowded with black lines over patches in different colors. He would point to a spot. The children would laugh. Then they would not laugh any more and would ask him to stay in their big town instead of going back to that small green boot on the paper. He would make them understand that he would not go back. The children never doubted his sincerity. They had become familiar with his gestures, his mannerisms, and the expression in his eyes. His dignified countenance helped him to maintain a respectful distance between himself and the children; otherwise they would have made him a laughing stock like the blind Toku. The children liked him the way he was and didn't want him to change. The grownups could not accept him as easily. They slandered him, but eventually surrendered to him. The children kept betting over his next job. They thought of everything except what he finally took up five days after he had photographed Zeinab.

Agha Julu took to the streets, singing and dancing. As Zeinab's father put it, the neighbor of the religious Mirza Hasan turned into a common street performer. The children were bursting with anticipation. They knew Agha Julu was not so foolish as to forfeit his dignity for nothing. The first night Mirza Hasan was lying in his mosquito net on the roof and had just blown out the lamp, when Agha Julu started singing in the street below. Dolu quietly sneaked past his parents' mosquito net and went down the stairs into the courtyard and opened the street door. He squeezed through the children, who had gathered in a circle in front of Zeinab's house. In the middle of the circle, Agha Julu was dancing and snapping his fingers. Toku played the clarion, his cheeks nearly bursting with air. Occasionally he would stop playing and would sing "Oh wine seller woman, how much is your wine?" The children would pick up the chorus and sing along. Then Toku would sing again "The moon is out tonight, how much is the wine?" Agha Julu sang too; but when he did, the children would stop singing, and would only laugh at him. You couldn't help laughing at his singing. The empty arrack bottle on the ground harmonized all that discord. When Mirza Hasan pushed his way into the circle, Dolu was caught by surprise. He did not have the chance to disappear among the children. Mirza Hasan took him by the hand and slapped him, shouting, "Go home, you bastard." Then he cursed Toku. "The way this blind beggar has taken to this crazy Julio!" he shouted.

"Say *Agha*. *Agha* Julu!" Dolu said.

"Get home, you bastard," his father shouted.

III

Dolu left the window open that night, using the heat as an excuse. His father had not let him sleep on the roof. His mother brought his bedding down from the roof the next morning. Dolu was at the window, listening. Suddenly he heard Toku's clarion wailing not too far away. Dolu looked out of the window and saw Toku and Agha Julu turn the corner and stagger into the alley with their shadows. The children were following them. Dolu ran to the door and turned the knob, but the door did not open. He felt a lump in his throat, as a child does whose parents have refused to take him along to a wedding. He went back to the window. Agha Julu and Toku were in front of Zeinab's house. The children were clapping. The newcomers melted into the moving circle of flesh. Agha Julu was dancing and singing in the middle of the circle. Now and then, when he took a gulp from the bottle in his pocket, Toku's loud clarion and the children's happy cry made up for his silence. A while later, Dolu saw his father rush toward Zeinab's house, where the windows were lighted indicating that the occupants were not asleep. He knocked and shouted for a long time, before they opened the door. He went in and returned not long after with Zeinab's father. They knocked a few more doors and other old men joined them. Then all left the alley together. Dolu tried to open the door again, but failed. Suddenly the noise stopped. He went to the window. The men had returned, led by Kadkhoda, whom they followed at a respectful distance, as if awed by his old pistol. The men broke into the circle, or maybe the children let them in. Kadkhoda said something to Agha Julu, and the latter went with him without a word. The men waited there angrily, until the children returned to their homes.

That night Dolu heard his father cough louder than on previous nights. He coughed as he turned the large beads of his rosary between his fingers. "What a brave man!" he said to his wife, mocking Agha Julu.

"You were too many," Dolu cried, unable to control his anger.

"Kadkhoda will stay with him all by himself tonight," Mirza Hasan said.

"Then he'll show you," Dolu said angrily.

"Shut up, you bastard," Mirza Hasan shouted.

IV

For the children, the next day's sun was the slowest sun that ever rose on the rooftops. They all woke up earlier than usual. Even Delbad woke up on his own, before his father could awaken him with a kick in the spine. Normally the children found excuses not to do the shopping for breakfast. But that day they volunteered to go. On the way to the market, however, none went beyond Kadkhoda's house. Two men were carrying Kadkhoda out of the mud-brick hut that had served as the town's prison since the night before. Kadkhoda was drunk, quietly singing "Oh wine seller woman." (Thereafter, whenever Kadkhoda wanted a drink he would take a gulp from Agha Julu's bottle, when no one was watching.)

The old men whispered together. Their expressions intrigued Dolu and he listened to them attentively.

"Won't you say this wishy-washy Kadkhoda has proved he

can't handle Julio?" Mirza Hasan said to Zeinab's father.

"Julio is a crafty fox, but I'm not going to let him get away with this," Zeinab's father said angrily.

"Don't kid yourself. We ought to think of something that'll work," Mirza Hasan said. Dolu thought his father had come to his senses.

"What sort of thing? He is disgracing me," Zeinab's father said.

"You aren't thinking of giving in to him, are you?"

"I don't know. I've got to do something."

"What do you want to do?"

"It was my fault to turn him down. Mirza Hasan, do you think if Julio gets married, he..." Zeinab's father said quietly, too embarrassed to finish. A knowing smile wrinkled Mirza Hasan's face as if he had tasted bitter tea. "But with one condition," Zeinab's father added quietly.

Dolu did not wait. He ran to Agha Julu's prison and the children followed him, screaming. Agha Julu threw the window open in terror.

"Agha Julu!" the children yelled.

"Agha Julu, hurry up before it's too late."

"Hurry up!"

He shouted at them. They quieted down and turned to Dolu. Dolu looked at them importantly, as if about to reveal a big secret.

"They want to make you a Moslem," he said to Agha Julu. The children saw the color return to Agha Julu's face and his laugh lines reappear deeper than usual. He laughed aloud. The children stared at one another. Agha Julu shut the window. They stood outside the hut, amazed.

"Did you see that?" Mamu said. They all turned to him.

"His face. His face was a funny color," one said.

"Why, he was just laughing. That's all," Dolu said.

"I'm not talking about his laughing. I think he's scared of something. Isn't he?" Mamu said.

"He isn't scared of anything," Dolu said.

"We'll help him, if it's necessary, won't we?" Mamu said.

"If he isn't worried, why should we worry?" Dolu said.

"Well, aside from all this, is he going to become a Sunnite or a Shiite?" one asked.

"A Shiite, of course," two answered together.

V

That afternoon the men took Agha Julu to Sayyed Mohammad Sadegh, the *mujtahid*. He read from the Koran. The children didn't understand a word he said, not even Delbad, who had gone to mosque school for two years. Then Agha Julu repeated Sayyed Mohammad's words, his accent making them even less comprehensible. It was because they were worried about him that they didn't laugh.

The wedding was celebrated the night after. Toku played the clarion, his cheeks swelling larger than anyone remembered. Agha Julu went around happily in his khaki shorts and T-shirt with a bottle of arrack in his hand, dancing. From the roof, the women tossed sweets and coins over his head. The men found excuses to call him by his new name, Engineer Agha *Javad*. It was the happiest night in the children's life.

After getting married, Agha Julu settled down a bit. He drank more than before, but people said he had grown more sensible. When the women passed him in the street, they wouldn't pull their black *chadors* over their veils any more. He had become part of the community. But the children stopped going to his house. They cleaned their playground, took out their fishing rods and waxed the lines. When they met him on the street, they would just say hello and walk by, then turn and watch a man who was no longer their playmate. He was a husband.

A few weeks passed in peace (like all the weeks the children remembered before Agha Julu came to Langeh), until Agha Julu began his new occupation. This time the nature of his work was a mystery to all. Whenever he smoked imported cigarettes and carried imported liquor in his back pocket, the children would know that a new ship had arrived. They would gather on the shore to watch it. That month two ships anchored near the port. The porters said it was a good month. The tugboat had brought two oil barges and the freighter had come for the shellfish for the second time that year. Meanwhile, once every few days Agha Julu would deliver something in boxes of photography paper to the ships and return. The children made bets and thought hard and long, but could not guess what was in those boxes. They saw him burn something on the roof of his house twice. They recognized the smell of film paper and the big fire led them to assume that Agha Julu's business was prospering. He did not buy the old Ford, but would rent it now and then. His honking called the children out, and the dust in his wake exasperated the shopkeepers. The laugh lines in the corner of his mouth were deeper than ever, until one night things changed. The neighbors heard sharp cries and loud voices from the house and after a series of separations and reconciliations, Zeinab returned to her father's house for good. Zeinab's father seldom left the house after that. The cause of the divorce was still a mystery when Agha Julu married again, this time no less a bride than Kadkhoda's daughter. The children enjoyed the second wedding celebration as much as the first. But this time the marriage lasted only a couple of weeks. One night Dolu was at the window, when he heard shouting from Agha Julu's house. He heard a scream and saw a shadow on the window of Agha Julu's room which was lighted by two or three lamps. The shadow looked like a naked woman's. Dolu turned his face and did not look again. The woman's screams were loud and resonant. Then Dolu heard the sound of breaking glass. A black box was hurled through the window. It broke when it hit the ground. The woman ran to the window again. Pieces of paper and cardboard whirled in the air. Agha Julu rushed out of the house, and collected everything. When he went inside, the fight resumed. Shortly afterwards, Kadkhoda's daughter rushed out and ran to her father's house.

Early in the morning, Dolu and Delbad found a stained photograph in the sludge in front of Agha Julu's house. Dolu hid it in his pocket quickly. It wouldn't be nice if Agha Julu found out that the children had seen his first wife's nude picture.

Dolu and Delbad stared at each other in amazement.

Delbad turned his face and began to walk without a word.
"Delbad," Dolu said.
"What?" Dolu asked.
"I won't tell anyone, either," Dolu said quietly.

VI

Later in the evening when silence and sleep had fallen on the small town, the children left Mosallah's coffeehouse and began to walk toward their homes. One by one they left the main road and turned into side streets, until Dolu was left alone. The moon was out. The shadows scared the solitary child and quickened his step. Before reaching home, he heard Agha Julu's voice. He was speaking in his own language. Dolu did not understand. Agha Julu was sitting, facing the wall. Dolu did not know who he was talking to. "How are you, Agha Julu?" he said, standing behind him.

Agha Julu did not look at him; he raised his bottle, took a gulp, and frowned. Dolu hadn't seen that kind of bottle before. He decided the arrack was of poor quality. But Agha Julu licked his lips and smacked his tongue against his palate. Dolu realized that the more the arrack made you frown the better it was. Agha Julu began to talk again, still facing the wall. The shadow on the wall made no response. 'Sometimes it's better if you don't say anything, like the shadow,' Dolu thought. But he couldn't leave. He tapped Agha Julu on the shoulder until he turned his head. Dolu sat on the doorstep before him. "Agha Julu," he said quietly. They looked at each other. Dolu said nothing. He discovered that Agha Julu didn't look like a husband any more. He stretched his arm, holding the photograph. "Here. We found this in the sludge. I swear we only looked at it once. Delbad promised he wouldn't tell anyone."

Agha Julu took the photograph. The wrinkles on his forehead persisted. He put the photograph in his shirt pocket and smiled, pressing Dolu's hand lost between his own large hands. He stood up. His shadow slid down the wall and entered the house before him. Dolu heard him sing the chorus in his drunken voice. He waited until the light was put out. He continued waiting until all sounds had died down in the house.

VII

It was the fifth month of summer—Langeh's long summer, when the nights are so short that the sun rises before the moon has completely disappeared. That day, the sun's first rays had just turned the mountain tops and the tips of the ventilation towers golden. In the cool morning fathers awakened their sons with a tap on the head or a kick in the spine, and sent them off to market before they had washed away the sleep from their eyelids with a splash of cool well water. Dolu saw something new on the way to the market. The sight of a pea-green jeep circled by children drove away the heaviness of sleep from his eyes. "What's going on?" he asked Mamu.

"I don't know. We saw a few gendarmes go into Kadkhoda's house."

"Let's go in," Delbad said.

"No. If I'm late with the bread again, my father will kill me," Dolu said.

"All right. Go and get the bread. If something goes wrong, we'll let you know," Delbad said.

Dolu went to the bakery with Mamu. The baker spread the dough expertly. His hand and arm would enter the red mouth of the oven and come out sweaty. Dolu saw the dough rise with small bubbles and darken. He was thinking about the jeep. The gendarmes would not come to the town for no reason. He heard his name and turned. Delbad was running toward him and calling his name. They ran together, bumping into people who were in their way. The wall of flesh was harder to penetrate than before, yet somehow they ended in the middle of the circle and saw Agha Julu held by two gendarmes, his hands handcuffed before him. The gendarmes' bayonets flashed in the children's eyes. They couldn't believe what they saw. Agha Julu's face was like that day when Mamu had said he seemed afraid of something. He was quiet, his head bent down. When he looked at the men, they turned their faces from him. He turned to the children and looked them in the eye one by one. He stood before Dolu, with those same laugh lines, placed his handcuffed hands on Dolu's head, and thrust his fingers in his hair. Agha Julu's smile was not gay. His eyes pointed to his shirt pocket. Dolu understood. Sheltered by Agha Julu's large body, he thrust his fingers into his shirt pocket, took out the photograph, and hid it in his own collar without looking at it. Agha Julu laughed. Dolu's hair was pressed with a pleasant pain.

The corporal emerged from the house with two more gendarmes carrying Agha Julu's belongings. The children could not look the corporal in the eye. Their eyes would not go beyond his mustache. "The son-of-a-bitch, every place he opens up shop he destroys all the evidence," he said to Kadkhoda. He turned angrily at Agha Julu, who was laughing. His hand went up. The children closed their eyes and heard the blow in the dark. Mamu nudged Dolu. "Shouldn't we do something?"

"Shhhhhh," Dolu said, watching the bright metal handcuffs dig into the red flesh of Agha Julu's wrist. He knew Agha Julu could break the handcuffs with one move if he chose to. He hadn't done so for a reason. The corporal shouted, and the gendarmes pushed Agha Julu toward the jeep.

"Sir! Captain, you can't. We won't let you take him away," Delbad shouted, no longer able to control himself. The corporal frowned, like a captain who has been addressed as a corporal. Delbad was tongue-tied. Even the children's encouragement could not make him speak again.

Everybody was silent, until the jeep disappeared in the column of dust it left behind.

"Who on earth was he?" Kadkhoda said as quietly as the settling dust. He felt as if he had seen a passerby for the first time.

"He was a strange creature," Mirza Hasan said.

Dolu ran toward his house. He wanted to cry. In the room, he shut the door firmly, put the photograph in the box with his eyes closed, and pushed it under the bed. He threw himself on the bed, lying on his stomach, and hot salty tears burned the corners of his mouth. He heard the people stoning Agha

Julu's house and breaking the windows. He did not go to the window to look.

1965

Why Do They Go Back?

NADIR IBRAHIMI

"Sha'ir Khan, are you really going back?"

"Stop bothering me, old man. Why do you keep asking? I've told you a hundred times, I'm going back. You can see for yourself the direction we're riding."

"No, Khan, you're kidding your servant. No one would believe that Sha'ir would go back—go back and surrender."

"Sha'il, who would believe that Sha'ir Khan would deliver Akbar Mirza and not go back? Who would believe that?"

"No one, Khan. No one."

"Then shut up, old man. There's nothing else to be done."

The night was like the description of night in stories about outlaws. The two horsemen rode oblivious of darkness, or of the small, mist-covered lantern of the moon at night's end.

"Sha'ir Khan, I have a right to know, don't I? For sixty years I've fought for you and for your father. For sixty years. Now you tell me you're going back. Don't I have a right to know why? Has everything been straightened out? Is there no more reason to carry a gun?

"Old man, you don't understand."

"That's what I'm saying, Khan. But I must understand. I mustn't be kept in the dark. If something has changed, if something has been straightened out, tell your servant . . ."

Sha'il, it has changed. Lots of things have changed."

"Too bad . . . too bad."

Sha'ir Khan turned and looked back at the mountains that moved almost imperceptibly farther away from them. The mountains were his clothing and his shelter; in the plain he was naked.

The wounded moon, in the eyes of the old man, was like a lantern about to die out.

"Khan, tell your servant why you're going back. Have you heard something I don't know?"

Sha'ir Khan was fingering his mustache, teaching it to stay up as he rode down the slope. The wind spread the bitter scent of poppies.

"Old man, the smell of opium. Don't you like it?"

"No, Khan. I only like the smell of gunpowder."

Sha'ir Khan laughed. "You old outlaw . . . it's all finished. That sort of talk belongs to the good old days. Once we wash and hang up our guns, you'll forget the smell of gunpowder."

"No, Khan . . . you don't mean it."

"Tomorrow, at sunrise . . ."

"If you've surrendered by then . . ."

"Mashhadi Sha'il will also surrender himself."

The old man made no answer. He struggled against doubt, disbelief, anger — but his age and his faith in the Khan would not let him rebel. 'Does it really mean we're going back to surrender?' he wondered. 'What will they do to us? Will they reward the Khan and give him a medal for surrendering his gun? Will they give him his land back and praise him for having come round? But, no . . . they're sure to hang him."

"Sha'ir Khan, they're sure to hang you," he said.

"What? What did you say?"

"I said they're sure to hang you. They'll hang you up like an old gun, they'll print your picture in the paper with your head bent to one side and your tongue sticking out."

"And what's wrong with that? How long do we have to roam around like this? How long can we fight without knowing what we're fighting for? Do you remember when I came back from England? I was my own man, full of ideals, full of plans. But my father . . ."

"God bless his soul."

"Yes...my father convinced me that we had to fight. Maybe what he said was right — thirty years ago. Thirty years. Do you remember it all? Homeless, our guns on our shoulders . . . now we'll go back. We'll rest, smoke opium to our hearts' content, then stand against the wall and tell them to finish us. That's all."

"You don't make the rules, Khan. They'll hang you."

The Khan rubbed his mustache and laughed. "No, old man, they'll listen to me. I'll beg them to shoot me."

"Sha'ir Khan, you will beg?"

"Yes, what's wrong with that?"

"No. No . . . Khan."

"Sha'il you think like the outlaws three centuries ago. Can't you see we're becoming extinct? One by one. Some get killed, some give up.... Today or tomorrow, what difference does it make?

"Too bad. Too bad I'm not like the outlaws three centuries ago. If I were, I'd stand here until you'd moved a hundred steps from me . . . and then I'd shoot you."

Sha'ir Khan laughed aloud and patted the old man on the back.

"Old man, I wish I were twenty again. But we're men without a cause. That's the trouble with us . . . men without a cause."

Mashhadi Sha'il tried to understand. He thought about past years and past days. 'What does it mean? For all those years the Khan had held his life in his hands and had never once talked like this. Why? Had he always silently regretted that he'd come from England with those ideals and had ended up a wanderer with a gun on his back? He had sacrificed Akbar Mirza, and had not gone back. Why now? Why did he want to beg them not to hang him . . .?"

"Do you think they'll kill me?" asked the Khan suddenly.

"Yes, certainly."

"No. There's no reason why they should. If I go back and tell them, 'I'm here, and I've come on my own,' they won't kill me. Once more we'll all be together. I'll plant wheat. All with machines. Not like the old days. I'll plant every inch of the land."

"What land, Khan? You no longer have any land."

Sha'ir smiled as he replied, but he feigned anger. "What? I don't have any land? All that land is mine. I can grow wheat wherever I want. Abdollah has protected my land like a watchdog."

Mashhadi Sha'il stared at him. "Abdollah? You're talking nonsense, Sha'ir Khan! Abdollah is working for himself, on his own land."

"His own land? Where's his own land?"

"Sha'ir Khan, you know what I'm talking about. You're making fun of me. I can tell from your smile. You sound like an outlaw who hasn't even heard the radio. No one is working for you anymore. Everybody is working on his own land. They're even given the grain they sow. If you go back you'll disgrace yourself. The only way you can save your honor is by remaining an outlaw, far away; by refusing to go back. Why won't you admit it?"

"Are you saying that even my wife doesn't want me? Is she planting on her own land too?"

"I didn't say that, Khan. No. I know Sa'ideh Khanom loves you. Those days, every time you went to see the children she was so happy to see you . . ."

"So? Do I get a piece of the land or don't I?"

"No, Khan. Outlaws don't get anything."

"And what about the sheep? Those are my own."

"Right, the sheep. You're going to become a shepherd in your old age, Khan?"

"My old age? Shut up, old man. Sha'ir Khan will never get old."

"When you go back, you'll be old. So old you won't have the strength to carry a gun and walk."

"Nonsense. I still can carry the cannon on my back. But why should I? Why should I go on killing for no reason? I'll go back. If they don't give me land, I'll raise milk cows."

The old man was on the verge of tears. He wanted suddenly to say something that would hurt the Khan, that would burn his heart.

"They'll mock you in verse, Sha'ir Khan," he said. "They'll mock you in verse all over the South."

107

Sha'ir Khan laughed again. "What kind?" he asked. "Wait . . . let me make one myself, and you can give it to them to recite . . ."

He smiled, humming the words under his breath, searching for rhymes.

"Sha'ir Khan is going back, disgraced and old,
Sha'ir Khan is going back, back to the fold.
Sha'ir Khan fought aimlessly many years,
Sha'ir Khan, Oh, Sha'ir Khan, Oh Sha'ir Khan . . ."

"No, old man, I can't do it. You'd better find someone and give him a couple of sheep to write some decent lines.

The old man gave no answer. The farther they went, the sadder he became. From the corner of his eyes he watched the Khan, who kept running his fingers over his mustache, and smiling. He remembered the year the Khan swore that he would never go back unless he'd won the war. Now he was going back, and he was smiling.

"Khan, if you had planned to go back and surrender, why did you kill those two people by the road? Couldn't you have surrendered to them?"

No, Sha'il, no. I needed a little time. If I'd surrendered to them they would claim they'd fought with me and caught me. They should've stayed out of my way. It was their own fault."

When they reached the Zobeir, the old man broke the darkness with the sad color of his voice. "Do you remember this spot, Sha'ir Khan?" he asked softly.

"So?"

"Do you remember?"

"Hosein was killed here."

"Not Hosein alone. They killed Hasan and Fatemeh here too. Your children, Khan."

For a moment the weight of sorrow tightened the eyelids of the Khan, his sharp glance cut through the night. He swallowed a sigh.

"Well, they had to kill them. The soldiers were shooting from up there, weren't they?"

"Yes, Khan. From up there."

"Were they good shots?"

"No, it took them many shots . . ."

"Don't belittle them like that, old man. I've seen some of them. They're good shots."

"They shot one after the other . . ."

"What's the difference? What's the difference, old man? Why shouldn't an outlaw get killed? Weren't my children outlaws? Weren't they?"

"Yes, they were. But they fought for Sha'ir Khan, their father, and they were killed for Sha'ir Khan, their father—the same man who is now going back to raise and milk cows. Who is breaking his vow . . ."

"Sha'il, remember what I'm saying: no one should fight for the sake of his father. To fight for your father's sake is to fight for something old and worn out. He should know himself what he's doing, what he wants, what he's getting killed for. If they fought only for my sake, then they deserved to die in their youth."

The old man looked at a rock. "Hosein was shot here, behind this rock," he said.

"Bravo, Hosein! Bravo! So he was behind the rock and he still got shot?"

"Khan, it doesn't suit you to talk like this."

"Look, Sha'il, didn't you say I sounded like outlaws who haven't even heard the radio? Well, hadn't my children heard the radio? Hadn't they? Didn't the newspaper reach them? Didn't they know that they would get killed if they didn't surrender?"

"What about Akbar Mirza? He surrendered."

"No, they caught him. I didn't want to go back for someone who had been taken captive."

"Sha'ir Khan, we are at Zobeir. We don't have very far to go. Think it over. You're making a mistake, Khan."

Sha'ir Khan hummed under his breath:

"Sha'ir Khan is going back disgraced and old,
Sha'ir Khan is going back, back to the fold,
Sha'ir Khan and his servant, Mashhadi Sha'il.
Sha'ir Khan, Oh Sha'ir Khan, Oh Sha'ir Khan . . ."

"How many children did I have, old man?"

"Seven."

"And were they all killed?"

"No. One died—Abedin Khan."

"No, none of my children had a right to die," Sha'ir Khan shouted. "None! Not peacefully, in a bed!"

"But Abedin Khan died. He died, with sores all over his body."

"Yes . . . now I remember. But they put a curse on him, he died of their curse. That in a way was like getting killed."

"Yes, Khan. They put a curse on him."

"I remember. He gave everybody a hard time... everybody. By the way, how old was my wife when we hit the mountains?"

"Thirty or so."

"Yes. She was thirty."

Later:

"You're tired, Sha'il. You're very tired."

"No, Khan. I'm not tired."

"Then why are you dozing?"

"I'm not dozing, just thinking."

"About what, old man? Still asking yourself why I'm going back? Listen, Sha'il; I'm going to talk to you. You must learn to accept that everything has changed. This time they're not joking. They've done a lot of things. Things you and I can't judge. They've built schools and towns for you. You told me this yourself, you can't deny it. Abdollah is working on his own land. What am I supposed to fight against? What? They didn't take my land for themselves, they didn't take my sheep for themselves. They divided them among the people. Not only didn't they take anything, they even gave something of their own. They fought those who opposed them. They had a right to. And many of their own people were killed. People who fought in their own country against their own kind—against you and me and my children. Who is going to tell me what all the fighting will come to? Who's going to help Sha'ir Khan? Why fight? To please a handful of people who sit in their cozy rooms in cities and like to hear about outlaws? Or to impress a bunch of weakling city kids who think of us as wild animals who starve in the mountains, yet somehow survive? When they hear we've broken a siege they applaud us in the safety of their rooms. 'What strange animals!' they think. Is this enough, old man? Is it? Not once in all these years did you ask me what we're fighting for, who we're fighting for. But for over a month now all day long you ask why we're going back. Be patient, old man. I've thought it over. It's because I have thought it over that we're going back. You're like an outlaw who has lingered on from the time of Nader Shah. An outlaw who thinks he can win Shiraz by battle, take Isfahan and Tehran, and become sole ruler. An outlaw who doesn't know which way the wind is blowing; who is a great shot, but doesn't know why he's shooting; who can tumble on the horse and spread-eagle himself, clinging to its belly, but doesn't know why he's doing these things."

Tears were rolling from the old man's eyes. Sha'ir Khan was shouting now. "Maybe you know what you're fighting for. All right. Then tell me. Tell your master so he'll follow you wherever you want to go. But don't tell me we're fighting against injustice and that sort of thing. We're nowhere near fighting injustice, Sha'il, nowhere near that."

The Khan lowered his voice and spoke more kindly. "Being an outlaw has become a tradition with us. A tradition that must remain—but for how long, it's not clear. You think I have become tired? You think I've become reconciled? You think I'm scared? Sha'ir Khan scared? No. It's like I told you, what's wrong with us is that we don't have a cause. We don't know. Abdollah doesn't know. My children didn't know."

Sha'ir Khan rubbed his mustache as he talked, and the mustache was like a white bird he'd caught in his mouth, a white bird with its wings stretched out. He was smiling, as if he'd heard his own speech and liked it.

"Sha'ir Khan is going back, back to the fold,
Sha'ir Khan is going back, disgraced and old.
Sha'ir Khan with his servant . . ."

"All right Khan," the old man said sadly. "I've no objection. No objection at all. You should have said this before."

"I haven't said anything yet. I only asked you to think and be patient, old man."

"All right. But you said you wished you were twenty. Why did you say that? You claim you'll never grow old, so why did you say that?"

"You caught me in a contradiction, old man. I said that because I thought if I were twenty I would understand why one should fight."

"Khan, here's the river. Finish with what you are saying."

"No, old man. There's no more. I hope they won't trap us here. Let's camp until morning."

On the other side of the river, the plain, with its lonely dim lights looked like the resting place of glow-worms.

"Get up, old man!"

"Where are we, Khan? Where are we?"

"Get up, Sha'il. Hurry up! Get your gun, let's go."

"It's still night, Khan. We didn't get any sleep . . . where are we going?"

"Anywhere. Get up."

The old man tied his cartridge belt, shouldered his gun. They mounted their horses.

"Goodbye, Sha'il."

"Goodbye."

"Goodbye, old man."

"Sha'ir Khan, have you changed your mind?"

"No, old man. I hold to what I said. We aren't fit to be outlaws. I'm sorry I killed those two . . ."

At daybreak the two outlaws crossed the Zobeir.

"How old did you say my wife was when we hit the mountains?"

"Thirty, Khan, thirty."

They heard a shot from the mountain top, and then more shots.

The Khan and Sha'il jumped off their horses and took shelter behind two rocks.

"I told you it was useless to kill them, didn't I?"

"Yes, Khan, you did."

"They've trapped us."

"You're right, Khan. They've trapped us."

Another shot echoed. The Khan's horse knelt, then rolled to the ground. The Khan watched the horse sadly. "Old man," he cried. "Do you think my wife could still have children?"

"Certainly, Sha'ir Khan. 'Til fifty, maybe even more."

"Good. She's not over fifty, is she?"

"No, Khan, she's not."
"Where are they shooting from?"
"Facing us, from up there."
Sha'ir Khan took his gun and looked.
"Why aren't you shooting, Sha'il?"
"I don't see anything. They're too far away."
"You too have stopped being an outlaw, old man."
More shots. The bullets whistled over the rock that sheltered the Khan. Sha'ir Khan answered the volley aimlessly. The old man was glad.
"Look, Sha'il. They mean business—one of them made a hole in my back."
The old man stretched his neck to look at Sha'ir Khan's back. It was soaked with blood.
"They hit you, Sha'ir Khan."
"They shoot well."
"But it takes them too many shots."
"Oh, come, Sha'il. Leave off. You keep belittling them. They're like us. I like them. I like them . . . a . . . lot . . ."
The Khan's voice was a broken boat, sinking.
"They see better than you . . . Better than you . . . And they have a cause. They're fighting the outlaws."
"Sha'ir Khan!" the old man shouted.
And Sha'ir Khan's head was on the ground. More shots snapped through the valley; blood leapt everywhere from his body. Still he hummed in the silence of his head . . .
"Sha'ir Khan is going back, back to the fold,
Sha'ir Khan and his servant, Mashhadi Sha'il . . ."

1965

The First Day in the Grave

SADIQ CHUBAK

For that which befalleth the sons of men befalleth beasts; even one thing befalleth them: as the one dieth, so dieth the other; yea, they have all one breath; so that a man hath no preeminence above a beast: for all is vanity.

All go unto one place; all are of the dust, and all turn to dust again.

Who knoweth the spirit of man that goeth upward, and the spirit of the beast that goeth downward to the earth?

Wherefore I perceive that there is nothing better, than that a man should rejoice in his own works; for that is his portion: for who shall bring him to see what shall be after him?

Ecclesiastes, iii, 19-22

And now the autumn sun was almost pleasant. Summer had sucked out its strength and life-blood, licked the color from its face, and left it. All summer the planes and maples, which were planted all the way from the foot of the walls to the vast pool in the middle of the garden, had not allowed a drop of sunshine to reach the earth. But now, pale and losing their leaves under the autumnal morning sun, they leaned against the sky, numb and tired, drinking the lukewarm sun, too weak to spread their canvas of leaves under its rays.

Hadj Mo'tamed was taking his morning walk around the pool, aided by his walking stick. Everyday, morning and evening, he walked around the pool until he was exhausted. The pool was beautiful. It was vast. The quadrangle surface was covered thickly with waterlillies, leaf lying upon leaf, and flowers resting side by side. In its center pure well-water bubbled from a generous subterranean canal that quenched the thirst of the ten thousand square meter garden all year round.

The garden was in Absardar. Hadj Mo'tamed had bought it forty-five years ago. In it, he had built a big house with separate quarters for men and women, a hall, a guest-house, a bath, a servants' quarter, and a stable. He was only forty then and strong as an ox, not like now, when he was as feeble as the setting sun.

Near the pool was a low wooden platform bordered by short, delicately carved wooden bars and covered by a fine, deep red, paisley Kashan rug. On it stood a cut-glass Fath'alishah waterpipe with a beaded, emerald-green bowl, and a silk hose embroidered with pearls. A crystal tea-glass and an enamel sugar-bowl were on a silver tray, next to a leather-bound volume of Hafiz.

Hadji would sit here after the evening prayer all by himself, and drink arrack. His nocturnal drinking was a long-standing custom. They would fix him a tray of toasted *sangak* bread with yogurt and spinach, yogurt and cardoons, boiled lima beans, mashed meat, cheese with mint and greens, or yogurt and cucumbers, according to the season. An unchanging part of the tray was a crystal decanter of strong arrack in which a whole citron floated.

The tray was his panacea. He would take hours, sipping the arrack slowly in the light of a single candle which spread its rays through a crystal globe. Now and then he would quietly hum a line of poetry. He drank a lot in his youth, but now he barely had more than two or three drinks. This solitary drinking was his only joy.

Hadji had finished his tea, smoked his waterpipe, and read his Hafiz. Now he was walking slowly, aided by his walking stick, his rosary in his hand.

"I wait on the shore of the sea of extinction;

Hurry, Cupbearer, for the lip is not far from the mouth," he sang quietly, his voice roughened by asthma. 'Time to sing the swan-song and say good-by to all this luxury,' he mused. 'Eighty or ninety years! Where did it all go? What came of it? What did I gain from all that struggle? It was a dream. A dream full of fear. And this is the end. For what? Life!'

He stopped before a majestic plane tree. 'I must start saying good by to you. Do you know who planted you? I know I don't. When I bought this garden you were here just like you're now. A lot of other trees were here too. Some didn't survive. You and a few others did. But your time will come, too. I don't know how old you are. A hundred years? Five hundred? Who knows. If they leave you alone maybe you'll live to be a thousand, like the plane in Imamzadeh Saleh. But what then? You've got to go. You send your roots down, you eat our hearts and guts, and you get bigger until your turn comes. Who knows, maybe some day they'll build a street here, with dingy shops and radios screaming all day long. I bet the minute I die the bastards will take the pick and cut the garden to shreds and each take a piece. They won't give a damn about you. Then where will I be? Where will you be? We all travel the same path. Your father could become my coffin, and you my children's.

A fresh, half-open tea rose on a straight green stem caught his eye. The wide petals curled out, like lips open in a smile. 'What are you up to? Do you think your beauty could console me? Do you know what shape you'll be in this time tomorrow? Even if I set someone to guard you so no one picks you, you'll wither. Your petals will fall, and bugs will tear up your heart. But you're lucky. You don't know what's waiting for you. You're proud and you show off to the garden, but I know you're only an overnight guest. No. I lost hope in life little by little in these eight or nine decades. You can't change that.

The well has gone dry and digging won't help. But the thought of not seeing you next spring scares me. You'll bloom again, and people will look at you, but I won't be here to see you. You won't smile at me. You can't give me hope, but I'm used to you. Who knows, maybe they'll put you on my grave.

"The rose is dear, prize its company
It enters and leaves the garden in haste."

'Why are you prized? Why loved? So they'd put you on my grave? I wish you'd never come into the garden, so you'd never have to leave. You all sow separation and death in my heart. I wish I didn't have any of you. No house, no land, no garden, no tree, no flower, no wife, no child, no grandchild. Then I'd have no sorrow.'

The steward, born and bred in Hadji's household, appeared through the trees, bowing respectfully as he approached. When he reached Hadji, he bowed to the ground and stood before him, folding his arms on his breast. He was lean and had a shrewd, boney face. Hadj Agha was taken by surprise. He turned from the tea rose and fixed his questioning eyes on the steward's sad face.

"Sir, the burial place is ready. When will you honor the site with your presence?" He bent down his head. His voice still rang in his own ear when Hadji shouted.

"You son-of-a-bitch! Honor the site, indeed! Are you asking when I'll die, so they'll take me there?"

"Sir, I'd sooner lose my speech than be so presumptuous. I meant to ask you when you wanted to see the structure."

"Today. This afternoon. Now, go."

The steward took a few steps backwards, still facing Hadji and bowing constantly, then left. Hadj Agha turned to the tea rose.

'Did you hear what he said? The burial place is ready. My burial place. Do you now see the difference between us? I know my grave is ready, but you know nothing about yours. My whole life the thought of this grave has melted me down like a candle. But you stand there without a care, oblivious. That's why you're loved. You're loved because you're innocent. Now I must find out what kind of hell this hole is.'

117

Hadj Mo'tamed's family tree began with himself. No one knew his parents, not even himself. He had never seen them, and no one had ever told him who they were, or what they did. His early years were in Borujerd. He did not know who had taken care of him. He vaguely remembered begging and hanging about in the streets. But he recalled his apprenticeship quite well. He was ten or fifteen then. That was a long time ago. Later he joined Zel ul-Sultan's staff. He became an officer, a steward, and finally earned a title and governorship and joined the ranks of the great. He bought so much land and so many villages that he lost track of them. He became one of the established rich and no one dared to bring up his origin.

He had confined himself to his house for many years now. In the beginning, every once in a while he would attend the memorial service of a friend, or the religious gathering during the Ashura* at the house of his friend and next door neighbor, Jalal ul-Sultan. But he had given up attending even these functions. Now his next door neighbors were strangers to him. The houses had changed hands several times. Some of them had been replaced by shops and stores, or had made room for roads; strange tall buildings with florescent lights and noisy radios had taken the place of others. The new face of the neighborhood was hateful to him.

Hadji had seven sons each of whom had two or three wives and half a dozen children. Once a year, on New Year's Day, his sons reluctantly paid him a visit only to observe the tradition. Hadji's sons, their brides, the grand and great grandchildren would crowd the house and their noise would drive Hadji to distraction. They would all kiss Hadji's hand. Unwillingly, he would give each grown up a gold coin, and each child a silver coin. That was the limit of Hadji's generosity to his sons: a gold coin once a year.

This year, Hadji had been sitting at the pool in his fur cloak, smoking the waterpipe and watching the children, who had invaded the garden and were plundering the blossoms. An eight or nine year old boy was sailing a paper boat in the pool.

---

*An annual period of mourning for Muslims.

Hadji had not recognized him and had asked the steward who the boy was. "Sir, he is Agha Taghi's son by the daughter of Mash Akbar, the rice merchant," the steward had said. Hadji had frowned and ordered the steward to send the boy away from the pool. Agha Taghi was his second son and had several wives. Hadji Agha disliked him more than his other sons.

Hadji Agha and his only wife, Hadjiyeh Khanom, lived in the vast garden in the shadow of its tall, ancient trees and were attended to by a host of servants and maids. But husband and wife were bitter enemies. They lived at opposite ends of the garden and did not see each other from year to year. Hadjiyeh Khanom had been an invalid for many years and could not move by herself.

In spite of fifty years of marriage and seven children, Hadji and his wife could not bear each other's sight. Hadjiyeh had nothing but curses for her husband. The two never met face to face or sent each other messages. The sons lived their own lives and hated one another. Because of his strange habits, Hadji's neighbors referred to him as "Crazy Hadji." He had heard this nickname and attributed its origin to Hadjiyeh's evil tongue.

The steward ran the house in such a way that it was unnecessary for the husband and wife to come in contact. With his innate intelligence and his shrewdness acquired through experience, he had succeeded in keeping both happy, and, having his wits about him, had caught large fish in muddy waters. He had secretly put aside a handsome sum of money for himself.

Hadji's newly built burial place bathed in the dying afternoon sun, in a secluded corner of the courtyard. Gol Agha was sweeping the courtyard, gathering the twisted plane leaves, and preparing the burial place for Hadji's visit. Bent double, she had been sweeping for a long time and was tired. She took a deep breath and stood erect. She switched the broom to her other hand and began to scratch her body. Under her dress, which was stiff with sweat and dirt, her skin was covered with sores. Her face and the back of her neck were also full of sores. She had had them for a long time and had tried to cure them at first, but had left them alone when she was told they were only eczema. She would take barberry juice, which she thought beneficial, whenever she could to cure them; but so far it had failed. The sores were dry and itched constantly. The skin around them peeled in thin layers.

'When the damn thing starts itching it makes me wish I were dead,' she thought. 'You'd think I was a leper, the way everybody avoids me. They tell me I got syphilis, chancre, pox, what not.'

She put the broom down and began to fill the burlap sack with leaves. 'What a season! You keep gathering the leaves, and they fall again like rain. God wouldn't let them fall if they'd any use. I'd like to know why it doesn't rain money instead. Would that be against the Koran? I wonder why old people kick the bucket in autumn and winter. Hadji is very old and he's got his grave ready. Maybe it's time for him to go. God knows best. He's got a lot of heirs. There'll be plenty of rice and halva for a few days. But God forbid! He's not a bad man. Who knows, his sons probably won't give me even the little he gives.'

The site had not been a burial place originally. On it, once stood two shops, belonging to an engraver and a pen-case maker, and a small courtyard filled with lumber. Hadji was happy that he had built his tomb on virgin land. He had bought the site dearly, had cleared it, and built a resting place for himself and his family. But during the time the burial place was under construction, he had not wanted to visit it even once, and it had been completed without his supervision.

Gol Agha was sitting on the doorstep at the entrance of the tomb, grown impatient at the crows' noise. A cluster of crows stained the sky like a dark cloud. She wished Hadji would come and leave soon, so that she could go to the coffee house and smoke opium, drink strong tea and listen to the storyteller. 'The sly Dervish!' she thought. 'Last night he put off Sohrab's death for tonight. I don't think he'll get to it even tonight. He'll go on milking us all he can, before he does.' Then she saw Hadji in the distance, jumped to her feet, and stood with her arms folded on her breast, bowing again and again.

Fat and of medium height, Hadji arrived at the burial place, followed by the lean steward. He stopped, placed his walking stick behind him, gripping its silver-sheathed head with both hands and leaning against it. He was breathing hard. His eyes hovered over the tomb as the sound of his asthmatic breath and palpitating heart beat against his ear-drums. Five years ago he had liked and bought the site. Now that it had been transformed into a burial place, whose first guest he knew would be himself, he disliked it. He looked at the tiles and the frieze. Lines from the Koran were inscribed in fine hand above the entrance. "All shall taste of death," he read the line several times and his stomach sank. The frieze was well done, but the windows were small and low, blocked by metal bars. They looked dreary. Hadji could not breathe.

"Why are the windows so small and low?" he asked the steward without looking at him. "With this strong brick wall you could've made the windows much larger. A southern exposure must have large windows. The place looks like a jail." He turned his head slowly and looked at the door and the walls. His mouth was dry.

Ordinarily, Hadji would not have dropped the matter so easily. It was unusual for him to speak softly, without cursing and using obscenities, especially when he was dissatisfied with something. But now that he had seen the tomb and knew his death was near, he was in no mood to make a fuss. The steward, who knew Hadji's temper, thought it best not to answer him. Silence buried Hadji's words. As if awakened from a deep sleep he mused: 'A faultfinder even here! You'll sleep in the grave—what difference will the size of the window make?' Then he thought, 'What are you saying! I paid all that money for this hole. My dignity depends on it. They'll all come to see it tomorrow, enemies and friends. I want something decent.'

"Well, the outside isn't much, let's see what the inside looks like," he said aloud, as he crossed the narrow corridor and entered the tomb. He looked for his grave, which he had ordered to be dug. The open mouth of the grave—the only one yet—sent shivers down his back. A cold sweat broke on his forehead and the back of his neck. It was as if they had erected a gallows to hang him. This was the grave he had prepared for himself. At its head a green slab of marble leaned against the wall, the inscribed side facing it. "Turn it the other way. Let's see what it looks like," he said to the steward gently.

The stone was light and thin. 'God is living and does not die. Here lies the forgiven, cleansed, resident of heaven al-Hadj Ali-Akbar Mo'tamed ul-Saltanah, died in the month of ―――' The Arabic inscription was in fine hand, the date left blank.

'The stone will weigh a ton on my chest and take my breath away,' he thought. 'People will read the inscription and admire the handwriting. Maybe they'll say a prayer for me. But what good will that do? This is the end. They stuff you into a hole with no way out. "Resident of heaven!" What optimism! Ridiculous! He doesn't care what we say. He does what He wants. I should've told them to write "resident of hell." I wonder what date will fill the blank. What day. Well, I won't be here to read it.

The monument was spacious. The windows looked even smaller inside. They were tightly shut. The stuffy, dank air burned his nostrils. He turned suddenly, afraid that the steward had left him there alone, and was heartened by his presence. "It's quite roomy. I didn't think it would turn out this big. There are two rooms upstairs, aren't there?" Hadji asked after a few phlegmy coughs. He was trying to hide his discomfort. He knew well there were two rooms upstairs; he had ordered them himself. The builder had showed him the floor plan and explained it to him many times.

"Yes, Sir," the steward had answered respectfully. "One for men, one for women. There's also a pantry for tea and waterpipe." He was about to add 'for the mourners,' but stopped himself. He feared Hadji like a dog. Something clawed at Hadji's heart. A heavy pain wrung his insides. He stared at the grave, thinking.

'When I'm gone, they'll come here, drink my tea, smoke my waterpipe and eat my halva, cursing me in their hearts. The world will go on without me.

"Nothing was lacking, before we came.
When we depart, it'll be the same."

Tsk-tsk! This is my grave. My life ends here. I'll have to sleep here, food for worms.'

He turned from the grave and glanced at the ceiling, the walls, and the door in terror. The monument had turned into a single stifling grave. He wanted to escape. He went to the narrow veranda which led to a courtyard behind the monument. He stopped and glanced around him. The veranda was narrow and long, borne by two columns with Jamshidi cornices. Under a tall pine in the courtyard was a small pool. The courtyard itself was small, half the size of the tomb. A toilet with a crooked tin roof and a leaky wall, which made Hadji uneasy, was at its other end. From the adjacent garden, dusty medlar branches intruded over the wall. Their unripe, worm-eaten fruit clawed at Hadji's heart. Suddenly a host of crows rushed at the pine tree, chasing one another. The pine shook and filled up with their noise. Dry needles fell over the courtyard. Then the crows flew away, their croaking leaving black spots in the sky.

He felt a weight over his heart. His skin had stretched; something wanted to get out but could find no escape. His knees trembled; he was about to fall. With the aid of his walking stick he reached one of the columns and held onto it. Everything was dizzily turning. A painful loneliness had separated him from life. His mind was overcome by a sleepy forgetfulness. He closed his eyes. 'Where's your courage?' he thought. 'Who knows. Maybe you'll live to be a hundred and twenty. It isn't impossible. See! I lied to the tea rose. Hope is still there. It hasn't dried up. Yes. Lots of people have lived a hundred and twenty years. I'm feeling better now. I guess I'm a little bilious.'

He went back into the tomb. His grave yawned before him. He leaned against the wall, afraid of being alone. Yet, he asked the steward to leave. "I want to be alone for a bit," he said. "Go and close the door behind you. Don't let anyone in. I'll leave when I'm done. I have to get used to the place." The steward bowed and left.

The dry sound of the latch cut his breath short. His eyes traced the steward's steps. He looked at the ground, thinking of the silence and loneliness inside the monument. Near the ceiling, the walls ended in a tile inscription with lines from the Koran elegantly written in white against a navy background.

'It's quite roomy,' he consoled himself. 'There's room enough for me, Hadjiyeh, Hasan, Hosein, Ahmad, Taghi, Mahmud, Sa'id, and all their offspring. The rest don't concern me, and those who'll come later will have to fend for themselves. We didn't get along in life, but here we'll lie side by side, embracing. I hope the graves won't open up into each other, otherwise that vicious Hadjiyeh won't leave me alone even here. She should be buried at the other end. I'll mention that in my will.'

Long, narrow, and deep the grave sank in the ground. It looked like a country outhouse. Its walls and floor were lined with bricks which were not cemented, for they would have to be removed before interment. He leaned against the wall, at the head of the grave. 'They'll remove the bricks and lay me on the dirt. Come, opening your mouth like that! There's nothing new about you. Your mouth has been open at my feet my whole life. Now I've to sleep in you. We'll have to get used to each other, become friends. You'll be my future house. I'll have to lie down here until the Day of Judgment.'

He propped his walking stick against the wall, hesitantly crossed the two yards between the wall and the grave, and sat down slowly, his legs hanging into the grave. His feet were a long distance from the bottom. He tried to estimate the distance. 'After they remove the bottom bricks it will be even deeper. What difference does it make how deep?' Suddenly he looked at the door. It was closed, solemn, frowning. Copper filaments of sunshine entered through the windows, dyeing the inscription a ghostly gray. He no longer wanted to look at the dark inside of the grave. He closed his eyes.

'"The vissisitude of Fortune is common.

But your judgment, O Lord, will not change."

Eighty, ninety years! It was like yesterday! I'm lucky I've a grave and a tomb with a burning light. There are many who don't. But what's the difference? When they stuff me in there, what use is a tomb or a light? I hope at least they spare me any punishment in the other world. Haven't I suffered enough here? Is there any punishment worse than life itself? I've known nothing but torment since I can remember. But this is just the beginning. Lord, I've a long way ahead of me!'

His nostrils burned and his eyes grew moist. He blew his nose into the grave and shook the slippery mucus from his fingers. He wiped his eyes with his fur cloak, his heart-beat echoing in his temples. 'What was life all about? Enough! Whatever it was, it's over. Over in the blinking of an eye. All was torment. Both when I begged in the alleys of Borujerd and now that I've made my millions. What came of it all? Seven sons, each meaner and more ungrateful than the next. And I was cruel. I killed. I took people's property. And I prayed, fasted, and wept. What for? I see my life wasn't worth a red cent.'

His thick, white mustache reached the corners of his mouth and a short growth covered his face. His wrinkled skin was an unhealthy brown. His large eyes were bloodshot, but his eyesight was still good. His silky white hair stuck out of his sheep-skin hat in shiny threads. He had a large head and large ears. His face had harbored a frown for many years.

His eyes became accustomed to the grave's darkness. 'How deep it is! They must dig deeper than one's height, they say, so the stench won't get out. I should sit in there one night and drink arrack. Then I'll get used to it. The grave must get used to me too. This is my future house. I must get used to it. Trusting in you, o Lord. In the name of God.'

He began to slip into the grave, supporting himself on his hands. His shoulders ached. 'I wish I'd taken my walking stick. I can't take a single step.'

He stood in the grave, the edge far above his head. Terror struck him. The bottom of the grave was quite visible. He was at a loss how to lie down in the grave. He removed his false teeth and stuffed them in his vest pocket. 'O Lord, you know what I suffered for every single one of my thirty-two teeth when they were pulled. I almost died. Do you think life's joys are worth that kind of pain? His face was now smaller; the upper lip tight against the lower lip, the cheek bones prominent, the nose extended downward. He sat in the grave, then lay down, as if governed by a will not his own. The smell of lime burned his nostrils. The bottom seemed narrower than the top. The monument's ceiling seemed very high. It pressed heavily on his heart. He noticed the iron beams in the ceiling under the plaster. 'Four number 16 iron beams! What for? How many floors were they planning to build? Well, it can't hurt. If they get a big crowd in the upper rooms, the ceiling won't collapse. The hell with it if it does. I won't be alive then.'

He stared at the ceiling. The grave seemed as deep as a well. He was far below the floor level. His body turned cold. 'I guess I really must call it quits. I never took it seriously till now. What did I gain in this life? I don't want to die and be stuffed into this hole like a dog. A life full of torment, made hell by fear of death, ending in such an insult. Is there an insult worse than death? I haven't finished my work yet. I've a lot to do. I must sort out a trunk full of papers and tear up half the stuff. I don't know what the court will decide about my real estate in Kermanshah. Sons-of-bitches! They gave me such a hard time. I must see to my property. I could never bring myself to make a will. I kept putting it off. How much longer can I do that? I have to divide everything among these sons-of-bitches with my own hands. They'll take everything and shit on my grave.'

The rough earth hurt his back, but his head rested comfortably on the sheep skin hat and his neck and shoulders did not touch the ground. He had always liked a high pillow. He slept on a high pillow at night. But the ground felt unfamiliar. 'One doesn't feel these things then. How will it come? Is it like falling asleep—when one doesn't feel anything? I don't think so. We kid ourselves. All our lives we know we'll die, and we know we're dying the moment death comes, and, worst of all, when we die, we know we are dead and cut off from the living. We feel the separation at the moment of death. One has to leave everything. I'll be truthful. I have no love for my wife or any of my children. But I've grown used to this house, the trees, the pool, my clothes. It's hard to leave the sun, the moon, the stars, the spring, summer, autumn, winter, the clouds, the snow, the wind, the rain; most of all, it's hard for me to leave myself. I think you remain aware of your surroundings until they put you in the grave. They say when they put the heavy rock over your breast and pour the dirt over it and fill the grave, you jump up and yell, "Take me with you! Don't leave me here!" Then your head hits the rock and breaks, and that's just the beginning. The beginning of a new world. The angels will test your knowledge of religion. Then the fiery club, the flames of hell, and eternal punishment. How long does it take before they decide where to send you, to heaven or hell? Do I have to wait till the Day of Judgment? What will I do till then? Just lie down? Or will I be tortured? And what about the righteous? Do their souls wander until the Day of Judgment before they go to heaven? Forgive me, Lord, but your territory seems to be as helter skelter as ours. I can't figure how it works. Maybe the archangel will blow his horn tomorrow. No one knows but you. Why should I lie, Lord? I'm really afraid of you. I'm not certain you exist. With this uncertainty you've put in our hearts, you've dragged the world to war and bloodshed. Who has seen you? How can you be nothing and everything? You've sent all these prophets, they say one hundred and twenty four thousand of them, to prove that you exist. But you know well not one of them has proved that. We haven't much of a choice. You sent the Prophet to earth, gave him a sword and said, "If they believe, well and good; if not, their lives and property are yours." Why? Isn't everybody your creature?

"He is not compound, material, visible or confined in space;
He has no partner, the mighty Lord beyond mind's grasp."

This is you. I for one haven't been able to know you from this description. The description itself shows that such a being can't exist. I don't know whether you exist or not. But because I'm afraid of you, because I shake with rage, I force myself to believe you exist. I say to myself, if there's a God, let Him be; if not, I haven't lost anything. I'm afraid of you because I'm accustomed to your fear. O Lord, I know my sins are too many; too many even for your boundless mercy. I'm too guilty to ask for forgiveness. You know I've killed, not one or two, but nine people. But you also know I couldn't help it. What I regret most is that I didn't even know them and they hadn't done me any wrong. They were probably good people. You're the Omniscient and know who prompted me to it. Do you remember? You had a small god on earth, he was a prince, and I was *his* servant, not yours. I was young and ignorant. I'd suffered so much cruelty from people that I'd become like them. But why should a prince, your agent on earth, commit murder? I don't understand. He killed a thousand. Whose fault was that? Forgive me, Lord, could anyone kill a louse if you didn't want him to? Take that poor girl, bless her soul, whom I ruined—the daughter of Mashdi Abbas, the corn dealer. Was it my fault? Was it her father's fault? He left her in my care when he died. But his shroud wasn't yet dry when I slept with the girl, got her pregnant, and robbed her of everything she had. You know how sorry I was for her later. But it was her fault not mine when later she ran away from my house to the brothel. Then I couldn't take her back. Now that I think about it I wasn't guilty in seducing her. I was young; she was young, too, and beautiful. I'd never seen such a lovely woman. I wanted her and she wanted me. We were like fire and cotton, the two of us. You know how I grew to love her after I slept with her. I was mad with love for her. I wanted to marry her. But when her belly began to rise, she ran away, straight to the brothel, afraid of what people would do to her. If I'd known where she had gone right away, I would've brought her back before anyone had touched her. But it was a week before I found out and by then she was like a rotten fruit. When she disappeared, I thought she had killed herself. I asked after her, but no one knew where she was. I had all the wells and pools searched. Finally, she turned up in the brothel. Still, I went there after her. Everybody found out about us and I was disgraced. She had aborted the child. Her eyebrows plucked, her face rouged and powdered, she spread herself under one mule-driver after another. She was no good any more. "Why the hell did you do this?" I asked her. "People made me feel so ashamed, I couldn't face them any more," she said. But this wasn't my fault; it wasn't her fault either. You consider both of us sinners. But we would have never met if you hadn't willed it. You're responsible. But let me pay for her sin as well as mine. She was innocent. I was responsible. No. You and I were responsible. If you're just, you'll take responsibility for this sin. I wish I knew where she is now. I'd go to her. She was a good girl. Let all her sins be mine and give her credit for all my fasting and praying. All of it. If I could find her I'd give her all my possessions. I want you to know I never loved anyone as much as her. At first she became loathsome to me. But now, after all these years, I love her the way I did in the beginning. Could my pilgrimages to Mecca and Karbala wash away her sin? All my sins together are not as bad as the way I treated that helpless girl. This sin has weighed heavily on my conscience. Aren't the tortures of this life enough? Must we burn in hell, too? Don't we burn enough here? Do you need to invent all those punishments for us to look forward to? You sit up there and take notes in your book. Did you write that she was like an angel? She was engaged. You sent cholera and killed off her parents, her young man, and thousands more. Then she was left with me and what shouldn't have happened did. All those innocent people you wiped out that year. The dead piled up in the street like garbage. You keep preaching, "You are all mortal." "You must leave everything and depart," you say. We keep burying our friends, our loved-ones, our relatives—the wolf gets the sheep one by one. And they continue grazing peacefully. You sit up there and watch, and we can't do a thing. Tell me, don't you have a god to answer to? Don't you have to explain why you do away with so many people? You know my life. What was it, except pain and torment? I never had a will of my own. Consider the Prince. He had money and land, and was a ruler. People's lives and possessions were in his power. He could say just one word and have a hundred people hanged. How many people do you think he killed? How many virgins did he rape? Didn't they belong to you? Their only sin was that they had no power, no free will. They were captives. Why did you create a prince whose food was human blood? Remember how he had the heart of that Hadji plucked out as he was still alive, because he had complained about him to the king? And what happened to the prince? He died peacefully in his soft, warm bed, surrounded by his wives and children, and was buried in Najaf. His offspring divided his possessions among themselves, and nothing happened to any of them. I don't want to bring up other people; they'll have to answer for themselves. I don't know what you're going to do with me. You're the boss. I can't stop you. You can do with me as you please. I've always been your captive. I had no will of my own. Whatever I did was with your will and your help. If there is to be punishment, it must be for both of us. You aren't going to leave this world pure and unstained. You're happy that you'll live forever to do unlimited injustice. It hasn't occurred to you that your immortality is worse than our mortality. We die and after a while our names, and our vices and virtues are forgotten. Think of yourself: generation after generation will taste your injustice and pass away. And this shall be eternal damnation upon you. In case you're interested, everybody hates you. They flatter you and bow before you because they're afraid of you. But in their hearts, they curse you. Man is a strange animal. Forgive me, I'm talking too much. Forgive me, Lord. I have committed a thousand sins, but I guess I was never able to talk to you until today. I talk to you in my prayers everyday, but not the way I'd like to. I speak in Arabic, without understanding what I say. I wish I could open my heart to you like this. But I was told the daily prayer included all of this. So I say my prayers, but they never satisfy me. I don't know what I am saying when I pray. And I have a lot to tell you, things that aren't found in the prayer. Sin weighs on my heart like a mountain. Why should you understand Arabic only? Lord, let me speak to you in my own language. I have a lot to tell you, to tell you in this world—there may not be time in the next, with all those crowds on the Day of Judgment and the sun descending as low as one's head. I couldn't talk to you then. Who knows, maybe on that day you'll speak a language even harder than Arabic, and we won't understand a word. You run the show. Always have. Maybe after death I'll lose my reason and won't be able to defend myself. Let me say what I have while I'm alive. The insults and torments are suffered here, why should the interrogation and trial be somewhere else? Forgive me, Lord, I can't hide from you what is in my heart. You know what is at the bottom of our hearts. The longer we live, the more we sin. I got used to sin. The more I sinned, the bolder I became. When I see all the injustice in the world I can't help thinking you're responsible. I wish you would do something so people would stop doing wrong. Evil is like a chain around our necks and we aid each other in wrongdoing. With all the prophets you've sent, why does evil still surpass good? If you exist, so does the Devil; and he quarrels with you all the time. Why did you make him? I am lying in my grave and I know I can't escape from death. My fate is in your hands. But I know you're behind every war, every killing, every famine, every epidemic. I sinned because you willed it. We were partners in sin. I did not kill those men at the prince's command single-handed; you participated in every murder. You and I together sowed the bastard seed in that girl's womb. How come the Devil can share in the begetting of bastards and you can't? You shouldn't be less than the Devil. Lord, if I'm speaking out of ignorance, forgive me for my lack of understanding. But if I'm in the right and speak with understanding, then you must not punish me. I have suffered your hell and your punishment in this world. My life was all torment. I've done some good deeds, deeds which you reward. I've said my prayer, fasted, gone to Mecca, fed the poor. But I myself don't consider these good deeds. And I have a mountain of sins, which you hurled over my back. I was destined to sin; there was no escape. You made me this way. How can one go to the next world, relying only on your mercy? From now on I want to do some good—what *I* consider good deeds. Now I realize you are closer to us than anyone, because I could never say these things to anyone else. Now I know what to do. I have to leave this world with a peaceful mind. I lived wrong. I never knew what it was like to be humane and show compassion. I was cruel to my wife and children. This grave has enlightened me. For the first time I can see all my faults. I only thought of amassing money. Once I learned that Mohsen and his children were destitute for their daily bread, and I didn't give a damn. That's how mean I was. Hadjiyeh Khanom's hair turned gray in my house; she bore me nine children, and I tormented her and never let her tears dry. I've done too many wrongs. You've probably recorded them all and know about them. But I want to change my life.

After I leave this place, I'll go directly to my wife, kiss her hands and feet, and apologize for the past. Then I'll call my children together and make it up to them. I'll build schools, hospitals, mosques—no, not mosques. There are too many of them around and they do no good. I'll leave endowments for schools and hospitals, then I'll divide what's left among my children and servants. I'll divide the villages among the farmers. This house will make an excellent hospital. I'll live here in a little corner until the day you're satisfied with me. Not a cent of this wealth belongs to me. Why should I leave anything for my children? It isn't mine, so how could I leave it to my heirs? Damn them, let them work and earn a living. They've been waiting for me to die, so they can eat up my money. I hope they choke. I'm not coming back to the monument again. Why should I? Why did I build this edifice and make a fool of myself?'

He felt free. An unfamiliar joy had bloomed in his heart. After a life of inner blindness a new and satisfying thought had blossomed in his heart and was bearing fruit instantly. It did not take him much effort to rise. He stood up, his face beaming. The walls of the grave were about a foot higher than his head. He raised his hands and grasped the floor on opposite sides of the grave's edge. But his body was heavy and numb, his arms could not support his weight, his feet were cemented to the bottom of the grave. He was cold. It had grown dark outside.

Suddenly his hands began to tremble, his legs froze and the cold numbness shot through his thighs. He tried several times to lift himself out of the grave. His fingers were bleeding. His insides were frozen; he felt nauseated.

Frozen blood slipped down in his head and excruciating pain shot through the left side of his chest. An ominous, deathly chill rose from within him and numbed his mind. He wanted to shout. He shouted. His voice echoed in his head and blood blocked his throat. His hands loosened their hold. His knees folded, his back cracked, his heart broke loose inside him, and he knew he was dead. His body swung and turned. He fell on his back, his eyes fixed at the steward's terrified eyes. 'Get me out of here! I'm alive!' he repeated in his mind. The steward had genuflected in the grave. "There is no God but Allah," he repeated.

Scattered lights sent their rays in through the window and the consumptive shadow of the window bars coughed blood on the tomb's floor.

1966

The Warm South
BY SHAPUR QARIB

The doctor lit his cigarette and pushed away his dinner tray. He had no appetite. The driver watched him curiously. "Something is the matter with him, and he doesn't want to show it," he said to himself. The doctor took off his shirt and lay on his cot, naked to the waist. At night, he enjoyed the breeze which rose over the fruitful palms. Lying in bed and smoking the local cigarettes which still tasted unfamiliar, he felt miles away from the South's unbearable heat, and from the filthy, fly-infested cottages of a land burned and dried up by the sun. Yet, opening his eyes, he would feel a deep attachment to the high hills, the black cottages, and the beautiful view, where one's eyes rested on the open umbrellas of palm in every direction. He was in love with Tala, the old man's daughter. The thought of leaving her behind had killed his appetite. He could not speak of this to the driver, who would not keep it secret. The old man eyed his cigarette pack like other nights. Ashamed of his forgetfulness, the doctor pointed to the green pack.

"Take some. You don't have to wait for me to offer them to you."

The driver watched the old man with contempt. He had abandoned his pipe and grown used to smoking free cigarettes. He lit the cigarette with a piece of charcoal and sucked the smoke avidly. The doctor liked the way he prevented any of the smoke from going to waste.

"It was fate, old man," the doctor said, leaning toward him affectionately. "In which cottage would we be staying now, if we hadn't come across you that evening?"

The old man blinked.

"In the cottage of *Kadkhoda*, the head of the village," said the driver, his mouth full.

His sarcasm annoyed the doctor. The old man knew where the shoe pinched. They could have stayed at Kadkhoda's cottage for free. The doctor closed his eyes to discourage an argument between the two. It pained him that he had failed to make peace between them. The old man pressed another piece of opium on his pipe and sucked the smoke with pleasure. The numbing smell of opium lingered in the air over their heads. The doctor loved the smell. It soothed his nerves and helped him temporarily forget the sad faces of the country people. The driver was still at his dinner tray. He looked glum because the fried eggs had not filled him. He played with the bread and dates, frowning. The doctor worried that eating too many dates would get him into trouble. He was always after women. When they would return to the port after being away on assignment for a few months in villages, the first thing he would look for was a prostitute. Late at night he would come back to the clinic and lie down in a corner, chewing the cud of his memories.

"Are you listening, doc? What a great piece, doc . . ."

The doctor would feign sleep to discourage him. Finding him unattentive, the driver would growl.

"The rotten stink! He neither likes women, nor wants to talk about them. And he thinks he is a man!" Then he would take his tale to the hospital caretaker.

The doctor took a deep breath, inhaling the opium smoke. His head bent, the driver considered his empty gasoline cans and decided to sell them that night. They would make noise and take too much room if he took them to Minab. If he didn't get rid of them that night, he would have to sell them to the old man at his price. He didn't want just to give him the cans. He was fed up with the shrewd old man, who pocketed half of what they gave him for their living expenses, and used his daughter to get around the doctor. The driver had gone to the torrid South to make money and was not about to spend his earnings to pay for the old man's addiction and his household expenses. He blamed himself for having let the old man trick them the evening they arrived at the village.

"You Americans, master?" the old man had asked, taking off his hat.

He wished he had said something nasty to the old man. Instead he had been flattered.

"Yes, we're American, old man. Where does the Kadkhoda live? I want a clean cottage for the doctor," he had said.

The old man had humbly placed his hands on his eyes.

"You can have my cottage, master. Over there, up the hill."

When they reached the top of the hill, Tala, who was sitting in front of the cottage, rose politely. The driver's eyes moved from the spindle in her lap to her round breasts and black eyes.

"Looks rather nice," he had said. "What do you think, doc?"

The doctor turned his glance from the palms at the foot of the hill and shook his head coldly.

"Forget the cottage," the driver whispered. "Look at that piece. She really turns you on."

The doctor put a cigarette to his lips. The driver struck a match, trying to persuade him to stay.

"A paradise, doc," he said. "In the evening, after tea and cigarettes, up here it'll be really nice."

The old man had gone to the jeep happily, trying to end their hesitation by unloading their suitcases.

"Hey! Wait a minute. Who said we were going to stay?" the driver had shouted.

"Leave him alone," the doctor had said quietly. "Let the poor man make some money."

The driver had smiled and turned confidently toward Tala, as if to say, "You owe this to me." The old man had placed the suitcases at their feet, panting.

"You don't have to kill yourself for the Americans," the driver had said.

"It's a servant's duty, master."

"Is that your daughter?"

"She's your slave, master."

"God keep her. She's first rate, like the dates around here."

He had pulled his cap over his eyebrows and mused, "I'll make her tonight." But when he had carried the suitcases to the cottage with the help of the old man and made the cots, he had not found Tala. He had been annoyed with the old man's trickery and his daughter's cleverness. That was why he took every chance to annoy him. He decided to sell the empty cans down the hill for any price he could get. Oblivious to the driver, the old man was carefully drawing lines on the floor, his pointed chin on his knees.

"Is this some witchcraft, old man, or have you become an architect?" asked the driver, staring at the floor.

The old man prepared for more of his gibes.

"What are these lines?" the driver asked again.

"You mean the coffee-house?" the old man raised his head.

"Did you say 'coffee-house'?"

"Yes. If I can get it together, I'll be in clover. No question about it." He smiled, hopeful and confident that his wish would materialize, heartened by the money he had saved during their stay.

"No one has ever thought of opening a coffee-house at the chromium mine," he added, his lips dark from opium.

"So this is the plan of your coffee-house, is it?" the driver asked hesitantly.

The old man moved back and pointed at the floor.

"The large cottage is the coffee-house, the one over there is the outhouse. The other cottage is for me and my kids."

The driver spat the date stones on the floor and licked his sticky fingers.

"Are you planning to take them along?"

"I couldn't run the place single-handed. Tala is a great help."

The doctor, who had been listening to them, suddenly sat up in his bed.

"Are you serious?" he asked the old man, surprised.

The old man raised his head, staring at the doctor's glasses, a hopeful smile on his face. The doctor was convinced that he was just daydreaming and chatting, high on opium.

"You smoke too much and then start making up stories," he said.

"Why should I make up stories, doctor? I've had the idea for two years now."

"Why haven't you built the place then?" the driver asked.

The old man bowed his head, selecting a glowing piece of charcoal to smoke his third piece of opium. The coffee-house with its arched ceiling, samovar and teapot loomed in his mind.

"The truth is, I didn't have the means," he said, breathing calmly. "I had the idea, but where was the money?"

"Don't you have the money?" the doctor asked, frowning.

"Doctor, if I had the money, would I be here?"

The doctor put his head on the pillow. He realized why whenever he had talked about Tala the old man had evaded him. "Tala isn't worthy of you, doctor," he had said. He wondered how he had failed to figure out the old man during the weeks they had lived in his cottage.

The driver lit a cigarette. His failure to win Tala had grown into an obsession. He was ashamed to have been put down by a country girl. He took his eyes from the smoky kettle.

"Well, if you don't have the money, why don't you give up?" the driver asked.

The old man shrugged. The driver turned the bitter smoke in his mouth and blew it at the old man.

"You crafty old man! I bet you invented this cock and bull story to sponge on us," he said contemtuously.

The old man smiled, then sadness invaded his face. The driver was used to these changes.

"Don't get depressed. Carry on with the story. I bet you'll succeed in fooling one of us," he said.

The old man paid no attention to him. He didn't want to spoil the effect of the opium for no reason. He drank up the strong tea in his glass and turned his eyes to his drawing on the floor. The doctor rose. He glanced at the foot of the hill. The cottages were marked by a few dim lights. In the course of the few weeks he had been lodging on the hill, he had grown weaker day by day. He would lose his composure and chain smoke when Tala would come for the trays after supper, but he was careful not to blunder and betray his secret to the driver. The old man filled the glasses with tea. The driver put a sugar cube in his mouth and swallowed his sweetened saliva. He had a tendency to tease the old man when he was high on opium.

"Old man, the day we rented your cottage folks down there told us nasty things about you. They said you were a crafty old buzzard."

"They hate my guts," the old man said.

"For no reason?"

"No. They think I am robbing you up here."

"Well, you probably are. Otherwise they wouldn't say you were."

"No. It's an old grudge, belonging to the time when the government prohibited the planting of opium poppies. They all stopped planting, but I kept at it."

"Even after it was prohibited?"

"I had no choice. How could I make ends meet with just a few date palms, which sometimes didn't bear fruit? The government didn't know what it was like. I had five daughters. If I'd had a boy, that would've been something. Like other families, I could send him to Kuwait and Dubai to smuggle goods. But God hadn't willed it. Anyhow, I planted a piece of land in Tang Goraz and the gendarmes never found out about it."

"Did the people?"

"No. Not exactly. But when the opium smoke didn't stop rising from this cottage, they became suspicious. Then the Kadkhoda caught on to me."

"Did he tell the gendarmes?"

"No. We worked it out, the two of us. He would come over whenever he had the urge and say he had seen the gendarmes around. I could take a hint. I knew I had to leave him alone with my daughter, the older one, in the cottage."

"You were in a jam."

"What a jam! I didn't mind being a pimp, but the son-of-a-bitch played a new tune every day. One day he stood outside the cottage and complained, 'Even a donkey gets tired of eating at the same trough everyday.' That did it. I knew even if I gave him Tala he would still want the others."

"So he told on you?"

"Yes, he informed the gendarmes in the port. When they set me free a year later, all I had was the rag on my back."

"Why didn't you plant again? Were you afraid?"

"No, it wasn't fear. I just didn't have the strength to struggle with the soil and fight the Kadkhoda. Besides, the village wasn't what it used to be. Everybody had left to work in the mine or build roads. I started thinking about building the coffee-house."

The doctor stood uneasily before him. "How much money do you need?" he asked.

"Two or three hundred tomans, doctor."

The old man held his chin up, awaiting the doctor's generosity. With his official jeep and fat wallet he certainly could afford to give him that sum. But the doctor was thinking of Tala. He hoped to reach an agreement with the old man later that night, when the driver wasn't around. He was sure the old man would give up Tala for the coffee-house. The driver looked at the doctor's tea and reminded him that it was getting cold. The doctor shrugged. The driver put another sugar cube in his mouth, waiting for Tala, who generally came up the hill after dinner.

* * * * *

In the dim lamp-light the doctor had been reading, but he could not follow the story. His mind was occupied with Tala and with the next day's departure. He was going to ask her father for her hand that night. His silence told the driver that he was preoccupied with something. Oblivious to them, the old man was examining the pile of empty gasoline cans like an expert junk-dealer. He shook his head with dissatisfaction to lower the value of the merchandise, watching the driver from the corner of his eye. The driver was not paying him any attention. He was kneeling before his disorderly suitcase, wondering where to put all the contraband merchandise he had bought to sell at a profit. The old man held up a can and examined it carefully.

"Do you see this? They're all like that. They get full of holes," he said nasally, hoping to persuade the driver to sell him the cans. He could make a good profit if he succeeded. But the driver was cross. He enjoyed teasing the old man. He continued packing the cologne bottles at the bottom of his suitcase.

"If you're thinking of selling them down the hill, forget it," the old man said. "They smell of gasoline and date syrup slips right through their seams."

The driver glared at him. "Even if I sold them to you at cost, it wouldn't do you any good. So forget it."

The old man returned the can to the pile, disappointed. The air smelled of night and of ripening dates. He missed the noisy date-picking seasons when the aroma of dates and date syrup filled the air. The young men would climb the palms, the women and children would watch them cut the high heavy bunches of dates. But now the village no longer marked the date-picking season. The mine had made the date-palms worthless. The wages paid by Americans and Italians left no incentive for anyone to stay in the village. The dates remained on the tree, ripened, and went to waste. The old man lighted his pipe, saddened. The sharp smoke reached the driver.

Tala came in to pick up the dinner trays. The driver fixed his eyes on her breasts. His face and chest warmed up as when he drank the date arrack. He looked for an excuse to chat with her. The doctor pulled the sheet over his naked body, bending his head to avoid her eyes. But he knew she was washing the tea glasses in the lukewarm water, her toes covered by her long dress.

Every night, Tala's arrival would stop the conversation. In the silence, the dizzying sound of the crickets agitated the doctor. He would turn silent and motionless. The driver would watch her lustfully.

Her head modestly bent down, Tala began to gather the supper trays. When she stooped to collect the date stones, the driver inhaled the scent of her body hungrily. He had waited every night for her and tried to win her, but she had given him no encouragement. His failure had led him to think that there was something between her and the doctor. When they had arrived, she had looked at the jeep with the joy and curiosity of a child and waited for them to take her for a ride. Why did she avoid him now? They were leaving the next day. He thought of having to leave Tala's untouched body for the rough hands of the village men, and cursed the doctor, whom he considered responsible for his failure. He covered the cologne bottle with local handwoven curtains to protect them from breaking. Tala glanced at the curtains.

"Well, we're finally leaving and you haven't traded your curtains with me. I wonder who will have them," the driver said.

Tala suddenly reeled. The driver jumped to his feet, ready to catch her in his arms. But she pulled herself together. The driver wondered why she had reacted in that manner. "Maybe she has given the curtains to him," he thought, his eyes searching for the doctor's suitcase. If he found the curtains there, he would know what to think. The old man offered him his pipe. The driver wiped it and inhaled deeply.

"Old man, this is the last time I'm smoking your pipe."

The old man smiled, not taking him seriously. He was sure he could talk him into selling the cans after he had smoked. The strong tobacco overcame the driver. He wanted to cry. He admitted to himself that he had failed with the girl, and was tempted to torment the doctor.

"What time are we leaving, doc?" he asked.

The doctor looked up.

"If we don't start early, the sun'll destroy us," the driver continued. The doctor said nothing, his eyes fixed on Tala. The lump in her throat had burst and she was trembling. She left the room with the trays.

"Where are you going tomorrow morning?" the old man asked. The driver bent down his head. He thought he had been tricked and was angry at the doctor. He would start a quarrel if he weren't afraid of the consequences; it could cost him his job. The old man, who was familiar with the driver's ugly mood, turned to the doctor.

"Doctor, do you mean to say people here have all been cured and don't need a doctor any more? I'm still sick," the old man said, coughing to win the doctor's sympathy. He sat on the floor, holding his head in his hands. Then he jumped to his feet, hearing a crash, the sound of trays and aluminum plates.

"What was it?" the driver called out, holding up the lamp. The old man joined him and looked down.

"It's that clumsy fool, Tala," he said.

"Are you all right?" the driver called out. This was a good excuse to join Tala down the hill, he thought, but the old man was in the way. He turned down the lamp which was smoking.

"With all my smartness, the doctor got the better of me," he thought. "That very first evening, when I was setting up the cots, I should've realized the sneaky doctor had stolen her heart." He spat on the ground.

"You were kidding when you said you were leaving tomorrow, weren't you?" the old man asked, his face catching the light from the lamp.

The driver walked away without answering. The old man took his hand.

"Say something," he pleaded.

"Leave me alone. Don't be such a pest," the driver shouted impatiently.

Behind the cottage, the old man was left alone in the dark. He was sour. Had he known that his boarders meant to leave so soon, he would have stolen more. The cans rattled, turning his attention to the driver. He was tying the cans in stacks to take them down the hill for sale.

*   *   *   *   *   *

The doctor sat before a suitcase full of books, lacking the energy to pack and take them to the jeep. He had been travelling in the South for a year. The hot southern sun had darkened his skin. He had lived in many villages and left them with no pangs. But now his heart sank when he thought of leaving the next day. Tala's tearful eyes, the thought of the old man's refusal, and the villagers who made a mountain out of a mole-hill agitated him. He sat with his arms folded around his knees like the old man and lighted a cigarette, trying to stop his thoughts. The old man had followed the driver down the hill. The lamp had run out of kerosene; the doctor rose. He turned the wick down until it fell into the bowl. He approached the bed listlessly. The night air mixed with smoke from distant cottages filled him with pleasure. He dropped into the sunken center of the cot. Alone in the hot South, working and living in dirty fly-infested villages, and feeling sorry for people who lived like animals, yet were satisfied, he was worn out and his nerves were frayed. He inhaled the smoke. Was it for this he had lost sleep and studied hard to become a doctor? In these villages he had forgotten how to practice medicine. Not having the medicine he needed, he had been reduced to a show-man. He went around in his American jeep, putting on a show and lying to diseased and decrepit villagers. He was a shrine devoid of miracles. At night, he would fall on his bed, tired, remembering Tehran, the neon signs of its movies, the lively music of its restaurants. In a few days he could spend a month's vacation in Tehran, stand at the counter of its bars, and forget himself and the South's endless sandy deserts in glasses of ice-cold beer. He wondered if the beer could wash away the memory of Tala. If he stopped seeing the scorched villages and their half-naked inhabitants, he might succeed in making peace with his memories. But the South would remain with him for many years. The people and the memory of Tala would last and fester like an incurable sore.

A sound outside the cottage caught his attention. "Who's there?" he asked, uneasy. The sound, which had stopped, grew louder. His heart sank. He rushed out of the cottage. Tala was sitting on the ground, crying. He put his arms around her, knowing why she wept.

"Get hold of yourself. You knew all along I would leave some day, didn't you?"

Tala was aloof. He blamed the driver's loose tongue. He kissed her long hair. He had grown used to the country smell of her body and it gave him pleasure. She had brought him the curtains she had woven.

"Are they for me?" he asked.

She did not answer. He wiped her eyes.

"I'm going down tonight to ask your father again."

"Don't. He is obstinate."

"But now I know how to handle him."

"You don't know him. If he weren't so obstinate, the Kadkhoda . . ."

"Kadkhoda was after you."

"Did he tell you all that? Did he say what became of my sisters?" she stared at him, surprised.

"No."

"When he grew penniless, he sent them to Shaghu."

"He didn't tell me that. He didn't say he sold his daughters."

"He hasn't told anyone. But people who had been to the port said they had seen my sisters in Shaghu."

The doctor closed his eyes. His nose itched from the smell of salt on Tala's skin. She had bathed in the salt-water stream that afternoon.

"He'll soften when I give him the money tonight."

"No, he will take me along to run the coffee-house," she said.

This upset him. He took her hands.

"My father isn't alone. The driver is with him," she continued.

"How come? They were fighting a minute ago."

"My father got the cans from him. He is in the cottage, smoking opium."

The doctor sat down on the ground.

"What he'll make on the cans won't be enough. I'll talk to him when he comes up."

She put her head on his breast. He smelled of alcohol and the injections he gave the villagers everyday. She had never known anyone as kind as he. She was in love with him.

"Don't cry, girl," he said, kissing her. "I'll take you to Tehran. You'll become my wife and learn to live in the crowded city."

"I'll become your wife here, tonight."

The doctor laughed quietly, caressing her long hair. Her childishness dispersed the clouds on his mind. Tala was

145

begging him, rubbing against his aroused body.

"Get hold of yourself. I want you to be my wife."

"If father learns that I became your wife here, tonight, he will relent."

He tried to free his lips from the warm pressure of her mouth. They rolled over the curtains. Her hard, heavy body filled him with pleasure. He tried to hide his excitement. He laughed, amused by her childishness. She became bolder, trying desperately to break his resistance. Hearing the driver, they both turned motionless.

"They've come after me," she said, afraid.

"Who?"

Tears prevented her from answering. She ran down the hill. He hid Tala's curtains under the pillow, lay down on the bed, and closed his eyes, depressed. He was in no mood for the driver's chatter. As soon as the driver fell asleep, he would go to the old man. This time he knew how to handle him. The driver's suitcase snapped shut. He went down the hill, humming. The doctor sat up, surprised.

"Whereto?" he called out.

"To a party, doc. The old man has invited me to a party."

The doctor lay back, powerless. His unlit cigarette slipped from his fingers.

* * * * * * *

The driver had one foot on the fender and held the wheel lightly, letting the jeep drive itself. The sustained silence of the desert and the sudden flight of the locusts reminded him of the opium, and Tala's virginal body the night before. The jeep rocked gently. His eyelids grew heavy, his body languid with remembered pleasure. He longed to share his memories with the doctor, but the latter was in bad humor and in no mood to listen to him. The driver decided to postpone his account until they reached the port. He yawned and began to hum a song he had learned from the old man. The doctor fixed his eyes on the dashboard, paying no attention to the driver or the dirt road which disappeared in the sand. The driver was familiar with the doctor's long periods of silence.

He could go on without saying a word until they reached the port. The driver stopped humming.

"I just thought about him," he said.

"Thought about whom?"

"The old man."

The doctor said nothing, listening to the monotonous sound of the pebbles hitting the fenders.

"He was hard to figure out," the driver resumed. "Sometimes he would go through the eye of a needle, sometimes the city gate was not big enough for him."

The doctor pulled his hat over his glasses and slouched in his seat. But the driver was not discouraged.

"Where shall we have breakfast?" he asked, lighting cigarettes for himself and the doctor.

The doctor did not answer. Fried eggs and barley bread did not move his appetite. He could not even taste the cigarette. The driver realized that he did not want to talk.

"Why don't we wait and have lunch at Shaghu?" he suggested. "If we stop there, we can look up the old man's daughters." He watched the doctor from the corner of his eye.

"I hope they are as good as Tala," he added.

"Who told you about them?"

"Last night the old man bored my head off, doc."

The doctor did not answer. The driver began to hum again. He was restless and wanted to talk to the doctor at any price. But the doctor continued frowning. He had not slept the night before. At dawn, the driver had returned to the cottage and collapsed on his bed. Early in the morning he had turned the engine on and waited for the doctor, yawning. The doctor had delayed their departure, hoping to see Tala. The driver had watched the red sun rays over the tight knit surface of the palms and urged him to hurry before it grew hot. The villagers had gathered to see them off. As always, the children followed the jeep as far as their legs could take them. The doctor looked through the back window, hoping to see Tala. At the turn of the road, he closed his eyes in despair. Since they had left the village, he had been preoccupied with the old man's disappearance and Tala's absence in the morning. The driver stopped the jeep at the side of a sandy hill. Several trucks passed by. The jeep filled with dust. They both began to cough. The doctor lit a cigarette and waited for the dust to settle. The road gradually loomed through the thinning dust. The driver started the engine, planning to follow the trucks to Shaghu at a distance. Then the doctor spotted the old man.

"It's him! The old man!" he cried joyfully.

The driver stopped the car. The old man looked at them as the doctor ran toward him. He bowed his head and greeted the doctor.

"What are you doing here?" he asked the old man.

"Trying to earn a living, doctor."

"In the desert? Have you lost your mind?"

"This isn't the desert. They call this place the Mine Road."

"Where is your daughter? If you give your consent, I'll give you the money for the coffee-house," the doctor whispered, holding the old man by the shoulders.

"I couldn't run the place single-handed. Tala will have to help out."

"But without the money . . .?"

"I got the money, don't worry."

"But you were complaining last night that . . ."

"That was last night. God sent me the money."

"You mean last night?"

"If I didn't have the money would I be here instead of getting your breakfast ready and seeing you off this morning?"

"Do you want me to take you back to the village?" the doctor asked kindly, wondering whether the old man was in his right mind and hoping to see Tala again.

"Doctor, I started before dawn to get to the mine on one of the trucks on their way back from the port. Now you're telling me to go back?"

The doctor said nothing. The old man took a bit of opium and paused, gathering his saliva to swallow it.

"Was she in the village when you left?" the doctor asked quietly.

"It was better for her not to see you."

"Why? Didn't she believe I wanted to marry her?"

"She believed you all right, but she still does as I say."

The trucks entered the side road. The old man jumped on, grinning happily. In the jeep the driver had taken off his shirt and was fanning himself. The doctor sank in his seat and took the cigarette he offered him. He watched the truck which was taking the old man away.

"Well, he finally got his coffee-house," the driver said, laughing.

"Have you too lost your mind? Where did he get the money all of a sudden?"

"I was his prey, doc."

The doctor sat straight in his seat.

"I was going to tell you when we reached the port," the driver continued.

"Why there?"

"Because there it would be too late to do anything if you got mad. But the old man told you what happened and messed up my plans."

"He didn't say anything. He didn't say he got the money from you."

"Last night, when I came down the hill he followed me, wagging his tail, and when we reached his cottage he said, 'Why do you want to throw your money away in Shaghu?' My mind was on Tala. I said, 'You got a better idea where I should spend it?' He chuckled and talked me into it."

"He made you sell him the cans?"

"No, he got them for nothing, plus a hundred tomans."

"What for?"

"For the girl. The crafty devil, he knew how to get round me."

The doctor sat back in his seat, weakly.

"What about her? Did she go along?" he asked, his voice hollow and sunken.

"No, doc. She resisted. They quarrelled outside the cottage and went to the palm orchard. I didn't think he would get anywhere, until he came back exhausted and breathless, and winked at me, rubbing his forefinger and thumb. He wanted his money in advance. When I went up the hill with the money, she was in the cottage with you. She gave you the curtains, didn't she?"

The doctor said nothing. The driver laughed hard.

"I thought you were screwing her. I said to myself, 'I pay the dough, the doctor has the fun.'"

The doctor remembered how she had pleaded with him. The driver had warmed up. He wanted to give all the details, like the times when he returned from his night out with prostitutes. The doctor turned his face, his eyes fixed on the sandy desert that shimmered in the sun.

"You hear me, doc? I'd never spent so much on that, but when I got down to business I saw it was worth it. The old man hadn't lied. She was a virgin!"

1967

Of Weariness

BY AHMAD MAHMUD

Hasan was frowning.
"This thing has really gone too far," he said.
Ata was clowning around.
"So what?" he said.
"Hasan is right," I said, gazing at the ceiling, my hands under my head. The ceiling was sagging. White termite marks lined the reddish beams. The hot breeze curled through the ventilator in the ceiling and burst into the room, beating against the walls.

Outside, there was the voice of the sea and sailors.
Kazem arrived. He was like a large, red hornet, sharp and red-haired.
"Why are you moping?" he asked.
We smiled, our smiles lifeless.
"Seriously, why are you so glum?" he repeated.
We told him why we were glum. Ahan had come to the house, shouting and screaming, and had chided us. The night before we had gone to Poshteh in our drunkenness. We had carried Ahan's benches over our heads to the house, and thrown them down one on top of another, roaring with laughter. Ahan had come while Kazem was out to buy fish. After shouting and cursing, he had gone to fetch porters to take the benches back.

Kazem burst out laughing; I followed suit. Hasan became angry. "It's a disgrace," he said.

I went into the corridor and lit the stove. I put the kettle on the stove and returned to the room. Kazem picked up the knife. "I couldn't find any Sangsar or Gabab, so I bought a Sarkhu," he said at the door, going to clean the fish.

"Sarkhu doesn't taste good," Ata frowned.

"It tastes rotten; like sludge," I said.

Kazem squatted in the corridor. He held the fish by its tail and scraped the scales. The scales had brown veins. The head of the fish was on the ground. It looked like a shark's head with a wide mouth.

The stove was roaring. The wind whirled into the room. I got up and walked to the window. The sea faded in a yellow dust. The sun was a golden tray over the spread of blue water dappled by the boats. The air smelled salty. The waves beat against the algae-covered foundation of the house restlessly.

I closed the window; the sound of the sea was muffled now.

Ahan returned with two Negroes. He was sweating heavily and grumbling. "For heaven's sake! You're educated. You come from a big city. And you do things even a lunatic wouldn't do."

"That proves we're sane," Ata retorted, laughing.

"Really!" Ahan said angrily.

I laughed. Ahan glared at me, cross-eyed, sweat shining in his eyebrows. He smelled like quick lime steaming in muggy weather. He looked at the benches. "How did you carry them all the way from the Poshteh? Didn't you get tired?" he asked.

"Liquor," I said.

"Levity," Ata said.

"Lunacy," Hasan said.

"I couldn't agree more," Ahan said to Hasan, wiping his brow before the sweat dropped into his eyes.

The Negroes tightened their loincloths around their waists. They hoisted the benches over their shoulders, turned, and walked out of the room.

"This is the bad part," Hasan said after Ahan left.

"Where's the salt?" Kazem asked.

"Which is the bad part?" I asked. Ata got up and gave the salt to Kazem.

"This," Hasan said. "You get drunk, lose your heads, and go

around the town, making fools of yourselves. The next day you feel ashamed on account of the people. I wish at least they were worth it."

"We've been putting up with a lot," Ata said.

Kazem sprinkled the sarkhu with salt and stuck it on the hook. He washed his hands and joined us in the room.

"What became of the tea?" he asked.

"It'll be ready in a minute," I said.

"It may not matter to you, but I feel embarrassed," Hasan said.

We felt embarrassed, too. The memory of the night bothered us in the morning.

"Hasan is right. This thing has gone too far," Kazem said, then laughed.

"Don't make fun," Hasan said.

"I'm serious," Kazem said.

Then we talked it over. Hasan had his say, we had ours, and we decided 'Once a week; only once a week.'

* * * * * *

In the afternoon, there was no wind, and no sound from the sea. Kazem was studying English. He was lying on his stomach, fiddling around with the dictionary, spelling and writing. Ata was reading a book. Hasan was writing in his diary. He had started it in Jahrom, where we were given permission to have pen and paper. He wrote in chapters; so far he had completed forty-two chapters in three one-hundred sheet notebooks: "Sakhlu," "Prison," "From One Town to Another," "Prison within a Prison," "Banishment," "Freedom in the City"....

I left the house. I wanted to go to town and walk around.'Once a week....Only once. I have to find a way to pass the evenings, the nights,' I thought.

* * * * * *

The wind had died down. The sound of the sea had died down. Here and there were empty abandoned houses with crumbling walls. The doors, made with inlaid wood, were marked by termites. Rusty locks hung from the latches, like large nose-rings. Adnani's words came back to me. "They all left at night.... They went to Qatar, Dubai, Sharjeh..." Adnani was a happy old man with laughter in his voice. His teeth were sound, white, and regular. "When the veil and *chador* were forbidden they all left. Langeh became a wilderness, a desert." A boy was approaching from a narrow alley that curled through the abandoned houses. He was singing, his voice tired and desolate.

The Massah bazaar was hot. The ground was covered with fine dust. It was muggy; the damp air made breathing difficult. I walked between sacks of date pits that lay on the ground in front of the corn-dealer's shop, and went to Mohammad Mashhadi's coffeehouse. I smoked the water pipe. Then Mohammad Nur arrived and sat near me. He took some tobacco out of his vest pocket and began to chew. He spat the thick juice, asked for *ordok** and chewed it with his tobacco.

"How much longer?" he asked me.

"Eleven months and three days," I said.

"You keep count of the days, too?"

He spat the yellow tobacco juice against the mud-brick pillar. 'I keep count of the hours as well,' I thought. 'Eleven months, three days, and two hours.'

It was five in the afternoon. The days were long. The sun was over the ruins, over the wide Massah Street, which lay before me, over the dusty palms that grew among the ruins. 'Once a week,' I said to myself.

'How? How will I spend the night? How can I sleep, if I don't drink?'

'You mustn't drink. You promised your buddies.'

Hasan had had his say, we had had ours, and we had decided 'Once a week. Only once a week.'

'Suppose I didn't drink tonight. What about tomorrow?'

'Only once a week.'

'But that's impossible.'

---

*A substance mixed with chewing tobacco.

'Well, you can't drink every night. You have disgraced yourself. Everybody knows you.'

'The hell with them. Who cares?'

'The hell with them? Aren't they the same people you defied danger for and got yourself into trouble?'

'It wasn't for the people; it was for my own ego. I didn't want to accept defeat. It was the same with Hasan. The same with Kazem. The same with Ata. We didn't want to break down. We wanted to show we were strong.'

The cows came out of the alley, sniffing at the sacks of date pits, their long shadows stretched before them.

"How about some cherry tea?" Mohammad Mashhadi asked.

"The water pipe has gone out," Mohammad Nur said.

I took a puff. I watched the sun over the ruins through the blue smoke. People walked by, their shadows before them. They wore one piece of cloth around their heads and another around their loins. Their lips were red and swollen—like flesh bulging through a cut in a buffalo's hide—the white of their eyes yellow, their faces like broken black mica.

I finished smoking and got up.

I was thinking of going to the covered bazaar and chatting with Gilan.

I was thinking of going to Alidad and chatting with him until evening.

I was thinking of going to the beach after it became dark and sitting there with the sea until late, then going home to sleep.

"Where to?" Mohammad Nur asked.

"I'm making Ceylon tea. Wait and have some. It has a great aroma," Mohammad Mashhadi said.

"I'm not in the mood," I said.

"Ghadam will be here any minute now. He's loads of fun."

Ghadam's buffoonery had lost its novelty for me. The same jokes, the same anecdotes. The same big, black body. In the beginning even the way he talked was amusing.

"I may come back by the time he gets here," I said.

* * * * * *

I went to the covered bazaar. It was hot and stuffy. I went to Gilan's shop, sat at the door, and thumbed through old girly magazines.

"Hasan took one of the pictures," Gilan said.

"Which one?"

"The one kneeling, with her bottom up in the air."

I looked for the picture: a woman in red bikini, with golden hair and pink skin, against a blue sky. But the picture was missing.

"Shall I make tea?" Gilan asked.

"I just left the coffeehouse," I said, looking at the pictures.

Beams of light pierced the gloom through the ventilators in the bazaar's arched ceiling. The smell of tobacco, different perfumes, and hot spices mingled together. The shade was not cool. A warm breeze blew through the bazaar's entrance, wafting the smell of burning dry palm branches and dung. Alidad had just lit the oven in his bakery. I thumbed through the old magazines and looked at the pictures of half naked women. I got up.

"Whereto?" Gilan asked.

"I'm taking one of the pictures," I said.

"Stay."

"I don't feel like it."

"Are you going to Poshteh to Ahan's coffeehouse tonight?"

"I don't want to drink tonight."

I folded the picture and put it in my pocket. In the shops, they sold perfume, sneakers, plastic slippers, sugar, different kinds of tea, fish oil, cooking fat, mangoes, bruised fruit, and limp greens.

I left the bazaar.

Alidad had just lighted the oven. I sat behind the counter. He placed the dry palm branches in the oven with a long pair of tongs. The flame blew out of the oven's mouth.

"I hope you're not exhausting yourself!" he said.

"Same to you," I said.

He moved his head, dodging the flames.

"Don't you get tired of doing nothing all day long?" he asked.

"I can come and help you every morning after I report in. I

can knead, bake, do anything."

"Do you know how?" he smiled.

"No. You can teach me, though."

He placed the first baked loaf on the counter. It smelled of white flour. I got up.

"Sit down. Let's chat. I'll make tea," he said.

"I don't feel like it."

"Where are you headed?"

"I'm going to the sea-shore."

* * * * * *

The sun had grown pale. I didn't go to the sea-shore. My mind had grown sticky. It was sticking to everything. It was sticking to the crumbling mortar walls, to the dust-covered, deserted alleys, to the spears of palm leaves.

I went to the pond. I talked to a dark-skinned woman who was drawing water. She poured the water into my cupped palms and I drank. I entered a long alley, turned many corners, and got out at the border of the town. The ruins cast pale shadows on the yellow earth made damp by the moisture in the air. The shrubs spread their thin, knotty branches on the dirt. I walked along the hedge enclosing the palm orchard, my boots sinking in the dirt up to my ankles. 'Twelve months and twenty-seven days have passed. I'm sick of it. The Massah Bazaar, old magazines, sarkhu fish...' My shadow beside me was folded double against the hedge. The crickets were chirping. Then came the sound of pigeons taking off together and landing on the dusty palms.

I watched the pigeons. I looked at the palm orchard. The dark slender woman wasn't at the concrete pool where she sat every day and poured water over herself with a copper bowl. I lit a cigarette. I was tempted to set the shrubs on fire, so that she would come out of her mud-brick shack in the corner of the orchard. The match went out. The air was damp.

I watched the shack's door. The sun was setting. My shadow was growing pale. The woman came out of the door. My heart pounded. She sat by the pool. She lifted her skirt to her knees, but did not take her clothes off. Darkness fell. I began to walk.

'How are you going to spend the night, man?'

'I'll manage somehow.'

'Somehow? How?'

'Stop thinking about it.'

'You're being stubborn and foolish again.'

'I'm not being stubborn.'

'Yes you are. Actually, all of you are foolish. Why else would you be the only ones who resisted? The only ones out of five hundred and thirty. How come they all said yes and you didn't? Wasn't that stubbornness? Or were you wiser than the rest?'

It had grown dark. I had reached the end of the orchard. I crossed a stretch of land paved with mortar and passed the crumbling stone pillars. Adnani's words came back to me. "They left at night. When the veil was forbidden, they all left. Then the railroad reached Mohammareh, and Langeh lost its importance. Langeh used to be peerless."

The waves clamored. The air was sticky and smelled of live fish. I sat on a rock embedded in wet sand, its uneven surface covered with velvety moss. Sea shells lay in the sand at its foot.

The stars began to shine one by one. The moon rose from the sea in the distance.

Night began.

On the sea, the boats' lights were like distant stars. Twelve months and twenty-seven days had dragged by. Long, hot days, and dark, stuffy nights. We had told each other everything. We had nothing to say any more. I had sought refuge in arrack. Then Kazem came. Then Ata. Hasan had not changed. And now we had decided to drink only once a week. The moon rose high; beneath it the sea like dark, wavy silk. The sea was latticed with the reflection of the stars. The moon made furrows in the water. The sea neighed. My mind wandered to the clamor of the crows and to the fields behind the bars that first day, when they had looked us over, gnashed their teeth, and sent us in. In the evening, we leaned against the wall and watched the fields through the window bars.

The mountain was covered lightly with snow that had fallen the night before. The crows flocked in the field here and there, their clamor suspended in the air. The grass was turning yellow. The poplar leaves were like melted gold, and the field was dusty behind the bars....

I was pressing my cheeks to the bars, when a loud command broke the silence. It was a military command, then the drums, then the trumpet, and six hundred and twenty-six voices as if coming from one throat:

"Infinite thanks to God, who..."

And the day faded, and the mountain loomed like a dark monster against the sky. The bar's chill against my cheeks, the night's darkness in my eyes, as fear inched its way into my heart.

My mind stopped wandering. I looked at my buddies.

Kazem was sitting at the window, smoking.

"My last cigarette. You can't imagine how good it is. I feel like smoking it slowly to the very end," he said.

"I still have a pack," I said, taking out the unopened pack from my pocket.

"I wish you hadn't said that. The last cigarette is always the best. You spoiled it."

Ata was sitting in a corner, the rug creased under his feet. Hasan paced back and forth. Their eyes were cold. I sat on the window ledge. The frying pan had been left near the door since lunch.

Hasan was dark and had a black mustache. Ata was fair, had green eyes and wide cheeks. Kazem was like a hornet: sharp, cutting and red.

We discussed what to do. We thought of running away—behind the bars were the field, a warm place to sleep in, a warm body to embrace. In the distance were the wooden watch tower and the neighing of horses leaving the stable. We have to stay alive, we said. This is more important than anything else. But life without freedom? And now we were alive, sitting on the shore. The sea was latticed with the reflection of the stars.

The voice of the sailors came from the sea. The fishermen

had set sail in the dark, to return at dawn with their catch, noisy and clamorous.

I heard Kazem's drunken singing. His voice mingled with the sound of the sea. He and Ata emerged and disappeared among the mortar pillars of the ruins like two dark shades. Hasan staggered behind them. All three joined in, singing the chorus.

They walked out of the ruins. I called them. I began to walk toward them.

"Are you there?" Ata called out.

They began to run. The sea shells crunched under their feet.

When we came together, Hasan put his arms around my neck.

"Where have you been, man?" Ata asked. He sounded drunk.

"We looked for you every—everywhere," Kazem said. Then pop, the cork flew out of the bottle. Ata had been shaking the bottle and hitting its bottom with his palm.

"Take a drink.... Just tonight," Ata said.

"And every night." Kazem said.

I took the bottle and drank until I was breathless. My throat burned. My insides burned. My eyes teared.

I wiped my eyes. Hasan was lying on the sea shells. Kazem was sitting on the moss-covered rock, his arms folded around his knees, staring at the sea. The arrack ran in my veins and warmed me.

The boats were gaining distance from the shore. The sea was growing louder. Broken stars scattered diamonds on the water and the moon made furrows in the sea.

I sought refuge in the bottle again.

1969

The End of the Passion Play
MAHSHID AMIRSHAHI*

It was the year of the heat wave, or the year after that when Kal Abul showed up in the Aminuldowleh Park District. He bought the vacant shop three doors down from Abul Kuseh's grocery and there he opened a vegetable and fruit store.

Kal Abul was big and mean. He wore a long, gray denim tunic and wrapped a stained, white shawl around his waist. He tried himself to dye his rough, graying hair with henna and the result was that his head—with its patches of red and black hair—was like a soot-covered copper pot. But it was a peculiarity of Kal Abul's physique which immediately caught the eye of the children in the Park District, for his right leg ended at the ankle. The dry ankle bone extended into a can of galvanized iron, and around it, so that it would fit into the can, were wrapped many layers of rag. The cords which joined the can to his shin climbed up his leg like ivy round a tree, and it was impossible to tell just where they ended.

This iron leg delighted the boys of the District from the very first moment. They were tired of pinning the women's *chadors* together as they waited in front of the butcher's or the baker's, and after Hasan's death had no one to tease but Idiot Esmayil and old Kuseh.

*Translated by Minoo Southgate and Bjorn Robinson Rye.

161

Rumor had it that if you goosed the Idiot the earth would shake. Because of this the boys called him Shaky Idiot and circled constantly around him, waiting for the chance to test the truth of this important matter. So long as Idiot had worked as furnace-man in the bakery across the park they'd followed him to and from work each day, and had made that trip a misery for him. But since he'd burned his eyes taking care of the furnace he was obliged to roam the streets all day hunting for old junk, and was at their mercy from dawn to dusk.

Idiot couldn't see the kids until they were within a foot—by then it was too late for him to run away. If they attacked him near the house of Taghi's mother, the widow of Mullah Ali, he'd take shelter in her doorway; otherwise he'd stagger, half-blind, to the nearest wall and press against it to stop the boys from getting behind him. With his back against the wall or from the doorway, where he was sure the widow would protect him, he'd hurl his never changing curse at his tormentors.

The widow of Mullah Ali, hearing this commotion, would bring him inside and shut the door. In the cool safety of the house she would sit him beside her son's cradle.

"Mind Taghi while I rinse the wash—may you be rewarded, Idiot Esmayil," she would say. Or, she would say "I'm glad you came, Idiot. Do bring me a bucket of water from the well while I change the baby, and may your hand never ache for the favor." She would always find some excuse to keep him so long that the boys would finally lose hope.

They would wander across the District then and, sooner or later, would end up before old Kuseh's grocery. There they'd pass some time tormenting him with a chant they'd made up:

Mint and cheese and milk and bread,
Kal Kuseh, we must be fed

The second line of this song was traditionally sung in a deep, growling voice like old Kuseh's own.

The shop-keeper would sit behind his counter and watch the street as though he were just idly looking out the window, as though what was going on was no concern of his—but his beads would be turning faster in his hand.

The District boys never bothered old Kuseh beyond this

because his shop was so dirty that none of them felt like snatching any of the food. His tray of rice pudding was black with flies, his roasted chickpeas smelled musty and his dry plums and cherries were little more than worms and stones. Besides that, the neighborhood's flags and banners, which were used in the somber mourning rituals and processions of the month of Moharram, were stored in the shop. This awed the boys a little, and made them hesitate to go in.

After that there wasn't much to do. The youngest would find some sticks and start a game of *alak dolak* in the street, the eldest would play dice, and those who were too old for the one and too young for the other would watch. But before the death of Hasan the days had been more exciting. Harassing Hasan had been more fun than either Shaky Idiot or Kuseh: he was grumpier than the shopkeeper and his curses were juicier and more varied than Idiot's had ever been.

In the bakery where Hasan worked, the long, flat loaves of bread were baked over hot pebbles in an open oven, and it was his duty to stir the pebbles so that the heat would be evenly distributed. This he did with a long, iron poker, using a rag to protect his hands from the hot metal.

The boys would wait until his back was turned, and then would stick gum on the poker just at the spot which slid through the rag. They knew that in the dim light of the tallow lamps he wouldn't notice the bit of gum.

When Hasan turned to make sure the bread was baking well he would take up the poker, move back, balance on one leg, and attack the furnace. After two of these rhythmic forays the poker would heat up enough to melt the gum, which would then stick to the rag. With the third attack the rag would slide with the poker from beneath his palm, leaving him with a hand full of hot iron. Then he would holler and curse and jump up and down as though the floor itself were on fire. With his first cry the boys would run to hide behind trees or inside the arch of the drinking fountain across the street. From there they would hoot with laughter as they watched the furnace-man shake and shout.

Because he could never catch them, Hasan would take out

his fury on the customers. He would keep them waiting in the summer heat or winter cold for so long that they'd finally settle for the stale bread on the counter to save themselves from his nastiness. His wrath spared no one, not even those who had no children or whose children were too young to roam the district and bother him.

Often Taghi's mother, babe in arms, would come and wait in the bakery until at last Hasan would throw her a miserable loaf with a good deal of frowning and grumbling. If Shaky Idiot were nearby then, he would come to her rescue. He would either take Taghi from her arms to lighten her load, or, since he had once been in charge of the furnace and knew the baker, he would go inside and buy a well toasted, perfectly browned loaf for her.

When Hasan finally died from drink and orneriness the people of the District were liberated from his tyranny, but the boys lost part of their entertainment. They were left with Shaky Idiot and Kal Kuseh, who weren't much fun. Naturally, then, the appearance of Kal Abul with that iron foot of his seemed to promise great new possibilities.

The first thing they did was nickname him "Abul Canfoot." The name spread across the Park District like wildfire and the newcomer was, in effect, issued a new identity card. Every kid cut a branch to make it his cane and pinched a copper pot from the kitchen or an empty can from the garbage to play 'Canfoot.' The game soon became the most popular in the District.

The first day, as Abul Canfoot took down the boards and swept out his shop, the boys were watching and biding their time. As soon as his back was turned two of them made their foray. One swiped a handful of dry cherries while the other earned himself a melon.

But the boys had misjudged Abul Canfoot; he wasn't like Shaky Idiot or Hasan the poker-man. The two hadn't taken a step before Kal Abul, with the tip of his cane, hit the melon out of one thief's hand and started beating the other.

"You bastards!" he shouted. "A few cherries is nothing, but today you steal an egg, then a camel tomorrow. Do you want to become thieves? Run, you sons of a jinn. Run before I cut your bellies open with my can!"

The two disappeared, and the boys who'd been watching realized that Abul's iron foot was no laughing matter, but rather a dangerous weapon that could cut stomachs open. That was it. Abul Canfoot had seized the cat by the tail. A few of the rougher boys still tried once or twice to bother him, but they soon realized that it wasn't in their own interest. Even if they managed to escape without bruises, they'd be left out of the nightly distribution of cucumbers, plums and apricots. But Abul Canfoot didn't bribe the boys with the left-over fruit from his shop like some of the other storekeepers. Instead he would gather the better behaved boys at the end of the day to sing the praises of his wares to passers-by, and then would pay each his wage in fruit.

Abul Canfoot stayed in the Park District. In fact, he did more than stay—his presence increased from day to day. After three months of shopkeeping he married Taghi's mother and took her to his house. He sold her own poor home (which was, in fact, Taghi's inheritance) and expanded his greengrocery. After he bought the local coffeehouse from the heirs of Mashhadi Bagher, he was firmly established as a pillar of the District.

Taghi was five when his mother married Abul Canfoot. The day after the ceremony Abul took Taghi by the ear and brought him to his shop. At first he only taught Taghi to sit beside the trays of berries or cherries to shoo the flies away. The other boys, passing by, would shout "Taghi! Taghi—shoo them towards Abul Kuseh's shop, they'll have a better time there!" Taghi would stare at them with open mouth and continue shooing the flies. If he put one plum, or even a cherry, into his mouth poor Taghi would get such a beating that he'd hurt for a week.

Drunk with sleep in the gray dawn, Taghi wouldn't want to go to the shop with his stepfather. Shooing flies and Abul Canfoot's blows could hardly equal the sweet morning sleep. Those first mornings, dragged from bed, he would cling to his mother and cry; he would hide his head in the folds of her *chador*, and even Abul Canfoot's cane, even the blows on his head, could not tear him from that safety. Taghi's mother

165

would be crying now too. "Karbalayi," she would beg, "it doesn't please God that you beat an orphan like this...let him be."

"Don't you want him to grow up right?" Abul Canfoot would rage.

"Of course I do."

"Woman..."

"Go to the shop, I'll bring him soon no matter what—or I'll get Idiot Esmayil to bring him. Please, Kal Abul."

Abul Canfoot would storm out and Taghi's mother would wash his tear-stained face and bloody nose and take him to the shop.

On the way, as they passed Abbas's opium-house, she would quicken her step and wrap her *chador* protectively around Taghi and say, "If you ever set foot around this place or I hear that you've been with Abbas I'll break your leg myself. Do you understand?" Taghi would look at the opium-house with terror in his handsome eyes. He'd heard rumors of what Abbas did with young boys.

"After you break my leg will you put it in a can?"

"Bite your tongue. Don't you ever say that in front of Karbalayi!"

And he would bite his tongue obediently.

Abul Canfoot kept the coffeehouse almost the way it had been in Mash Bagher's time; he made only a few changes. One of these was in the big painting, the work of Ghullar Aghasi, which had always hung opposite the entrance. The painting showed Mash Bagher and a fresh-faced, beautiful boy sitting by a stream. At their feet was a slice of red watermelon with large, black seeds, and underneath was written "Mashhadi Bagher and his Friend." But soon those who went to the coffeehouse discovered that Mash Bagher's 'friend' had grown a long beard and was wearing a white shroud like a Dervish, and that the slice of watermelon had been transformed into a *kashkul*, or begging cup. Underneath the picture was written, "Mashhadi Bagher and his Guru."

There were other changes as well. Kal Abul established a tradition of inviting all the Park District mourners who had gone to the mosque on the night of Ashura to feast at his coffeehouse afterwards on a stew which he provided. And he was finally able to convince Gholamhosein, the story-teller, to tell his tales in the coffeehouse each evening.

Perhaps because of these small changes—or perhaps thanks to the presence of Abul Canfoot himself—the coffeehouse became more and more popular. If you were to drop a pin at night it wouldn't reach the floor, the customers packed in so tightly. The night that the story teller told the tale of Sohrab's death seats were bought and sold for as much as one toman, four servants nearly broke their backs serving tea, and forty pounds of sugar was consumed.

But the more Abul Canfoot succeeded in his businesses, the heavier Taghi's duties became. At dawn he would go to the coffeehouse and help Mohammad, whose job it was to wash the cups and clean the tables and benches. Then he would check the stew bubbling in its individual pots, and skim the foam from the top. As soon as he had added the meat it would be time to hurry over to the shop. There Abul Canfoot would load a donkey with all the most wrinkled and bruised of his fruit and send Taghi to sell it outside the Shemiran Gate.

In the evening, when he returned, it was his job to sit behind a little display of yellow cucumbers, and every time Abul Canfoot cried "Tender cucumbers ... Cucumbers with blossoms still on them ... All these cucumbers for a dime," Taghi would echo "Cucumbers for a dime," in a sleepy, absent voice.

If he failed to sell the donkey's load or fell asleep beside the cucumbers, then Abul Canfoot would fall upon him with his cane and Taghi would wake quickly enough.

"I'll cut your belly open with this!" Kal Abul would shout, pointing down to his iron foot. "When are you going to shape up?"

At the end of the day Taghi would be given a few cucumbers or a handkerchief full of leftover fruit—whatever happened to be in season—and would start home with his stepfather. They did not, however, walk together. No matter how tired Taghi might be, he was always careful to keep a safe distance between them—especially on nights when Kal Abul was in an ugly mood. Without turning or looking back,

Taghi would maintain his distance by the dry tap of Abul's iron-foot against the pavement behind him.

Between Abul Canfoot's discipline and his mother's guidance Taghi grew up to be simple and honest. He would not do what he was told not to do, and did what he was told to do. He became a lithe, handsome boy of fifteen, yet not once had he pinched a melon from the shop or so much as a cup of tea from the coffeehouse. He had never bothered Shaky Idiot, who was now old and decrepit. He was almost unaware of the pranks of the District rough-necks, and he'd yet to pass Abbas' opium house without nervously quickening his step. Once when one of the boys had only pointed out Abbas in the street he slept badly for a few nights because he felt as though he'd somehow done something wrong.

Moharram was a good month for the boys in the Park District. In addition to fooling around with Shaky Idiot and pinning the women's *chadors* in front of the butcher's and baker's, they had other things to do. In Kheibar Alley they set up an enormous tent, which they covered in black cloth and prepared for the rituals of the holy month. As in previous years they would call themselves "The Assembly of Young Moslem Mourners," and take themselves very seriously.

There was a scandal that year, however, which marred the prestige of the "Young Moslem Mourners." One night when Abul Canfoot was returning late from the shop he heard suspicious sounds coming from the supposedly deserted tent. The next day found Ali, the head of the "Assembly" and Yusef, the nine year old son of Mashhadi Rajab, black and blue from Kal Abul's blows. Word flew around the district (everyone except Taghi seemed to know all about it) and for a while after that poor Yusef was called by the female equivalent of his name—Yusefah. As a result of all this Sayyed Mehdi, the district porter, was assigned to sleep in the tent for the rest of the holy month.

Moharram was an especially good month for Taghi because, in addition to the excitement of the nightly ceremony of the Imams, he had less work to do in the shop and coffeehouse. The adults were busy preparing the ceremonies, so instead of suffering Abul Canfoot's blows, he was free to watch the mourners beating their breasts and, sometimes, to enjoy the passion plays.

On the first of the month of Moharram, Taghi got ready to go to the mourning ceremonies, and was just leaving the coffeehouse when the waiter, Mohammad, who was standard-bearer for the Fakhrabad Mourners, called him over. "Taghi," he asked, "are you going to the mourning?"

"Yes," said Taghi.

"Wait a moment."

Taghi waited obediently, unaware that his stepfather had instructed Mohammad to keep him away from any possible contact with the scandalous "Young Mourners."

"Do you know the lamentation?" asked Mohammad.

"Of course."

"Let's hear you sing it."

"What for?"

"If you can do it, I'll take you to march in our group with me."

At first Taghi was so overjoyed that he was tongue-tied and the words wouldn't come.

"Well," said Mohammad, "I guess you're too young after all."

"Wait, Mohammad," Taghi begged. "I *do* remember...

O Moslems, wear the black of pain,
Let the mourning shawl cover our domain,
Karbala's been entered by King Hosein."

Taghi paused there, furrowing his brow with effort.

"What else?" asked Mohammad.

"Tonight Ali's house is parched and dry,
There is no sleep in Hosein's eye,
Take water to the children, hear their cry!"

"You have to sing that twice," Mohammad said.

"Take water to the children, take water to the children," sang Taghi hurriedly.

"That's enough. Good."

"Can I go with you, then, Mohammad?" begged Taghi.

"You can follow behind me when we march from now on. You don't have to go with the 'Young Mourners' anymore."

It was a great honor and Taghi was too happy to stand still, so he ran off to give his mother the news.

That year the Fakhrabad Mourners, which performed the passion play in the Park district, was in good shape. Before the play began, the man who played the part of Shemr, the villain who killed Imam Hosein, claimed that in his youth he had played the part of one of the two Moslem children. Taghi couldn't believe that. For him Shemr was Shemr and no one else. He was a wicked man with a helmet and a large, black mustache which stretched beyond his ears, and a big lion on the buckle of his belt which jumped up and down over his fat belly as he moved. Shemr was Shemr just as he had always been, but it was the entrance of Imam Hosein that Taghi awaited with the most excitement.

When the man who played Imam Hosein at last came on stage, Taghi was not in this world anymore. Imam Hosein was his favorite character, and the Imam Hosein of this play was the best Imam Hosein he had ever seen. Pale, broad shouldered, with a smooth, black mustache and a round, black beard, he was more like a representation of Amir al-Momenin*—but he had a look which was holy in its pure innocence and kindness, a look which could belong only to the saintly Imam Hosein.

Taghi thought at first that he had seen the Imam Hosein somewhere, but he forgot this as the stage, the audience, the whole district melted away in his absorption. Nothing was as real to him, not even Abul Canfoot's beatings, as this wonderful Imam Hosein.

When the play ended, Taghi was in such a trance that he didn't notice the people leaving. He sat still in his place as the tent emptied around him, his mind filled with the wonderful goodness of the Imam Hosein.

After the play the mourners gathered at the mosque, where they sat in groups around the trays of food. Abul Canfoot was standing at the door, welcoming everybody and ordering waiters to bring bread, greens and spices. He kept a look-out

---

*The Imam Ali.

for Taghi—finally everyone had arrived and there was still no sign of the boy. Kal Abul paced up and down for a few more minutes, his beads spinning through his fingers. Mohammad was passing with a tray of bread, and Kal Abul stopped him.

"Where the hell is Taghi?" he asked angrily.

"He'll come soon, Kal Abul."

"He was supposed to bring the club to mash the meat, damn him!"

People had already begun to complain. No one was willing to share the unmashed meat and peas for fear of getting the short end of the stick.

"Didn't I tell you to keep an eye on the boy? What's happened to him?"

"I swear he was with me at the play. I don't know...He'll come, don't worry."

"If he does, I'll cut his belly open with my can!" raged Abul. "How can we serve the meat?" Then something occurred to him. "Is there any hot water?" he asked Mohammad.

"The samovar is boiling."

"Bring me a kettle of boiling water."

Mohammad filled the kettle with boiling water and brought it to an alcove which was out of sight of the diners.

Abul lifted his iron foot. "Pour the water over it," he commanded.

Mohammad hesitated a moment.

"What are you waiting for? Pour!"

The water was poured over the galvanized iron can.

"Rub the dirt off with your hand...Good...Now put the meat in the big bowl and bring it to me."

Mohammad's eyes lit up with admiration. "You've really got a head on your shoulders, Kal Abul. You keep saying you'll cut bellies open with that can, but..." he laughed under his breath.

Kal Abul leaned against his cane, put his foot in the bowl, and mashed the meat and peas. When he had finished, Mohammad wiped clean his iron-foot, careful not to waste any of the meat.

"Now take it out to 'em!" Abul commanded.

Mohammad took the bowl to the impatient mourners.

Taghi started to leave the empty tent, still absorbed in his admiration for Imam Hosein. He moved like a sleep-walker, the club for mashing the meat forgotten where he had been sitting. Then, from close behind the tent, he heard a voice—the voice of Imam Hosein. His heart beat faster. If he could talk to the holy man, if he could...

He raised the corner of the tent with a trembling hand and looked into a sort of dressing area. Imam Hosein had his back toward him and was pissing in a flower pot as he talked to the Shemr.

"My piss is yellow as saffron, you should excuse the expression," he said without turning.

The Shemr was struggling to undo the lion buckle on his belt. "It's all the sun you've been exposed to, it's messed up your yellow bile," he replied. "You ought to see a doctor."

The good Imam Hosein turned, buttoning his fly. "I shit on doctors," he said. "The remedy of all the aches and pains in the world lies fifty yards away in my opium-house. Give me two pipe-fulls, a tight-assed little boy beside me, and the doctor can eat my balls!"

It was then that Taghi saw Abbas for the second time, and the world for the first. He did not stay to hear the rest of the words.

1970

The Historic Tower

KHUSRAW SHAHANI

In the middle of our town's main crossroad, there was a mudbrick tower whose origin and history was a mystery to us. Nor did we know what purpose it served in the center of the crossroad.

The tower was about twenty-five or twenty-six meters high. Holes in its upper parts indicated that at one time the inhabitants of the village which had grown into what was now our town had used it in their battles against their enemies. The tower could no longer be used for this purpose in our time, but it hadn't lost its martial potential altogether. When two people quarrelled, for example, amid the shouting and abuse, they would make the sign of the tower—forearm or finger firmly erect—and dispatch it to each other's mother and sister. A large hole near the foot of the tower served as its entrance. In the old days, the hole had let in warriors who battled the enemy; in our time it served as the entrance to an unofficial public toilet.

Pigeons and sparrows nested in the inner walls of the tower, in holes which marked the ravages of time. In the spring, when the tower served as a roosting ground, plundering the nests was a pastime of the town's young hooligans.

Another virtue of the tower was that it made giving directions easy and helped visitors find their way around our town. It was an integral part of the town, as if a tower with its characteristics had to exist or else something essential to the town would be missing. Maybe we found its presence so crucial because we were used to it. Anyhow, one afternoon a fat man, bearded and bespectacled, accompanied by two blond men wearing khaki shorts and burdened with cameras, tripods, and shoulder-bags—all obviously foreigners—marched toward the tower, followed by the town's supervisor and officials.

They stopped near the tower. The fat, bearded man looked up and down the tower, his left hand on his waistst. He scanned the edifice, now with, now without glasses, then thrust his head into the hole which led to the town's unofficial public toilet, drew back, and said something to his two companions, holding a handkerchief to his nose. They wrote down what he said, then stationed their tripods, and began to examine and measure the tower and to take pictures.

By this time, news had gotten around that the town supervisor and officials had visited the tower with a group of foreigners. People began to arrive from all directions. Climbing over one another, they were trying to beat the town officials and the foreign delegation in discovering the mysteries of the tower. We had passed by the tower for years, without so much as looking at it. Now, suddenly, the tower had become an object of great interest—as if it had never been there, but had miraculously sprouted out of the ground only half an hour earlier. When the fat bearded man, who was addressed as professor (later we found out that he was the head of the team of archaeologists), raised his head to look at the tower, our heads too turned up automatically, and we all scrutinized the broken crenels. When he lowered his head, we did the same en masse. When he turned his head to say something to his companions, we turned back to see what he was looking at. When he bent down, put his hands on his knees, and looked up at the tower from a special angle sideways, we imitated him, like his image in a full length mirror. But when the professor walked to the tower and touched its surface, we couldn't do the same because the policemen barred our way. Later, when the professor had left, we went to the tower and touched the places he had touched, but whatever *his* discovery, we couldn't make out anything.

For a while after that, the professor and his companions were busy photographing and filming the tower. In the interval, we weren't idle, but passed the time speculating about the importance of the tower, the history of its construction, and the reason for the archaeologists' visit. One believed that a treasure had been unearthed in the tower; another maintained that Darius had buried his jewels at its foot when he was fleeing Alexander. Some swore that the tower was built by one of the saints. Others said that an Imam who was buried under the tower had appeared to the bearded professor in Europe, and the professor had come to study the site after that vision. We talked about the existence of a buried treasure more than the other theories.

After some time, the professor and his companions finished their job and, one day, departed, leaving us with a bunch of rumors. That day, some of the townspeople waited until midnight and then secretly entered the tower and dug up its foundation, hunting for treasure. The search was repeated for many midnights, until the authorities were forced to send guards to protect the tower from treasure-hunters.

One day, about a month after the bearded professor had shown up in our town, we found a public notice, signed by the town supervisor, pasted on walls all over the town. It read something like this:

To the patriotic and honorable residents of the town of - - - - - - - - - Since the preservation of ancient monuments, which represent our glorious past, is incumbent upon us all, the township took it upon itself to invite an international team of archaeologists to visit our town's tower. Upon visiting this monument, the team identified it as one of the glories of our ancestors, built around the time of the Prophet Daniel. Since it is incumbent upon us all to protect and honor this Tower of Glory, we have established a fund to defray the cost of repair and restoration, and we invite you honorable fellow-townspeople to contribute what you can to this fund.

From that day on, the tower wasn't the same in our eyes.

Now we respected it and wouldn't aim it at our mothers and sisters any more when we quarrelled. We also stopped using it as a toilet and when birds sat on its crenels we scared them off, waving our arms, throwing up our hats, or hurling stones at them, lest they would ease nature on our Tower of Glory. Moreover, our zeal got the better of us, and we all contributed to the fund, eager to play a part in the restoration of the tower. The sight of the tower filled us with pride. We showed off our town's monument, dragging all visitors to the site to see it, and we felt especially proud of it when we visited towns which didn't have a tower of glory. Those were small towns without a history, and we somehow blamed their residents for this shortcoming.

The restoration began with the money contributed by the patriotic townspeople, but half way through, the funds ran out. We weren't to blame. We had given generously, but the money was not enough to cover restoration costs. One day, a second notice embellished the walls all over town. After an introduction like that of the first, the notice informed us that since the funds for the restoration of the Tower of Glory had proved insufficient, the town Council and the Governor's Office had passed a sales tax of two rials on a kilo of sugar, three rials on a kilo of bread, and four rials on a liter of kerosene and gasoline. The notice added that the tax was temporary and would be lifted as soon as the repairs it was to pay for were completed.

We couldn't very well oppose the tax; the tower, as well as our honor and dignity, was at stake. The cost was our responsibility. It wasn't proper that the government should pay for the restoration and we should reap the glory. It served us right. We'd made our bed, and we had to sleep in it.

The next day meat went up three tomans a kilo. The notice had said nothing about meat, so we asked the butcher why he'd raised the price. "Do you expect me to pay more for bread, sugar, and kerosene, and sell the meat at the old rates? What do you take me for?" he said self-righteously. He was right. We all agreed that the new prices for goods under government control had to be maintained; otherwise the repairs would be halted. Meanwhile, rent, bus fare, and all merchandise began to soar, while our incomes remained the same. But we were happy to share the glory bequeathed upon us by the tower.

When the restoration was finally completed, a new department was formed and our Tower of Glory was entrusted to its chiefs and staff. They set up an office at the tower, and charged the visitors two tomans. Shortly afterwards, those who left or entered the town were charged five tomans and issued a receipt containing a picture of the tower and the statement, "For the Restoration and Preservation of the Tower of Glory."

What a nuisance the tower had turned out to be! But what were we to do? Could we expect the government to pay for the new department, for its offices, and for its many automobiles driven by the heads of the General Bureau of National Glory? It was our town and our glory; why should the government pick up the tab? There's a limit to what your government should do for you.

Meanwhile the fame of our Tower of Glory spread everywhere and people flocked to our town to see it. They came, they saw, and they left, and their comings and goings didn't leave our lives unaffected. Rents soared at the inns, and shopkeepers demanded outrageous prices for their goods. If we protested, they'd simply say no one was forcing us to buy. And they were right. If we didn't pay those prices, there were plenty of tourists who would. We began to regard the Tower of Glory as a nuisance, while residents of other towns envied us and wished they had such a tower.

One day, rumors spread that the Tower of Glory had sunk and was leaning a few inches. Now try and straighten that out! After all that trouble, the tower was in danger of collapsing. We flocked to the tower three or four times a day, to make sure it was still there. The sight of our Tower of Glory leaning pitifully broke our hearts. We were trying to find a solution, when a second team of archaeologists came from the capital to see the tower. They warned us that unless something was done right away, the Tower of Glory would collapse. A specialist was called, the cost of repairs was estimated, committees were formed one after another, as we waited anxiously, wondering about the fate of our Tower of Glory. One day, the walls were once more covered with notices informing the honorable and patriotic residents that in order to save the tower from destruction, home-owners were to pay twenty rials a square meter in real estate tax each month. The notice added that the order was approved by the Governor, and those who disobeyed it would be severely punished.

This was the straw that broke the camel's back. True, the Tower of Glory had been handed down to us by our ancestors; true, it was several centuries old. But why should we have to pay for our ancestors' architectural blunders? Damn it, those who had constructed the tower should have built a garden or a mill, or dug a well, or put aside a piece of property to pay for the tower's maintenance, so they wouldn't have to plague their innocent descendants with all this trouble. Where the hell were we supposed to get the three or four hundred tomans every month to pay for the tower?

We gathered together, some of us led the way, and we walked to the governor's office, and, so to speak, held a demonstration. We said we didn't have the money, and as far as we were concerned they could keep the Tower and the Glory.

They said nothing that day and promised to reconsider the order. But the next day they arrested some of the demonstrators and made them sign a written statement to the effect that they would abide by the law. The rest of the demonstrators paid their six months' taxes in a lump sum in advance, willingly and on their own.

One gets used to everything after a while. We grew used to paying the tax, as we had grown used to the high food prices. But it was as if nature itself was at odds with us, for around this time an earthquake tore down some of our homes and cracked our Tower of Glory in the middle. The authorities sent for a team of archaeologists to examine the tower and estimate the cost of repair, and we prepared ourselves for the new taxes. The archaeologists arrived, and after one month of study and research concluded that the Tower was not built in the time of the prophet Daniel, was only seventy or eighty years old, and couldn't be the Tower of Glory the first team of archaeologists had been trying to locate. Apparently the European archaeologist-orientalist, the fat, bearded professor, had mistaken the site of the tower. The tower he and his team had come to look for was in Darkness County, where the archaeologists had resumed their search for the Tower of Glory.

Suddenly, the tower was divested of all its grandeur. The department and its offices were closed down, and the tower resumed the life of its inglorious days. It became a dog-hole, a public toilet, and an obscene missile aimed at the adversary in quarrels. The pigeons and sparrows returned to their old nests in the holes of its inside and outside walls. Its cracked middle opened wider, and it leaned more every day. The taxes and high prices, however, held their own and remained stable. We are still paying them. Rates which had soared with or without government sanction remained where they were.

We don't know whether the archaeologists and orientalists have yet discovered the Tower of Glory in Darkness County.

1970

The Game Is Up

BY GHULAMHUSAYN SA'IDI

Hasani himself asked me. He asked me to go to their hut that evening. I had never gone to their hut. He had never come to ours. I'd never asked him to, because I was scared of my pa. He was scared of his pa, too—a lot more than I was of mine. But that evening was different. I had to go. Hasani would feel hurt and get angry at me if I didn't. He would think I didn't like him any more and wasn't his friend. That's why I went. That was the first time I set foot in their hut. We always met outside. Our huts were in a cluster of squatters' huts. I'd stop by their hut in the morning and whistle—a pretty whistle he had taught me. This was our signal. It was like saying, 'Come Hasani! Time to go to work.' Hasani would pick up his bucket and come out of the hut. Instead of saying hello, we would fistfight for a spell—nice, hard blows that hurt really good. We fistfought when we met, and we fistfought when we parted—except when we were mad at each other for some reason.

*

Hasani and I would walk past the huts until we reached the pit near the home where they washed the dead. The garbage trucks emptied the garbage in that pit. Hasani and I went to the pile every morning. Some days I would collect tin cans, Hasani would look for broken glass; some days he would look for tin cans, I for glass. Once in a while we would find something better, an empty margarine can, a pacifier, a broken doll, a shoe, a plastic pitcher, or even a sugar bowl with just a tiny crack. Once I found an amulet and Hasani an unopened pack of imported cigarettes. When we got tired we would go to the other side of the pit, past Hadj Teimur's kilns—which were not working any more and had been abandoned—and rest in the Kaffeh, a large piece of level ground, full of deep wells. Not just one or two, but a whole lot of wells. Once we decided to count them. We passed fifty, got bored, and stopped. We played fun games at the wells. We would lie down, lean into the well down to our chests, and make strange noises. The sound would echo and reverberate. Every well was different; it answered back differently. Usually we would laugh into the well, but instead of laughter we would hear weeping. Then we would get scared, laugh harder and louder; the well, too, would weep harder and louder. Most of the time Hasani and I were alone at the wells. The other kids seldom came to the pit. Their mothers wouldn't let them. They were afraid they'd fall into the well, or hurt themselves some other way. But because Hasani and I were big boys and went home from the pits with full hands, our mothers left us alone and never complained.

That evening, the day after I'd been to their hut, Hasani looked very glum when he joined me. He was frowning. His eyes were swollen; I could tell he had been crying. He didn't feel like doing anything. When we got to the pit, he just looked around, thrusting his stick into the garbage and cursing his pa nonstop. I knew what had happened. I could see the belt mark on his shoulders, and he had a black eye. His father had returned to the hut that noon in an ugly mood. He had quarrelled with his boss and had been fired. He had started beating Hasani the minute he had gotten home. We had heard Hasani scream. My mother had cursed his pa for beating the poor kid like that. Hasani's pa would beat him every night as soon as he got home from work, even before washing up and undressing. He would beat Hasani for as long as he could take it, kicking and punching, hitting him with a stick, whipping him with a rope or a belt, cursing him all the time. He would hit so hard, it made Hasani holler and scream. Then the neighbors would plead with his father and save him from his blows. Hasani's pa beat him every night, but my pa beat me once or twice a week, when he was in a nasty mood, like when he hadn't made money. Then he would take it out on my brother and me, and beat us all we could take. My mother would cry and holler, "You're going to kill them! You're going to cripple them." Then pa would turn and start on her. She would yell for us to escape. We would run out and sit some place quietly. Then he would calm down and sit in a corner, chewing his mustaches. Ma would say, "Call them in, so they can eat something."

But Hasani's father didn't bother his other kids. He only had it in for Hasani. And Hasani's mother never told him to run away, because his pa would block the door and go at him, punching and kicking, grabbing his head and knocking it against the wall. That day, for the first time, he had beaten Hasani at noon. Hasani was very glum. I tried to cheer him up. "Let's go," I said.

We climbed out of the pit and went to the wells and sat down near one. Hasani wouldn't speak no matter what I did. I lay down by the well, stuck my head in, and mooed, then barked, laughed, cried; I did everything I could think of, but Hasani just sat there, glum, frowning, beating his stick against his shin. At last I whistled to him, like saying, 'What's the matter?'

Hasani didn't answer. Then I yelled, "Hasani! Hey Hasani!"

"What?" he asked, raising his head.

"What will come of frowning like this?"

"I don't want anything to come of it."

"For God's sake stop frowning."

"I can't help it."

"Get up," I said, standing up. "Let's do something, so you'll feel better."

"Like what?" he asked, hitting his big toe with the stick.

I tried to think of something. I couldn't figure out how to cheer him up. "Let's go to the road and watch the cars," I said.

"What good would that do?" he asked.

"Let's count the hearses, like we did that day. Let's see how many pass by in an hour."

"What for? What do I care how many?" he snapped.

"Do you want to go up to Hadj Teimur's kilns and hurl stones?"

"I don't feel like it," he said impatiently. "You can go by yourself if you want."

I sat on the garbage pile. He wasn't going to do anything I suggested. "I've got an idea," I said. "Let's go to the square; it'll be lots of fun."

"What's fun about it?"

"We can look at the photos outside the movies. After that, we can watch Dervish Sagdast's street show."

"It'll be dark before we get there."

"We'll take the bus."

"Where will we get the money?"

"I've got twelve rials."

"Keep it for yourself."

"Let's get something to eat. Shall we?"

"I don't want anything."

I was at the end of my wits. I kept looking around, trying to think of something to say. We were near Shokrayi's garden. "Let's go and steal some walnuts," I said.

"Yeah! Haven't I had enough today? You want the gardener to beat us too?"

We sat for a while, neither saying anything. Two men showed up behind the kilns and came towards us. They hung around for a while, watching us, then went to the garden and jumped over the wall. There was some yelling, then we heard laughter from the garden. I turned to Hasani. "Why are you angry at me?" I asked.

"I'm not angry at you," he said.

We turned silent again, Hasani still hitting his big toe with his stick. "Stop hitting it! Are you crazy?" I said.

"It's all right. It doesn't hurt," he said.

"Why don't you say something?"

"I've got nothing to say."

"Come on! Don't overdo it. Let's go."

We got up and started walking. We went past the wells. "Hasani," I said.

"What?"

"I'll do anything you say. What do you want to do?"

"I want to lay hands on my pa and beat the daylight out of him."

"Well, why don't you?"

"I'm not strong enough."

"Of course you aren't."

He stopped suddenly. "The two of us together could do it," he said. I began to think. I was scared of his pa. Very scared. All the kids were scared of his pa. He never answered when we said hello. He'd turn back and just stare at us. My pa said he was crazy. He said the man was off his rocker, crazy as a loon. How on earth was I going to beat him? But if I didn't Hasani would get angry at me and stop talking to me.

"Don't you want to help?" he asked.

"Of course I do," I said.

"Then why aren't you answering?"

"How on earth are we going to do it?"

"Come to our hut in the evening. We'll hide in a corner and jump him when he comes to beat me. We can grab his legs, push him to the floor, then beat him."

"What then?"

"Nothing. Only he'll know what it tastes like, and I'll feel better."

I went to their hut that night. It wasn't night really. It was early in the evening, just getting dark. His pa hadn't come back yet. His ma asked us to fetch some water from the waterfountain. We filled the jug and hung around at the waterfountain until his pa showed up carrying a sack on his back. "Here comes the son-of-a-bitch," Hasani said.

We hurried and took a short cut back to the hut. His ma was sitting outside, cooking tomatoes. His younger brother was bawling. We crossed the courtyard, put the jug near the window, and went inside. The room was dark. "Light the lamp," his mother called out. Hasani lit the lamp. His sister was sleeping in a corner. "What do we do now?" I said.

"Nothing. Leave everything to me. Just sit there at the door."

I sat down and waited. Hasani sat at the opposite end of the room. "Don't forget. Grab his legs," he said.

"What will you do?" I asked.

"I'll punch him in the nose, then jump on him and push him to the ground," he said.

I was scared. I didn't know how things were going to turn out. Then we heard his pa hollering outside. "You dirty bitch," he shouted. "How dare you cook dinner before I get home?"

"What the hell am I supposed to do? You want to eat as soon as you get back," Hasani's mother wailed.

"Am I the only one who eats? Don't you and your sons-of-bitches eat too?" his pa yelled.

Then his ma began to holler: "Oh God! I hope you break your leg." Hasani whispered, "Did you hear that?"

"Hear what?" I asked.

"He kicked my ma, the crazy bastard."

Then his pa shouted, "Why is this good-for-nothing sleeping here?"

"Where do you want him to sleep?" his ma wailed.

"I don't know. Some other place. Any place," he shouted.

He entered the courtyard, lay down his sack at the door, and started to cough. He coughed for a while, spat the mucus, then swore. He took the jug, rinsed his mouth, and drank a few gulps. Finally, he came into the room. Hasani backed a few steps. His pa gnashed his teeth, raging. Hasani's back was against the wall. "What are you going to do?" he asked his pa.

"Nothing," his pa said. "What can one do to a big bully like you?"

Then he suddenly saw me. He looked me over, rubbing his mustaches.

I was numb with fear. I backed up as I was sitting. "Well, well, well! What the hell is he doing here?" his pa asked.

"He's my friend," Hasani said. "Abdol Agha's son."

"I don't care whose son he is. What the hell is he doing in my house?"

"I asked him in," Hasani said.

"Why? Doesn't the poor bastard have a place of his own?"

"Of course he does; better than ours."

"So what the hell does he want here?" his pa asked, then turned to me. "Get the hell out. Get out!" he shouted.

"He isn't going. He's staying," Hasani said from the end of the room.

Hasani's pa turned to him. "You've gotten so bold, you dare contradict me to my face?" he said, going toward Hasani, his arms spread out, so Hasani wouldn't get away. Hasani's sister woke up and ran out of the room, screaming. His pa lifted his fist, then Hasani yelled, "Get him!"

I attacked. His pa aimed a blow at Hasani. Hasani dodged. His pa's fist hit the wall. I grabbed one of his legs, Hasani grabbed the other, and we pulled. His pa fell over us, breathing hard, his punches landing on our heads, first on me, then on Hasani, then on both of us at the same time. We used all our strength and freed ourselves. Hasani was cursing. He kicked his pa in the ass, and we jumped out. His pa roared and ranted: "I'll kill you. Weren't you enough trouble by yourself, so you'd to bring this ruffian along?"

He ran after us. Hasani's ma was standing near her cooking-stove, terrified, at a loss what to do. We passed her by and ran out, taking a short cut to the pit. "Stop them! Stop them!" Hasani's father shouted. He chased us a short way, then stopped, cursing and grumbling. It had grown dark. No one had chased us. No one wanted us to be caught. We passed the water-fountain and got to the pit, panting. I took Hasani's hand and we watched for his pa, or any one who might be following us. "We'd better get out of the pit," I said.

"Yeah," Hasani said. "The son-of-a-bitch might show up with a stick and trap us here. Then we'll be in trouble."

We climbed out of the ditch and sat to catch our breaths. "That was a good get-away," I said.

"Too bad we didn't beat him much," he said.

"When are you going back?"

"Going back! Are you kidding! That's all he would want so he can beat the daylight out of me."

"Well, what are you going to do then?"

"Nothing."

"Where are you going to sleep tonight?"

"Nowhere. I've no place to go."

"Come to our hut."

"Yeah! So your pa can beat me? Sons of bitches! They're all the same. They have no feeling."

"Suppose you stayed out tonight, what will you do tomorrow and the day after? You got to go back."

"I don't know. Maybe I'll go some place."

"Like where?"

"Somewhere."

"What will you do?"

"I don't know. I'll do something. I'll become an errand boy, or a delivery boy."

"You're too young. No one will hire you."

"Why not?"

"Because there's nothing you can do."

"I can sweep the sidewalk in front of stores, can't I?"

"But you got to be with a grown up before they'll hire you."

"Well, if that doesn't work, I'll scrounge around for junk and sell what I can find."

"Where will you sleep at night?"

"Anywhere."

"It won't work. You can do this for a day or two, but not more. You could die of hunger. Something could happen to you."

"No, it won't. I'll beg and stay alive."

"That's what you think! They'll arrest you and lock you up in the beggars' house of detention. Don't you remember Asdol's children, or Reza's sister?"

"Well, what do you think I should do.?"

"I don't know. I guess it's best if you went home."

We grew silent. The moon had come up but the wells' mouths were dark as always. We could see the huts' dim lights in the distance. Hasani examined the surroundings. "I can't go home. He'll kill me if I do," he said.

We grew silent again, listening to the crickets. Suddenly Hasani jumped to his feet. "I got it!" he said. "Listen, you're going to run back to the huts, you're going to cry and holler, beating yourself and screaming, 'Hasani fell into a well.'"

I jumped to my feet. My stomach sank. "You mean you're going to jump into a well?" I stammered.

"What sort of a fool do you take me for?" he said. "You just tell them I fell into a well. Then you'll see how my pa will carry on! It'll be fun!"

"What then?"

"Nothing. I'll hide some place."

"Then they'll come to search the wells."

"They can't search them all. They'll get tired and give up. Then they'll get together and hold a memorial service for me, thinking I'm dead. My ma and pa will beat their breasts and cry."

"It isn't right."

"Why not?"

"Your pa could die of shock. Your ma could die of grief."

"That's what you think. I know them. They won't die of shock or grief. When they're mourning and beating themselves unconscious, you'll come and tell me. I'll run home and when they see I'm alive and haven't fallen into a well they'll be so happy, that pa will probably make up and stop beating me."

"But . . ."

"But what?"

"I'm scared of your pa. I'm scared he'll catch me and kill me as soon as I give him the news."

"You don't have to tell *him*. You can start yelling as soon as you get to the huts. Just beat yourself and carry on. Just yell 'Hasani fell into a well.'"

"What if I couldn't cry?"

"What an ass!" he said, looking me over. "Who'd know whether you were crying for real or not in the dark?"

"Well, what will you be doing?"

"I'll be hiding inside one of the kilns."

"You'll die of hunger."

"Why, won't you bring me bread and water? Won't you, really?" he asked, astonished.

"Sure, I will."

"All right, then. Go!"

I was hesitating whether to go or not. He took my hand. "Come, I'll show you where I'm going to hide," he said.

We walked in between the wells, toward Hadj Teimur's kilns. A couple of dogs attacked us before we got there and we hit them with stones. Then we circled the kilns until we reached the last one. It was a high kiln with a collapsed ceiling. No one would think anyone could hide there. "This is where I'll be hiding. All right?" Hasani said.

"All right," I said.

"Hurry up now. Don't forget. You must really shout and scream."

"All right, I will."

I had started to go when he called me. "Don't forget. I'm hungry. Bring me something to eat in the morning."

"Sure thing," I said.

I circled the kilns, walked between the wells, and reached the pit. The dogs ran away when they saw me. I climbed the pit and got to the water-fountain. My throat burned from dust. I drank some water. I remembered that I had to run and scream. I took off for the huts, hollering. A crowd had gathered in front of our hut. I didn't know what for. I started yelling and beating myself, like Hasani had really fallen into a well. The crowd turned to face me. Hasani's father was arguing with my pa, carrying a stick in his hand. "Hasani! Hasani!" I sobbed.

"What's happened to him? What?" his pa asked.

"He fell! He fell!" I said, crying. Really crying. Tears streaming down my face.

"Where did he fall? Speak! Where did my Hasani fall?" his father shouted.

"Into a well! He fell into a well!" I yelled.

Suddenly they all were quiet. Then there was a tumult, voices here and there saying, "Hasani has fallen into a well. Hasani has fallen into a well."

People began to pour out of the huts. Some brought lanterns and all began to run to the pit. I was sitting on the ground, crying. My pa bent over me and took my hand. "Which well? Which well did he fall into?" he asked. We began to follow the rest of the people, running. Before we crossed the road some of the men surrounded me and kept asking "Which well?" as we all ran. We passed the pit and reached the wells. The moon had risen higher and the wells looked darker and deeper. The crowd stopped. Hasani's pa was shaking like a willow. "Where is he? Where is he?" he asked, shaking me by the shoulders. He threw himself on the garbage pile and began to weep aloud before I could answer. Abbas Charkhi tried to calm him. "Don't worry, we'll get him out right away," he said. When Hasani's father quieted down, we heard another noise. The women arrived, crying, headed by Hasani's mother beating herself and scratching her face. "Hasani! My Hasani!" she moaned. She said other things but I couldn't make them out. Abbas Charkhi left the crowd and came to me. "Listen kid," he said, "Which well did he fall into?"

"I don't know," I said.

Hasani's pa rushed at me. "You bastard! Tell the truth! What happened to my son?" he yelled.

"Calm yourself," Agha Ghader entreated. "Let him explain what happened."

I swallowed my tears. "Hasani's pa beat Hasani and me," I stammered.

"Tell us where he is now?" Hasani's pa said.

"Yes, hurry up," my pa said.

"Give the poor kid a chance to talk. What is this?" Abbas Charkhi snapped.

"We ran away," I said, "and we came here. Hasani was a long way ahead of me. His pa wasn't following us. Nor was anyone else. So I yelled for Hasani to stop, but he kept running. He was running between the wells when suddenly he yelled and fell."

"Where did he fall?" Hasani's pa shouted.

"I thought he had just tripped, so I called him. He didn't answer. Then I started to look for him but couldn't find him."

"Which well did he fall into?" Hasani's pa shouted again.

"How could he know?" Abbas Charkhi said angrily. "Let's start looking. Be very careful." He said to the men.

They walked toward the wells in silence. No one was crying, or shouting. But Hasani's mother was moaning quietly. "Be quiet, sister. Don't make noise. They're going to find him and get him out," the women kept saying to her. "Shhhhh, shhhhhh, shhhhh," some kept saying, as if Hasani was asleep and they were afraid he would wake up. They went past a few wells, then Hasani's pa bellowed, "Hasani! Hasani! Hasani!" He was so angry, if Hasani was in a well and could come out, he would grab him and give him a sound beating. "Be calm! Be calm, man, and let's get to work," Abbas Charkhi said.

"We need some rope and a lantern," someone said from the dark. "You can't go down the well without a rope."

Some of the men began to run toward the huts to fetch rope and lantern. Two men offered Abbas Charkhi their lanterns. He lay down at a well and lowered a lantern into it. The men circled the well. "I don't think he's in this one," he said in a low voice, his head inside the well. They walked over to another well. This time Mosayeb lay down and lowered the lantern into it. "Where are you, kid. Where are you?" he called, like a street vendor. After the sixth well they broke into two groups, each taking one well, then a second, then a third. Then they broke into three and later four groups and continued the search. Those who had gone for rope and lantern came back. They tied the ropes together. Failing to find Hasani the men were beginning to lose their tempers. Then suddenly Abbas Chakhi called them and they rushed to the well he was checking out. "I think he's in there," he said excitedly. "I heard some noise, like someone was moaning at the bottom."

They all turned quiet. Some of them lay down and stuck their heads into the well. "You're right. He's in there," they said. Hasani's father began to shout, "Hurry up! Get him out! Get my child out!"

"Who's going to go in?" Mosayeb asked.

"It's an old well. Its walls might collapse," Ghader said.

"No they won't. I swear to God they won't. Go in and bring him out," Hasani's father entreated.

The men stared at each other. "Isn't anyone man enough? All right, I'll go myself. Pass the rope," Abbas Charkhi said.

"Not you! Not you! You can't! You don't know how," his wife called amidst the women.

"Shut up, woman. Mind your own business. I can't let the child die in there," he said angrily.

She pushed her way through the crowd, ran up to him and hung from his neck. "I won't let you. I swear to God I won't," she said.

Abbas Charkhi slapped her hard. "Get lost, woman. What a bother," he said. "Give me the rope," he called to the men.

They tied the rope about his waist and checked all the knots. "Be careful. Don't let go of me half way down," Abbas said.

"Don't worry, we'll be careful," some said.

Abbas took one of the lanterns, bent, and looked into the well. Then he passed the lantern to someone. "In the name of God," he said aloud. Everybody recited the *salavat*. Hasani's father raised his arm to the sky and called on all the Imams to help his son make it out of the well alive. Abbas leaned into the well, supported by his forearms. "Hold the rope tight and pull it up when I shake it," he said. His wife, who was behind me, began to cry. My ma tried to calm her. Then Abbas went down. Five or six men were holding the rope firmly, and releasing it little by little. They were whispering something. Hasani's pa was turning around like a chicken without a head. He was wringing his hands, biting his lips, and calling on God. I had forgotten that Hasani was in the kiln. Like the rest, I was praying for Abbas to find him and make everybody happy.

A few minutes passed. Then my pa, who was holding the rope with some others, said, "Pull it up! Pull it up!"

"What for?" Rahmat asked.

"Are you blind, or what?" Can't you see the rope is shaking?" pa said.

Everybody turned silent. They began to pull the rope. Hasani's pa stood on his toes, trying to see over the men's heads, looking for Abbas Agha to appear. Then Abbas Agha's hands grabbed the rim, he put his forearms on the ground and pushed himself up. He lay on the ground, panting. "Was he in there?" asked Ghader. Hasani's pa let out a cry and began to weep. Abbas Agha rolled and half rose. "I almost suffocated in there," he said.

"Was he dead?" Ghader asked.

"All I found was a stinking dead dog," Abbas said.

"Couldn't you be mistaken?" asked Mosayeb.

"Can't I tell the difference between Hasani and a dead

dog?" Abbas snapped. He stood up and untied the rope from his waist. The men got together again and went to another well. After the fourth well, they broke into two groups, then four, carrying lanterns and calling Hasani at every well. That was when I sneaked out and ran for the huts, trying to stay in the dark, so no one would see me. I drank at the water-fountain and went into our hut quietly. No one was there. I took some bread and an empty jug and ran out. I filled the jug at the water-fountain, went past the pit and Hadj Teimur's kilns to Hasani's hiding-place. I stuck my head in and called his name in a low voice. He did not answer. I got worried. Then I thought maybe he can't tell it's me. I whistled like I did when I called him in the morning. I heard him whistle from above. He was lying on the roof of the kiln, watching me.

"Hey, Hasani!" I said.

"Come up here quietly," he said.

I gave him the jug, grabbed the brick wall and climbed. We crawled forward quietly and sat near the kiln's chimney. "Weren't you supposed to be inside?" I asked.

"I wanted to see what was going on."

"Do you have any idea what will happen if they see you?"

"They won't. No one can see us." He began to laugh.

"Why are you laughing?"

"Laughing at my pa and the rest of them—the way they're running around!" He pointed at the wells. Some of the men were walking around, others stood fixed at the wells.

"We did a terrible thing," I said.

"Why?"

"Your pa is killing himself. You won't believe the shape he's in."

"Don't worry, he won't kill himself. What about my ma?"

"She's beating her breast and crying."

"Let her."

"Abas Agha went down a well and instead of you found a stinking dead dog."

"It was his father's carcass."

We laughed. Then I took out the bread, divided it in half, and we began to eat. I wasn't thirsty, but Hasani drank a few gulps from the jug. "Shouldn't we go to them?" I asked.

"What for?"

"To end this thing. They can't search all the wells."

"It isn't time yet. Let them search a bit longer."

"Someone could fall into the well and die."

"Don't worry. They all have nine lives like cats. Nothing ever happens to them."

"We're doing a wicked thing."

"Isn't it wicked of them to beat us all the time?"

"For God's sake, Hasani, stop it. Let's go to them."

"No."

"Why not?"

"What will I say to them?"

"Say you'd gone to Shokrayi's garden to pick walnuts."

"Then you'll get into trouble."

"I'll say I didn't know where you were. I figured you'd fallen into a well."

"No, they'll see through us. Then we'll really be in trouble."

"I swear to God they won't see through us. Come, let's go."

"I'm not going anywhere."

"Then I'll go and tell them you're all right, hiding in Hadj Teimur's kiln."

He gave me a straight look. "All right. Tell them. That'll be the end of our friendship. You'll never see me again."

"All right. All right. When do you want to go home?"

"During the memorial service. I'll burst in as they are mourning for me. That should be fun."

"What's fun about it?"

"I'll tiptoe in as they're beating their breasts and crying, suddenly jump in front of them and say hello! At first, they'll be terror-stricken. The women will scream. The children will run away, thinking I've come back from the dead. Then they'll pull themselves together, see it's really me. I am looking at them, laughing, moving my limbs. They'll get happy then. Jump up and down, hug and kiss me. You don't think that's fun?"

We watched the crowd which still went around the wells with lanterns. Once in a while we could hear the men and women shout. "I'm going back to the wells," I said.

"All right, but don't snitch," he said.

I crawled on all fours, watched my surroundings carefully, then jumped down. I passed the road, crossed the pit, and joined the men. They had gathered around a well. I ran to them. My ma was beating herself and screaming. Someone was in the well and the men were holding the rope. I pushed through the crowd and got to the well.

"He's shaking it. Pull it up! Pull it up!" Abbas told the other men.

"What for?" Ghader asked.

"Are you blind, or what? Can't you see he's shaking it?"

They became quiet and began to pull. Hasani's pa was behind me, calling all the Imams to his aid. Then I saw my pa put his forearms on the ground, pushing himself out of the well. He was panting, covered with sludge from head to toe.

"Lie down. Lie down and breathe," Abbas said. They supported pa under his arms and stretched him by the well.

II

No one went to work when morning came. They returned to their huts, dead tired. They hadn't found Hasani. Abbas had said it was no use to go on searching. They couldn't search all the wells. They had found deeper wells with tunnels between them. Sludge water ran from one well to the next. The men had discovered strange beings at the bottom of the wells. Habib had seen a creature as big as a bull, with four or five tails, holding the head of a dead man between his jaws. Sayyed had seen naked hairy people clinging to the wall of the well. They had jumped and disappeared into the stinking water when they had seen him. Mir-Jalal had seen enormous black wings hovering in the well. Weird noises, like cats moaning, invisible women laughing, were heard down in the wells; some had even heard cymbals and trumpets. Abbas had said Hasani had to be dead already and it was no use to go on looking. Then they had returned to the huts, tired and sleepy. They had all gone to bed, except for Hasani's father who kept walking among the huts, shaking his head and saying, "Did you see what happened? How I lost the poor child. How he died before his time." He wasn't crying any more, or yelling. He just stared at things. He stared at the hut's ceiling, at the decaying barrels that put side by side formed a wall, at the stains on the piece of burlap that hung at the door. Once in a while he would bend and pick up something, like a piece of glass or an old shoe, play with it, then throw it away. He would look around for something else. "Now they're eating him. It's all over. My son is gone," he would say under his breath.

I hung around where he was. He looked strange. He didn't see me. Or maybe he did, but didn't pay any attention to me. I went to our hut. Everybody was asleep. Pa was sleeping on his side, his muddy feet sticking out of the covers. I filched some bread and a handful of sugar cubes, which happened to be at hand, and left. It was quiet. Hasani's pa was behind a hut, scratching something off a wall. The sun had risen. It was light. I drank at the water fountain. No one was around. I crossed the pit, went to Hadj Teimur's kilns, and began to look for Hasani's hiding place. He was asleep. When I called him he woke up in terror. "Who's it? Who's it?" he cried.

"It's only me. Don't be afraid," I said.

He sat up. He looked different; his eyes sunken, his hands trembling.

"What's the matter? Something wrong?" I asked.

"I was dreaming I'd fallen into a well and couldn't get out no matter how hard I tried."

"Serves you right for this tomfoolery. Your pa has gone completely berserk."

He said nothing. We sat in the sun. I gave him the bread and a handful of sugar cubes. He drank a few gulps from the jug and splashed some water on his face.

"What's happening?" he asked, feeling better.

"They think you're dead."

"What did you do?"

"I didn't do anything, or say anything."

"What are they going to do now?"

"They aren't going to do anything."

"Aren't they going to hold a memorial service for me?"

"I don't know."

"I think they will. This evening."

"How do you know?"

"Remember when Bibi's grandchild died? They held the memorial service the next day."

"If that's the way it's done yours will be today."

"I hope it is. I'm getting bored."

"I hope so, too."

"Don't forget to come and call me."

"I won't forget. But brace yourself for a sound beating."

"Nothing like that. They'll be overjoyed to see me."

"That's what you think. You'll see."

"Want to bet?"

"All right."

"If they beat me when they see me, you'll win. If they are happy to see me alive, I'll win and you'll receive a sound beating at my hand."

"Bah! I worry myself sick over you, and you want to beat me on top of it?"

"I'm kidding," he said, laughing. "I'll buy you an ice cream."

"That's more like it."

He put some bread in his mouth. "What shall we do now?" he asked.

"Nothing," I said. "You'll just hide here. I'll go to the huts and see what happens."

"You'll come and call me if the memorial service is this evening, won't you?"

"Sure thing."

Hasani's memorial service was that evening. Abbas Agha had nailed a black cloth to a pole in the open space in front of the huts. The men sat on one side, the women on the other. Squatters in other areas had heard the news and were arriving in great numbers. They were strangers. The women would go to Hasani's mother, who was sitting in front of her hut, her face scratched and bloody. She was shaking her head and occasionally beating her breast, but not crying. The women would start weeping the minute they reached her. "Oh dear sister, dear sister! What you've gone through," they'd say, beating their breasts.

Hasani's pa was sitting in front of our hut, sprawling, rather, and staring vacantly. The men would walk up to him and say hello, since he was the dead boy's father. He wouldn't respond, and they would leave him, looking for a place to sit down. Abbas was on his feet, urging the crowd to recite the *Fatihah*.*

The men were reciting the *Fatihah*. Habib went among the crowd with a jug, giving water to the thirsty. Two old men, from another neighborhood, had come with a bag of tobacco and were hurriedly rolling cigarettes in pieces of newspaper and filling the tray which Ramazan would then pick up and offer to the crowd. Everybody was smoking and drinking water. Once in a while they would roll their tongues about their lips and spit on the ground.

After about an hour, a crowd appeared on the road and approached the mourners in haste. "The Black Mourners from Gowd-e Piran. Let's go to meet them," Abbas shouted. Some of the men went to welcome them. The Black Mourners arrived two by two, headed by a few shabby old men who were beating their breasts nervously. Many of the Mourners bore standards. In the middle of the Mourners was a thin, tall priest, wearing a small turban. The women followed last, barefoot and dusty. The Black Mourners were greeted by a loud *Salavat*. The women went to Hasani's mother, bawling. The men went to his father and the old men greeted him, but he did not respond. Then the standard bearers passed the standards to the boys, who stood behind the grownups at a distance. The priest sat on the step in front of our hut.

"Recite the *Salavat* loud and clear," cried Abbas Agha. Everybody recited the *Salavat*. "Sit down, all of you. Sit down. Let's recite the tragedy of young Ghasem in memory of this innocent poor child, and mourn his untimely death," the priest said in a hoarse, nasal voice. First he said a strange prayer, then began the tragedy of Ghasem. Suddenly the sound of weeping and moaning rose to the sky. Everybody was crying. The men, the women, the children. Even I was crying. Only Hasani's pa wasn't crying. He kept fidgeting in his place and rolling his tongue over his dry lips. The weeping grew louder and louder.

---

*A chapter in the Koran, recited when someone dies.

The Black Mourners rose and undid their shirts, exposing their breasts. The priest, too, undid his shirt. "Now, let's beat our breasts to please the Lord of the Martyrs, and to mourn the death of this poor child," he said and began the lamentation. The Black Mourners started to beat their breasts in harmony. The other men followed suit. The women were hugging each other, weeping and screaming louder and louder. I suddenly remembered it was time to call Hasani. No one was paying any attention to me. No one was paying any attention to anyone. I sneaked out, first tip-toeing out of the crowd, then walking faster, wiping my tears. I drank at the water-fountain, crossed the pit, then began to run. I ran between the wells. I was worried; a cold sweat covered my face and scalp. I finally reached Hasani's hiding place. He was lying on the floor, in the kiln. He came out as soon as he saw me. "What's happening?" he asked.

"They're having a memorial service for you."

"What are they doing?"

"People've come from all over and are mourning your death."

"What have you been crying for?" he asked, staring at me.

"For you."

"What an ass! You know I'm alive."

"Yes, but the priest the Black Mourners brought along made everybody cry."

"Then it's time, isn't it?" he said happily, rubbing his hands.

"Yes, I think it's time."

"Let's see who wins the bet."

"I hope to God you do."

"Let's go," he yelled, laughing.

He took off like a bullet. I followed, but he ran like he was flying. I couldn't keep up with him. "Hasani! Hasani!" I called several times.

"Boo! Boo!" he said.

Then suddenly something happened. I don't know what. I don't know how to describe it. Hasani stepped on the garbage pile and took off and fell right into a well. Right into it. At first I didn't think he had fallen into a well. I thought he had just fallen to the ground. I ran to where I thought he had landed.

He wasn't there. He had fallen into a well—a big well, bigger than all the rest. I couldn't speak. My lips wouldn't move. I wanted to yell, to call him. My voice was gone. My mouth wouldn't open. I tried hard, but couldn't say 'Hasani!'

I sat on the garbage pile and grabbed my shoulders. My breath was locked inside me. I knocked my head against the ground. Then I stood up. It was more like someone lifted me up and put me down on my two feet. I began to run. Faster than ever. Faster than Hasani. I wished I could jump and fall into a well. Then I reached the road. When I passed the water fountain, I could breathe again, and I could speak. "Hasani! Hasani!" I said quietly.

When I reached the huts, the mourners were sitting quietly. Ramazan was distributing cigarettes. Habib went around with a jug of water.

"Hasani! Hasani!" I yelled out. I beat myself on the head and rolled on the ground. Everybody got up and rushed to me. They surrounded me. Abbas Agha reached me before anyone else. He held my hands, so I wouldn't beat myself. "What's the matter? What's the matter?" he asked.

"Hasani! Hasani fell into a well," I cried. I rolled over and bit the ground. There was a tumult. Everybody wanted to calm me down. "It's all right. It's all right. God bless his soul. Be calm. Stop beating yourself," they said.

"He fell into a well just now. Just a minute ago. Hasani fell into a well," I cried.

My pa pushed the men aside and came forward. "Shut up, kid. Don't rub salt into their wounds," he said.

"He fell. He fell right before my two eyes!" I cried.

"I said shut up. Be quiet, you ass," pa shouted.

"I swear to God he fell in. He fell in the well just now," I yelled louder.

Father lifted me up and slapped me hard. Esmayil Agha pulled him away. "Don't beat him. Can't you see he's gone berserk?" he said to pa. Then he took me in his arms. "Be calm; be calm," he said.

Habib gave Esmayil Agha a glass of water and he splashed it on my face. I tried hard to free myself, but his arms tightened harder around me. Other men came to his aid, so I wouldn't run away.

"Hasani fell! Hasani fell into the well. Hasani! Hasani!" I yelled as loud as I could. Esmayil's large hand stopped my mouth. The men dragged me to our hut. As we went past his pa, I looked at him and motioned to the wells. He didn't look at me; he just stared into the air. "Be quiet, boy." Esmayil said to me inside the hut. "We all know you two were pals and liked each other a lot. But what can one do? God's will be done." I shouted again. "He fell in just now! just now!" I wanted to run out, but they stopped me.

"What shall we do with him? What shall we do?" pa asked.

"He's gone berserk. We'd better tie him up," Esmayil said.

They tied my hands and feet. I began to yell.

"What shall we do about his yelling?" pa asked.

"We'll gag him," Esmayil said.

They gagged me and threw me in a corner.

"What shall I do with him? Oh God! God! If he stays like this, what am I going to do?" pa kept saying, wringing his hands.

"Don't worry. I'll tell the priest to give him an amulet. That will cure him," Esmayil said.

"And if it doesn't, we'll take him to the shrine of Shabdol'azim," Habib said.

Pa kept turning around himself, moaning and calling upon the Imams. "Let's leave him alone. Maybe that will help," Esmayil said.

They left the hut, and closed the door. The crowd recited the *Salavat* again, and the priest began the tragedy of young Ghasem in his nasal voice.

1973

GLOSSARY

Agha: Mr., placed before or after the proper name. (Aziz Agha in Hidayat's story, however, is a woman).

Chador: A veil; a large triangular piece of cloth covering the head and the body.

Fatihah: A section of the Koran, recited when someone dies.

Ghandagh: Hot water sweetened with sugar.

Ghebleh: The direction of the Ka'bah, in Mecca. Moslems face the Ka'bah when they say their prayers.

Hadj, Hadji: Titles used before the name of a man who has performed the pilgrimage to Mecca.

Hadjiyeh: A title used before the name of a woman who has performed the pilgrimage to Mecca.

Kadkhoda: The head of a village.

Karbalayi: A title given to a person who has performed the pilgrimage to the shrine of Imam Hosein in Karbala, Iraq.

Khan: Mr., placed after the proper name.

Khanom: A lady; title placed after a woman's name.

Korsi: A wooden stand, covered by a large counterpane and heated by a charcoal burner, used to sit or sleep under in winter.

Lahd: Stone placed in the grave.

Mashhadi or *Mashdi:* Title used before the name of a person who has performed the pilgrimage to the shrine of Imam Reza in Mashhad.

Mujtahid: Title given to ecclesiastical dignitaries.

Nakir va Munkar: Two angels.

Salavat: Benedictions addressed to the Prophet and his people.

Sigheh: A contract wife; a woman married by way of a temporary marriage.

NOTES ON THE CONTRIBUTORS:

JALAL AL-I AHMAD (1923-1969). A daring stylist and the author of several collections of short stories, Al-i Ahmad also wrote a number of essays, novels and anthropological studies. He contributed to *Arash, Sukhan, Kayhan-i Mah, Ilm-u-Zindigi* among other journals. In the 1960's, he emerged as a particular favorite of the intellectuals. The present story, "A Joyous Celebration" (Jashn-i-farkhundah) was published in *Arash*, 1:1 (Aban 1340/October-November 1961).

MAHSHID AMIRSHAHI. Amirshahi has published several collections of short stories and contributed to *Nigin*. She writes about the middle and lower classes. Her female characters show her deep understanding of Iranian women. The present story, "The End of the Passion Play" (Akhar-i ta'ziyah), appeared in her short story collection *Ba'd az ruz-i akhar* (After the Last Day), Tehran 1969.

SADIQ CHUBAK. Chubak was born in 1916 in Bushire, a major port-town in Southern Iran on the Persian Gulf. He has written several novels and collections of short stories. Most of his work deal with the lives of the lower classes. He is a leading contemporary writer, distinguished for his mature prose style. The present story, "The First Day in the Grave" (Ruz-i avval-i qabr), appeared in the collection of that same title in Tehran in 1965.

SIMIN DANISHVAR. As author and translator, Danishvar writes sensitively about the Iranian woman and her life. Danishvar's most successful work is *Suvushūn* (The Mourners), a novel published in 1969. She has contributed to *Sukhan* and *Alifba* as well as translated some of the works of Shaw, Chekhov, Moravia, Hawthorne, Saroyan, and Albert Schnitzler. The present story, "A Land like Paradise" (Shahri chun bihisht), is the title story for a collection she published in 1962.

IBRAHIM GULISTAN. Gulistan was born in Shiraz in 1922. He is a translator, writer, and cinematographer. He made an effort to divorce his work from the climate of Hidayat's stories and was influenced by Hemingway, Faulkner, and Henry James. He translated *The Adventures of Huckleberry Finn* and several short stories by Hemingway. His films, "Fire," "The Wave, the Coral, the Rock," "Marlik Hills," and "The Mudbrick and the Mirror," have won him international recognition. The story, "The Carrousel" (Charkh-u-falak), was published in his collection of short stories *Juy va divar-i Tashnah* (The Stream, and The Wall, and The Thirsty), Tehran, 1967.

SADIQ HIDAYAT (1903-1951). The founder of modern fiction in Iran, Hidayat went to schools in Tehran and Paris. While in Post-World War I France, he was deeply influenced by European literature. He wrote several novels, six collections of short stories, and a number of plays. He also translated works from French and Pahlavi, and wrote critical essays on Omar Khayyam and Franz Kafka. The story, "Seeking Absolution" (Talab-i amurzish), is taken from Hidayat's collection *Sih qatrah khun* (Three Drops of Blood), Tehran 1932. An earlier version of the translation was published in *Iranian Studies*, IX (Winter, 1976).

NADIR IBRAHIMI. Ibrahimi is a committed writer and critic with several collections of short stories and a number of children's books to his credit. His short stories and literary criticism appeared regularly in *Payam-i Nuvin*. The present story, "Why Do They Go Back?" (Bara-yi chah bar migardand?), was translated from the text of the story published in *Payam-i Nuvin* (Azar 1346/ November-December 1967).

MAHMUD KIYANUSH. Kiyanush (b. 1934) is a prolific short story writer, poet, novelist, and critic. He has contributed regularly to *Sukhan* and *Nigin*, and has published several volumes of his works. The story, "Gowhartaj's Father" (Pidar-i Gowhartaj), was written in 1962 and published in Kiyanush's short story collection *Dar anja hichkas nabud* (No One Was There), Tehran, 1967.

AHMAD MAHMUD. Mahmud has contributed to *Payam-i Nuvin* and has published several collections of short stories. Dark despair is the prevailing mood in most of his works. The present story, "Of Weariness" (Az diltangi), was published in the short story collection *Za'iri zir-i baran* (Visitor in the Rain), Tehran, 1968.

JAMAL MIRSADIQI. A short story writer and novelist, Mirsadiqi (b. 1933) focuses on the lives of the poorer classes in most of his works. His novel, *The Length of Night*, however, deals with the conflict between the old and new mores in contemporary Iran. He has contributed to *Sukhan* and other journals. The story, "The Snow, The Dogs, The Crows" (Barfha, sagha, kalaghha), was first published in *Sukhan* (13 Isfand 1336/ February-March 1957). The present translation is taken from Mirsadiqi's collection *Musafirha-yi shab* (Night Travellers), Tehran, 1971.

SHAPUR QARIB. Qarib contributed short stories to *Jung, Arash*, and *Payam-i Nuvin*. He has published two volumes of short stories. Many of his stories are about life in Southern Iran. The present one, "The Warm South" (Junub-i garm), was published in *Jung* (Spring 1346/ 1967).

BAHRAM SADIQI. Sadiqi, a master of irony, published short stories in *Sukhan, Kayhan-i Haftah, Jung, Sadaf,* and *Firdawsi-yi Mahanah* during the 50's and 60's. These stories were later collected and published in his collection, *Sangar va qumqumah 'ha-yi khali*, Tehran, 1970. The present story, "Teaching in a Pleasant Spring" (Tadris dar bahar-i dil angiz), first appeared in *Kayhan-i Haftah* (28 Isfand 1341/February-March 1962) and then was reprinted in Sadiqi's major collection in 1970.

GHULAMHUSAYN SA'IDI. Sa'idi was born in Tabriz in 1935. While a psychiatrist, he is currently Iran's leading writer and one of the founders of Iran's modern drama and theater. He has written numerous plays, short stories, film scripts, and anthropological monographs. His criticism of the social and economic conditions in Iran caused his frequent incarceration, torture and the banning of many of his works. The present story, "The Game Is Up" (Bazi tamam shud), was published in *Alifba*, I (Tehran, 1973).

KHUSRAW SHAHANI. Shahani was born in Mashhad in 1929. He writes satirical short stories about conditions in contemporary Iran and has published several collections of short stories. The present story, "A Historic Tower" (Burj-i tarikhi), was published in Shahani's collection, *Vahshat abad* (Lonelyville), Tehran, 1969.

NASIR TAQVA'I. Taqva'i is a distinguished film director as well as a writer. He was nominated best director in 1973. His stories deal with life in Southern Iran and were published in *Jung* and *Arash*. The present story, "Agha Julu," was published in *Arash*, 2:1 (Tir 1343/1964).

A SELECTED BIBLIOGRAPHY OF WORKS IN PERSIAN AND ENGLISH

JALAL AL-I AHMAD

I. Author's Works:

Arzyābī-yi shitābzadah. Tabriz, 1344/1965.
Az ranjī kih mībarīm. Tehran 1326/1947.
"Ā'īn-i faṣal," *Payām-i Nuvīn*, 7:9 (Ābān, Āzar 1344/1965), 37–42.
"Chand kalimah bā mashshāṭah'hā," *Andīshah va Hunar*, 3:2 (Ābān 1337/1958), 92–97.
Dīd va bāzdīd. Tehran, 1324/1946.
"Dīd va bāzdīd-i 'īd," *Sukhan*, 2:9 (Mihr 1324/1945), 697–705.
Durr-i yatīm-i khalīj: jazīrah-yi Khārg. Tehran 1339/1960.
Gharbzadigī. Tehran, 1341/1963.
"Guldastah'hā va falak," *Ārash*, 2:14 (Bahman 1346/1968), 9–19.
"Guzārishī az Khūzistān," *Ārash*, 2:4 (Summer 1345/1966), 143–62.
"Guzarishi az kungirah-yi bayn al-milali-yi mardum shināsī," *Payām-i Nuvīn*. 7:1 (Azar 1343/1964), 61–72.
Haft Maqālah included in *Dīd va bāzdīd*, 2nd. ed. Tehran, 1334/1956.
"Iy la'mas' sabā," *Sukhan*, 2:6 (Khurdād 1324/1945), 452–59.
"Jashn-i farkhundah," *Ārash*, 1:1 (Ābān 1340/1961), 15–29.
Kārnāmah-yi sih sālah'ī, Tehran, 1347/1968.
Khasī dar mīqāt. Tehran 1345/1967.

"Mu'allim va darvīsh," *Arash*, 2:1 (Tir 1343/1964), 2–14.
Mudīr-i madrisah. Tehran, 1337/1958.
Nasl-i jadīd, unpublished.
Nifrīn-i zamīn, Tehran. 1346/1967.
Nūn va al-qalam. Tehran. 1340/1961.
Owzaran. Tehran, 1333/1954.
Panj dāstān. Tehran, 1353/1974.
"Pirmard chashm-i mā būd," *Ārash*, 1:2 (Day 1340/1961), 65–75.
"Safarī bih shahr-i bādgīrhā: dār al-'ibādah-yi Yazd," *Andīshah va Hunar,* 3:1 (Shahrīvar 1337/1958), 18–30.
"Ṣamad va afsānah-yi 'avām," *Ārash*, 2:5 (Āẕar, 1347/1968), 5–12.
Sangī bar gūrī, unpublished.
Sarguẕasht-i kandūhā. Tehran. 1333/1954.
Sih maqālah-yi dīgar. No place of publication, 1339/1961.
Sih tār. Tehran, 1327/1949.
Tātnishinhā-yi Bulūk-i Zahrā. Tehran 1337/1958.
"Vidā'," *Sukhan*, 3:4 (Mihr, 1325/1946), 272–75.
Zan-i ziyādi. Tehran, 1331/1952.
"Ziyārat," *Sukhan,* 2:4 (Farvardin 1324/1945), 283–91.

II. Translations and Reviews:

Al-i Ahmad, Jalal. "The Old Man Was Our Eyes," trans. by Thomas M. Ricks, *Literary Review*, 18:1 (Fall 1974), 115–128.

──────. *Owzaran : Iranian Village.* Trans. by I. V. Pourhadi. Tehran, 1955.

──────. "The Pilgrimage," trans. by D. G. Law, *Life and Letters,* 63:148 (December, 1949), 202–209.

──────. *The School Principal,* trans. by J. Newton. Chicago, 1974.

──────. "Someone Else's Child," trans. by T. Gochenour. *Iranian Studies,* 1:4 (1968), 155–162.

Barahini, Riza. *Qiṣṣah Nivīsī*. Tehran, 1348/1969.

Bihnam, Jamshid. (Review of *Tātnishīnhā-yi Bulūk-i Zahrā*.), *Rāhnāma-yi Kitāb* (Shahrīvar 1338/1959), 209–12.

Ibrahimi, Nadir. "Bāzdīd-i Qiṣṣah'hā-yi Imrūz," *Payām-i Nuvīn* (Urdabihisht 1346/1968), 67–69.

Jamalzadeh, A. M. (Review of *Mudīr-i Madrasah*,) *Rāhnamā-yi Kitāb* (Summer 1337/1958), 167–78.

Kamshad, Hassan. *Modern Persian Prose Literature.* Cambridge University Press, 1966.

Kiyanush, Mahmud. *Barrasī-yi shi'r va naṣr-i mu'āṣir dar āsāri az Jalāl Āl-i Ahmad, Ṣādiq Chūbak, Darvīsh, Akbar Rādī, Ghulāmḥusayn Sā'idī, Muḥammad Riẓā Shafī'ī Kadkanī, Sīyāvush Kasrā'ī, Jamāl Mīrsādiqī*. Tehran, 1353/1974.

Mahjub, Muhammad Ja'far. (Review of *Durr-i Yatīm-i Khalīj . . .*) *Rāhnamā-yi Kitāb* (March 1961), 733–36.

Milah, Kh. "Sūki bar Jalāl," *Jahān-i Nuv*, 26:3 (1348/1969), 1–8.

Nuvin, Farid. "Kāvushī dar dunyā-yi Hidāyat va Āl-i Aḥmad," *Nigīn* No. 83 (Farvardīn 1351/1972), 8–10.

Sabri-Tabrizi, G. R. "Human Values in the Works of Two Persian Writers (Al-i Ahmad and Bihrangi)," *Correspondence D'Orient: Actes*, No. 11 (1970), 411–18.

Tihrani, Maḥmud. "Dāstān-i buland va kūtāh dar īn sarzamīn," *Arash* (Winter 1342/1965), 144.

Yar Shater, Ehsan. "The Modern Literary Idiom," *Iran Faces the Seventies*. New York, 1971. pp. 305–308.

Zavarzadeh, Mas'ud. "The Persian Short Story Since the Second World War: An Overview," *The Muslim World*, (Oct. 1968), 311–12.

MAHSHĪD AMĪRSHĀHĪ

I. Author's Works:

Ba'd az rūz-i ākhar. Tehran, 1348/1969.

Bih sīghah-yi avval shakhs-i mufrad: majmū'ah-yi dāstān. Tehran, 1350/1371.
Kūchah-yi bun bast. Tehran, 1345/1966.
Sār-i Bībī Khānum. Tehran, 1347/1968.

II. Reviews:

Daryabandari, Najaf. (Review of *Sār-i Bībī Khānum*,) *Sukhan*, 18:4 (Shahrīvar 1347/1968), 457–460.
Sattari, Jalal. (Review of *Ba'd az rūz-i ākhar*). *Nigīn*, No. 69 (Bahman 1349/1970), 48–50, 56.

SADIQ CHUBAK

I. Author's Works:

'Antarī kih lūtīsh murdah būd. Tehran, 1328/1949.
Chirāgh-i ākhar. Tehran, 1344/1966.
Khaymah'shab bāzī. Tehran, 1346/1968.
Rūz-i avval-i qabr. Tehran, 1344/1965.
Sang-i Ṣabūr. Tehran, 1346/1967.
Tangsīr. Tehran, 1342/1963.
"'Umar kushūn," *Sukhan,* 11:5 (Shahrīvar 1339/1960), 578–82.

II. Translations and Reviews:

Avery, P. W. "Modern Persian Prose," *The Muslim World* (Oct. 1955), 322–23.
Barahini, Riza. *Qiṣṣah Nivīsī.* Tehran, 1348/1969. Pp. 652 ff.

Chubak, Sadiq. "The Baboon Whose Buffoon Was Dead," trans. Peter Avery. *New World Writing*, 11 (May 1957), 14–24.

_____ . "The Inquest," and "Yahya," trans. Henry D. G. Law. *Life and Letters* 63:148 (December 1949), 228–32.

_____ . "Monsieur Elias," trans. William L. Hanaway, Jr., *Literary Review*, 18:1 (Fall 1974), 61–68.

_____ . "Two Short Stories: Justice and The Flower of Flesh," trans. John Limbert, *Iranian Studies*, 1:3 (Summer 1968), 113–20.

_____ . "The Wooden Horse," trans. V. Kubickova and L. Kroutilova, and "The Cage," trans. by V. Kubickova and I. Lewit. *New Orient*, 4:5 (1965), 148–52.

Dastghayb, 'Abd al-'Ali. (Review of *Sang-i Sabūr*), *Rāhnamā-yi Kitāb* (Nov. 1967), 363–71.

_____ . (Review of *'Antarī kih lutish murdah būd,*). *Rāhnamā-yi Kitāb* (March 1963), 904–906.

Gulshiri, Hushang. (On *Sang-i Sabar*), *Jung*, No. 5 (Summer 1346/1967), 216–229.

Kamshad, Hassan. *Modern Persian Prose Literature*. Cambridge University Press, 1966. pp. 127–130.

Kiyanush, Mahmud. *Barrasī-yi shi'r va nasr-i mu'āsir dar āsārī az Jalāl Āl-i Ahmad, Sādiq Chūbak, Darvīsh, Akbar Rādī, Ghulāmhusayn Sa'idī, Muhammad Riza Shafī'ī Kadkanī, Sīyāvush Kasrā'ī, Jamāl Mirsādiqī*. Tehran, 1353/1974.

SIMIN DANISHVAR

I. Author's Works:

"Bikī salām bikunam?" *Alifbā*, 1:4 (1974), 171–179.
"Tasāduf," *Alifbā*, 1:2 (1973), pp. 142–51.
"Tīlah shikastah," *Alifbā*, 1:1 (1973), 99–118.
Shahrī chun bihisht. Tehran, 1340/1962.
Sūvushūn. Tehran, 1348/1969.

II. Reviews:

Anonymous. (Review of *Shahrī chūn bihisht*.) *Ārash*, 5 (Āzar 1341/1962), 88–89.

Dustkhwāh, Jalil. (Review of *Shahrī chūn bihisht*.) *Rāhnamā-yi Kitāb* (Nov. 1962), 628–29.

IBRAHIM GULISTAN

I. Author's Works:

Asrār-i ganj-i darrah-yi jinnī. Tehran, 1353/1974.
Āzar, māh-i ākhar-i pā'īz. Tehran, 1327/1948.
"Bā pisaram rūy-i rāh," *Jung*, 5 (Summer 1346/1967), 76–93.
"Guftār: tappah'hā-yi Mārlik," *Ārash*, 2:2 (Winter 1343/1964), 80–85.
Jūy va dīvār-i tashnah: dah dāstān. Tehran, 1346/1967.
Madd va mih. Tehran, 1348/1969.
"Māhī va juftash," *Ārash*, 2:1 (Tīr 1343/1964), 15–17.
Shikār-i Sāyah. Tehran, 1334/1956.
"Tūṭi-yi murdah-yi hamsāyah-yi man," *Ārash*, 2:4 (Summer 1345/1966), 1–26.

II. Translations and Reviews:

Barahini, Riza. *Qiṣṣah nivīsī*. Tehran, 1348/1969. pp. 450 ff.

Dastghayb, 'Abd al-'Ali. (Review of *Jūy va dīvār-i tashnah*.) *Rāhnamā-yi Kitāb* (Nov., Dec. 1969), 561–66.

Gulistan, Ibrahim. "Bend of the Road," trans. Karim Emami, *Kayhan International Supplement* (7 Oct., 1965), 10–11.

———. "My Neighbor's Parrot Died," trans. by Massud Farzan, *Literary Review,* 18:1 (Fall 1974), 85–103.

Tihrani, Mahmud. "Dāstān-i buland va kūtāh dar in sarzamīn," *Ārash* (Winter 1342/1963), 143–44.

Zavarzadeh, Mas'ud. "The Persian Short Story Since the Second World War: An Overview," *The Muslim World* (Oct. 1968), 312–13.

SADIQ HIDAYAT

I. Author's Works:

'Alaviyyah Khānum. Tehran 1312/1933.

Būf-i kūr. Bombay, 1315/1937; Tehran, 1320/1941.

"Du nāmah," *Sukhan,* 15:5 (Urdībihisht 1344/1965), 463–65.

Haji Aqa. Tehran, 1324/1945.

"Khaṭṭ-i Pahlavī va alifbā-yi ṣawtī," *Sukhan,* 2:8 (Shahrīvar 1324/1965), 607–16.

"Nāmah'hā-yi Hidāyat bih duktur Shahid Nura'i," *Sukhan,* 8:3 (Urdibihisht 1334/1956), 199–209.

Nayrangistān. Tehran, 1312/1933.

Sag-i vilgard. Tehran, 1321/1942.

Sāyah rawshan. Tehran, 1312/1933.

Sih qatrah khūn. Tehran, 1311/1932.

Vagh Vagh Sāḥāb. Tehran, 1313/1933.

Vilingārī. Tehran, 1323/1944.

"Yik aṣar-i muntashir nashudah az Ṣādiq Hidāyat," *Nigīn,* 41 (Mihr 1347/1968), 3–5; 43 (Āzar 1347/1968), 3, 72–74.

Zindah bigūr. Tehran 1309/1930.

II. Translations and Reviews:

'Alavi, Buzurg. "Ṣādiq Hidāyat," *Payām-i Nuvīn* (Ābān 1324/1945), 23–29.

Al-i Ahmad, Jalal. "Hidāyat-i *Būf-i kūr,*" *Ilm va Zindigi*, 1 (1951), 65–78.

Archer, William Kay, "The Terrible Awareness of Time," *Saturday Review,* (27 Dec. 1958), 24–25.

Bashiri, Iraj. *Hidayat's Ivory Tower: Structural Analysis of the Blind Owl.* Minneapolis, 1974.

Barahini, Riza. *The Crowned Cannibals.* New York, 1977. Pp. 19–84.

Beard, Michael. "Character and Psychology in Hidayat's *Buf-i Kur*," *Edebiyat*, 1 (1976), 207–18.

Blakeston, Oswell. (Review of *Blind Owl*), *Time and Tides* (22 Feb. 1958), 235.

Farid, Maher Shafik, *"The Blind Owl* by Sadegh Hedayat," *Afro American Writings* (Cairo), 1:4 (1970), 215–18.

Fraser, Eileen. (Review of *Blind Owl*), *The Twentieth Century* (May 1958), 490.

Hidayat, Sadiq. *The Blind Owl,* trans. D. P. Costello. New York, 1957.

―――― . "Daud the Hunchback" and "Cul de Sac," trans. Henry D. G. Law, 63:148, *Life and Letters,* (Dec. 1949), 255–70.

―――― . *An Introduction to Sadeq Hedayat*, trans. Deborah Miller Mostaghel. London, 1976.

―――― . "The Man Who Killed His Passions," trans. Jerome W. Clinton, *Literary Review,* 18:1 (Fall 1974), 38–52.

―――― . "The Mongol's Shadow," trans. Donald A. Shojai, *The Chicago Review* (May 1969), 95–104.

―――― . *Sadeq's Omnibus: A Selection of Short Stories*, Trans. Siyavosh Danesh. Tehran, 1972.

―――― . "Seeking Absolution," trans. Minoo S. Southgate, *Iranian Studies,* 9 (Winter, 1976), 49–59.

―――― . "Solitude," trans. D. P. Costello, in *Modern Islamic Literature*, ed. J. Kritzeck. New York, 1970. Pp. 196–201.

―――― . "Three Drops of Blood," trans. Thomas M. Ricks, *Iranian Studies,* 3:2 (Spring, 1970), 104–14. Also trans. Guity Nashat and Marilyn Robinson in *Hedāyat's "The Blind Owl" Forty Years After.* Austin, Texas, 1978. Pp. 60–67.

―――― . "Tomorrow," trans. by Lucien Ray, *New Left Re-*

view, 24 (March-April 1964).

———. "Trial by Cobra," from *The Blind Owl*, trans. D. P. Costello, in *A Treasury of Modern Asian Stories*. New York, 1961. Pp. 196-201.

Hillmann, Michael C., ed. *Hedāyat's "The Blind Owl" Forty Years After*. Austin, Texas: University of Texas Press, 1978.

Humāyūnī, Sadiq. *Mardī kih bā sāyahash harf mīzad*. Tehran, 1352/1973.

Kamshad, Hassan. *Modern Persian Prose Literature*. Cambridge University Press, 1966. Pp. 137–208

Katira'i, Mahmud. *Kitāb-i Ṣādiq Hidāyat*. Tehran, 1350/1971.

Khanlari, Parviz Natil. "Marg-i Ṣādiq Hidāyat," *Yaghmā*, (Khurdād 1330/1951), 106–13.

Komissarov, D., "Ṣādiq Hidāyat," *Payām-i Nuvīn*, 4:1 (Mihr 1340/1961), 66–72.

———. "Ṣādiq Hidāyat," *Payām-i Nuvīn*, 5:11 (Shahrivar 1342/1963), 1–6.

Kubickova, Vera. "Persian Literature of the 20th Century," *History of Iranian Literature,* ed. Jan Rypka. Dordrecht, Holland, 1968. Pp. 353 ff.

Law, Henry D. G. *Life and Letters* (Dec. 1949), 198, 252–53.

Maher, Farid Shafik. "The *Blind Owl* by Sadegh Hedayat," *Afro-Asian Writings (Cairo) 1:4 (1970), 215–218.*

Massé, Henri. *Persian Beliefs and Customs*. New Haven, Human Relations Area Files, 1954. Pp. 1–2.

Muhandisi, Manuchihr. "Hidāyat va Rīlkah," *Nigīn*, 88 (Shahrīvar 1351/1972), 22–25.

Nuvin, Farid. "Kāvushī dar dunyā-yi Hidāyat va Āl-i Ahmad," *Nigīn*, 83 (Farvardīn 1351/1972), 8–10.

Qutbi, M. Y. *In ast Būf-i kūr: tafsīrī bar būf-i kūr*. Tehran, 1351/1972.

Ricks, Thomas M. "Dū tarjūmah az asar-i Hidāyat bih zabān-i Inglisi," *Farhang-u-Zindigi,* XVI (Tehran, 1353/1974), 169–178.

Rypka, Jan. "Yādbūdhā-yi man az Hidāyat," *Sukhan,* 15:5 (Urdibihisht 1344/1965), 460–465.

Wickens, G. M. (On Hidayat). *Books Abroad* (Winter 1967), 43.

Yar Shater, Ehsan, " The Modern Literary Idiom," *Iran Faces the Seventies.* New York, 1971. Pp. 284–285.

NADIR IBRAHIMI

I. Author's Works:

"Afsanah-yi bārān," *Payām-i Nuvīn*, 7:5 (Khurdād 1344/1965), 20–24.
Afsānah-yi bārān: majmū'ah-yi davāzdah qiṣṣah. Tehran 1346/1968.
Arash dar qalamruv-i tardīd: dah dāstān. Tehran, 1342/1963.
"Bād, Bād-i Mihrigān," *Payām-i Nuvīn*, 9:2 (Āzar 1346/1967), 52–75.
"Barayi chih barmigardand?" *Payām-i Nuvīn*, 7:10 (Day 1344/1965), 1–10.
Bār-i dīgar shahrī Kih dūst mīdāram. Tehran, 1345/1966.
"Barkhurd," *Payām-i Nuvīn*, 8:12 (Shahrīvar 1346/1967), 72–77.
"Bāzdīd-i qiṣṣah'hā-yi imrūz," *Payām-i Nuvīn*, 8:7 (Day 1345), 89–95; 8:8 (Bahman 1345/1967), 78–83; 8:9 (Farvardīn 1346/1967), 66–72; 8:10 (Urdībihisht 1346/1967), 64–75; 8:11 (Tīr 1346/1967), 97–106; 8:12 (Shahrīvar 1346/1967), 85–98; 9:1 (Aban 1346/1967), 119–126, 131.
Dah dāstān-i kūtāh. Tehran, 1351/1972.
Dar sarzamīn-i kūchak-i man. Tehran, 1347/1968.
"Fārsī nivīsī barāyi kūdakān," *Payām-i Nuvīn*, 10:4 (Khurdād, Tīr 1352/1973), 1–12; 10:5 (Murdād, Shahrīvar 1352/1973), 26–36.
Fārsī nivīsī barāyi kūdakān. Tehran, 1353/1974.
Ijāzah hast, Āqā-yi Beresht? Tehran, 1349/1970.
In Mashghalah. Tehran, 1353/1974.
Insān, jināyat va iḥtimāl. Tehran, 1350/1972.
"Kā'ūchū," *Payām-i Nuvīn*, 8:2 (Khurdād 1345/1966), 24–35.
Khānah'ī barāyi shab: haft dāstān. Tehran, 1342/1963.
Kitāb-i namāyish. Tehran, 1346/1968.
Makānhā-yi 'umūmī: nuh qiṣṣah. Tehran, 1345/1966.

"*Muhrah-yi mār* va mas'alah-yi mas'ūliyyat-i nivīsandah," *Payām-i Nuvīn*, 8:2 (Khurdād 1345/1966), 81–85.
Muṣābā va ru'yā-yi gājrāt: hijdah dāstān-i kūtāh. Tehran, 1343/1964.
"Pāsukh nāpazīr," *Kitāb-i Haftah*, 88 (27 Murdād 1342/1963), 4–15.
Pāsukh nāpazīr. Tehran, 1354/1975.
"Rābiṭah," *Sukhan*, 17:6, 7 (Shahrīvar, Mihr 1346/1967), 677–684.
"Sharīfjān, Sharīfjān" *Payām-i Nuvīn*, 7:9 (Āzar and Ābān 1344/1965), 85–90.
"Sidā kih mīpichad," *Payām-i Nuvīn*, 7:8 (Mihr 1344/1965), 1–8.
Ṣidā-yi Ṣaḥrā. Tehran, 1348/1969.
"Tappah," *Ārash*, 2:3 (Farvardīn 1347/1968), 75–84.
Tazādhā-yi darūnī. Tehran, 1350/1972.
"Zabān-i dīgar," *Payām-i Nuvīn*, 7:7 (Murdād 1344/1965), 1–15.

MUHAMMAD KIYANUSH

I. Author's Works:

Ābhā-yi khastah. Tehran, 1349/1960.
"Ā'īnah-yi siyāh," *Sukhan*, 16:10 (Āzar 1345/1966), 980–88.
"'Alāmat'i su'āl," *Sukhan*, 23:7 (Khurdād 1353), 687–719.
"Ān rūz-i yikshanbah," *Nigīn*, 67 (Āzar 1349), 14–18, 59–60, 63.
Barrasī-yi shi'r va nasr-i mu'āṣir dar āsārī az Jalāl Āl-i Aḥmad, Ṣādiq Chūbak, Darvīsh, Akbar Rādī, Ghulāmhusayn Sā'idī, Muḥammad Riżā Shafī'ī Kadkani, Sīyāvush Kasrā'ī, Jamāl Mīrṣādiqī. Tehran, 1353/1974.
"Bihisht-i az dast raftah," *Sukhan* 18:7 (Āzar 1347/1968), 711–717.
Dar ānjā hīchkas nabūd. Tehran, 1345/1967.

"Dar majlis-i yādbūd," *Sukhan*, 17:8 (Ābān 1346/1967), 775–782.

"Dar ṣaḥn-i bihisht," *Sukhan*, 15:2 (Āẕar 1343/1964), 194–98.

"Dīvānigī dar sitāyish-i bīgānigī," *Nigīn*, 66 (Ābān 1349/1970), 22–28.

Ghuṣṣah'ī va qiṣṣah'ī. Tehran, 1344/1965.

"Gul-i surkh," *Sukhan*, 16:4 (Urdībihisht 1345/1966), 341–44.

"Jāy-i khālī-yi shawhar," *Sukhan*, 16:6 (Tīr 1345/1966), 546–48.

"Langarūdī," *Sukhan*. 17:3 (Khurdād 1346/1967), 283–88.

Māh va māhī dar chashmah-yi bād. Tehran, 1347/1968.

"Maqām-i maẓmūn dar shi'r," *Nigīn*, 114 (Mihr 1353/1974), 28–31.

Mard-i giriftār. Tehran, 1343/1964.

"Mawẓū'-i dāstān," *Sukhan*, 16:11 (Day 1345/1966), 1163–68; 16: 12 (Isfand 1345/1966), 1216–22.

"naqd-i kilāsīk," *Nigīn*, 110 (Tīr 1353/1974), 34–38.

"Qudamā va naqd-i adabī," *Nigīn*, 109 (Khurdād 1353/1974), 56–59; 112 (Shahrīvar 1353/1974), 42–45; 113 (Mihr 1353/1974), 37–41.

Sādah va ghamnāk. Tehran, 1341/1962.

"Shab," *Sukhan*, 18:8, 9 (Day, Bahman 1347/1968), 892–97.

Shabistān. Tehran, 1340/1961.

Shikūftan-i hayrat. Tehran, 1343/1964.

"Tavallud," *Sukhan* 17:5 (Murdād 1346), 500–505.

"Yāddāshthā'ī dar bārah-yi dāstān nivīsī," *Sukhan*, 15:9 (Mihr, Ābān 1345/1966), 899–905.

"Yik shahr-i kūchak bā dīvārhā-yi buland," *Sukhan*, 14:10 (Tīr 1343/1964), 902–13.

II. Reviews:

Dustkhwah, Jalil. (Review of *Shabistān*.) *Rāhnamā-yi Kitāb* (Oct. 1961), 653–59.

M. T. (Review of *Mard-i giriftār*). *Ārash*, 2:1 (Tīr 1343/1964), 163–68.

AHMAD MAHMUD

I. Author's Works:

"Barkhurd," *Payām-i Nuvīn*, 8:3 (Murdād 1345/1966), 12–34.
Bīhūdigī. Tehran, 1341/1962.
Daryā hanūz ārām ast. Tehran, 1339/1960.
"Dar tārīkī," *Payām-i Nuvīn*, 7:11 (Bahman 1344/1965), 17–22.
Gharībah'hā: majmū'ah-yi dāstān. Tehran, 1350/1972.
Mūl. Tehran, 1338/1954.
"Muṣībat-i kabkhā," *Payām-i Nuvīn*, 8:5 (Mihr 1345/1966), 26–30.
Pisarak-i būmī: majmū'ah-yi haft qiṣṣah-yi kūtāh. Tehran, 1350/1971.
"Sāḥilnishīnān-i kārūn," *Payām-i Nuvīn*, 5:5 (Isfand 1341/1962), 57–64.
"Ṭarḥ," *Payām-i Nuvīn*, 8:8 (Bahman 1345/1966), 62–70, 87.
Zā'irī zīr-i bārān: majmū'ah-yi dāstān. Tehran, 1347/1968.

JAMAL MIRSADIQI

I. Author's Works:

"Abrhā," *Sukhan*, 23:8 (Tīr 1353/1974), 917–20.
"Āmad va shud," *Sukhan*, 10:4 (Tīr 1338/1959), 422–28.
"Ān shab kih barf mībārīd," *Sukhan*, 10: 11, 12 (Bahman, Isfand 1338/1959), 1282–92.
"Āqā, Āqā," *Sukhan,* 23:10 (Shahrīvar 1353/1974), 1111–15.
"Azān-i ghurūb," *Sukhan*, 11:7 (Ābān 1339/1960), 803–809.
"Bābā," *Sukhan*, 10:7 (Mihr 1338/1959), 755–65.

"Barfhā, saghā, kalāghhā," *Sukhan*, 8:11, 12 (Isfand 1336/ 1957), 1127–35.

"Bih tamāshā-yi shikūfah'hā," *Sukhan*, 21:3 (Mihr 1350/1971), 252–57.

"Bisalāmatī," *Nigīn*, 93 (Bahman 1351/1972), 47–48, 59.

"Chāh," *Sukhan*, 20:12 (Khurdād 1350/1971), 1161–66.

"Chahārumī," *Sukhan*, 13:2 (Khurdād 1341/1962), 200–209.

Chashmhā-yi man, khastah. Tehran, 1345/1966.

"Darī rūy bidīvār," *Sukhan*, 11:4 (Murdād 1339), 482–92.

"Dar ma'nī uftādan," *Nigīn*, 80 (Day 1350), 45–46.

Darāznā-yi shab. Tehran, 1349/1970.

Dāstānhā-yi muntakhab. Tehran, 1352/1973.

"Davālpā," *Sukhan*, 21:5 (Āzar 1350/1971), 506–11.

"Fāji'ah," *Sukhan*, 12:12 (Nuvrūz 1340/1961), 1364–74.

In shikastah'hā. Tehran, 1350/1971.

"khālah," *Sukhan*, 9:4 (Tīr 1337/1958), 367–79.

"Lahzah-yi asīrī," *Sukhan*, 21:7 (Bahman 1350/1971), 735–38.

"Mard," *Sukhan*, 11:2 (Urdībihisht 1337/1958), 138–42.

"Marsiyah" *Sukhan*, 14:1 (Tīr 1342/1963), 97–101.

"Matrūd," *Sukhan*, 9:10 (Bahman 1337/1958), 987–1003.

"Musāfirhā-yi shab," *Sukhan*, 9:7 (Ābān 1337/1958), 657–67.

Musāfirhā-yi shab (the 2nd. edition of *Shāhzādah khānum-i chashm sabz*). Tehran, 1350/1971.

Nah ādamī nah sidā'ī. Tehran, 1354/1975.

"Naqshī," *Sukhan*, 16:12 (Isfand 1345/1966), 1225–29.

"Pardah-yi ākhar," *Sukhan*, 12:5 (Shahrīvar 1340/1961), 562–79.

"Parī-yi ā'īnah," *Sukhan*, 23:5 (Farvardīn 1353/1974), 536–40.

"Shab, shab-i tārik," *Sukhan*, 17:2 (Urdībihisht 1346/1967), 173–83.

Shabhā-yi tamāshā va gul-i zard. Tehran, 1347/1968.

Shāhzādah khānum-i chashm sabz. Tehran, 1341/1962.

"Shākhah'hā-yi shikastah," *Sukhan*, 14:3 (Shahrīvar 1342/1963), 320–25.

"Tah-i kūchah'hā-yi khalvat," *Sukhan*, 17:9 (Āzar 1346/1967), 871–78.

"Utāq-i rūbirū," *Sukhan*, 20:11 (Urdībihisht 1350/1971), 1029–34.

II. Reviews:

Komissarov, D., "Janbah'hā-yi nuvīn-i rumān-i mu'āṣi-i fārsī," *Sukhan*, 23:4 (Isfand 1352/1973), 415–417, 420–21.

Navvabpur, Riza. (Review of *Darāznā-yi shab*), *Sukhan*, 21:8 (Aban 1351/1972), 458–61.

Rahguẕar, M. (Review of *Chashmhā-yi man, khastah*), *Sukhan*, 15:9 (Āẕar 1345/1966), 1063–65.

Ṭahiri, Abū al-Qāsim. (Review of *Daraznā-yi shab*), *Rāhnamā-yi Kitāb* (July-Sept. 1971), 388–91.

Tunukabuni, Firaydun. (Review of *Chashmhā-yi man, khastah*), *Payām-i Nuvīn* 8:6 (Āẕar 1345/1966), 80–83.

SHAPUR QARIB

I. Author's Works:

'Aṣr-i pā'izī. Tehran, 1339/1960.
Gunbad-i Ḥalabī. Tehran, 1341/1962.
"Junūb-i garm" *Jung*, 4 (Spring 1346/1967), 47–64.

II. Reviews:

Mihrban, Kurush. (Review of *Gunbad-i Ḥalabī*). *Arash*, (Khurdād 1342/1963), 135.

Parsa, H. (Review of *Gunbad-i Ḥalabī*.) *Payām-i Nuvīn*, 5:11 (Shahrīvar 1342/1963), 86–89.

BAHRAM SADIQI

I. Author's Works:

"Dar īn shumārah . . .," *Sukhan*, 10:6 (Shahrīvar 1338/1959), 637–45.

"Dāstān barāyi kūdakān," *Sukhan*, 8:7 (Ābān 1336/1957), 664–69.

"Fardā dar rāh ast," *Sukhan*, 7:9 (Day 1335/1956), 889–98.

"Ghayr-i muntaẓir," *Sukhan*, 9:9 (Day 1337), 881–96.

"Haft gīsūy-i khūnīn," *Sukhan*, 11:2 (Khurdād 1339/1960), 207–28.

"Ḥulūl-i jinn," *Sukhan*, 12:2 (Khurdad 1340/1961), 192–206.

"Kalaf-i sardargum, *Sukhan*, 8:1 (Farvardīn 1336/1957) 63–67.

"Khwāb-i khūn," *Jung* (Winter 1344/1965), 21–31.

"Mihmān-i nākhwāndah dar shahr-i buzurg," *Sukhan*, 15: 11, 12 (Ābān, Āzar 1344), 1080–1100.

"Namāyish dar du pardah," *Sukhan*, 8:10 (Bahman 1336/1957), 969–83.

"Qarīb al-vuqū'," *Sukhan*, 10:9 (Āzar 1338), 987–96.

"Sangar va qumqumah'hā-yi khālī," *Sukhan*, 9:3 (Khurdād 1337/1958), 237–47.

Sangar va qumqumah'hā-yi khālī. Tehran, 1349/1970.

"Sarāsar ḥādiṣah," *Sukhan*, 10:2 (Urdībihisht 1338/1959), 183–207.

"Tadris dar bahār-i dilangīz," *Kayhān-i Haftah* (28 Isfand 1341/1962).

"Ta'ṣīrāt-i mutaqābil," *Sukhan*, 12:7 (Ābān 1340/1961), 806–811.

"Vasvās," *Sukhan*, 7:12 (Nuvrūz 1336/1957), 1171–1175.

II. Translations and Reviews:

Gulshiri, Hushang. "Si sāl rumān nivīsī," *Jung*, 5 (Summer 1946/1967), 205–15.

Ibrahimi, Nadir. "Bāzdīd-i qiṣṣah'hā-yi imrūz," *Payām-i Nuvīn*, 9:1 (Ābān 1346/1967), 122–26.

Sadiqi, Bahram. "Imminent," trans. Karim Emami, *Kayhan International Supplement* (2 Sept. 1965), 10, 12.

_____. "With Deepest Regrets," trans. Marcia E. Mottahedeh, *Literary Review*, XVIII, 1 (Fall 1974), 129–143.

GHULAMHUSAYN SA'IDI

I. Author's Works:

(Sa'idi's plays are published under the pen name Gawhar Murād.)

"'Arūsī: a play," *Ārash*, 1:3 (Urdībihisht 1341/1962), 17–24.

Āshghāldūnī. Tehran, 1352/1973.

Ahl-i havā. Tehran, 1345/1966.

Ā-yi bi kulāh, āyi bā kulāh. Tehran, 1347/1968.

'Azādārān-i bayal. Tehran, 1343/1965.

Bāmhā va zīr-i bāmhā: namāyishnāmah dar du pardah. Tehran, 1340/1961.

Bihtarīn bābā-yi dunyā: namāyishnāmah dar du pardah. Tehran 1344/1965.

Chashm dar barābar-i chashm. Tehran, 1350/1971.

Chub'bidasthā-yi Varāzīl. Tehran, 1344/1965.

Dah lālbāzī. Tehran, 1342/1963.

Dīktah va zāviyah: du namāyishnāmah. Tehran, 1341/1968.

"Du barādar," *Ārash*, 1:4 (Āzar 1341), 71–85.

"Faqīr," *Sukhan*, 13:11, 12 (Isfand 1341, Farvardīn 1342), 1177–78.

Faṣl-i Gustākhī. Tehran, 1348/1969.
Gāv, dāstānī barāyi film. Tehran, 1350/1971.
"Gidā," *Sukhan*, 13:8 (Āzar 1341/1962), 834–44.
"Gujah dūr, bākh, gujah dūr," *Ārash*, 2:5 (Āzar 1347/1968), 15–16, 106–107.
"Gumshudah-yi lab-i daryā," *Ārash*, 14 (Bahman 1346/1967), 33–49.
Gur va gahvārah. Tehran, 1945/1966.
"Intizār," *Ārash*, 2:1 (Tīr 1343), 111–114.
"Khānah'hā rā kharāb kunīd," *Ārash* (Winter 1343/1964), 3–33.
Kalātah gul: namāyishnāmah dar sih pardah. Tehran, 1340/1961.
Kārbāfakhā dar sangar. Tehran, 1339/1960.
"Khānah Barf," *Andīshah va Hunar*, 3:4 (Day 1337/1958), 250–59.
Khānah Rawshanī. Tehran, 1346/1967.
Khiyāv ya Mishkīn Shahr: ka'bah-yi yaylāqāt-i Shahsavan. Tehran, 1344/1965.
"Laylāj," *Sukhan*, 8:8 (Āzar 1336), 800–803.
Ma nimīshinavīm, Tehran, 1349/1970.
"Murgh-i anjīr," *Sukhan*, 7:4 (Tīr 1335), 372–77.
Panj namāyishnāmah az inqilāb-i Mashrūṭiyyat. Tehran, 1345/1966.
Parvārbandān. Tehran, 1348/1969.
"Qāṣidakhā," *Ṣadaf*, 6 (1959).
"Shabān-i Farībak," *Ṣadaf*, 10 (1961).
Shabnishīnī-yi bāshukūh, 2nd. edition, Tehran, 1349/1970.
"Shafāyāftah'hā," *Sukhan*, 14:4, 5 (Mihr, Ābān 1342/1963), 412–27.
'Shahādat," *Ārash*, 1:4 (Āzar 1341), 5–8.
"Shafā-yi 'Ājil," *Ārash*, 2:5 (Āzar 1345), 28–34.
Tūp. Tehran, 1347/1968.
Tars va Larz. Tehran, 1347/1968.
Vāhimah'hā-yi bī nām va nishān. Tehran, 1346/1967.
Vāy bar maghlūb. Tehran, 1349/1970.
"Ẓiyāfat," *Intishārāt-i Ārash: daftarī dar shi'r, qiṣṣah, namāyishnāmah, va ravāyat*. Tehran, Khurdād 1343/1964. Pp. 34–57.

II. Translations and Reviews:

Anvari, Ḥasan. (Review of *Ā-yi bī kulāh*). *Rāhnamā-yi Kitāb* (July 1968), 171–73.
Farzan, Massud. (Review of *Parvārbandān*). *Books Abroad* (Winter 1972), 167–68.
——.(Review of *Gūr va Gahvārah*'. *Books Abroad* (Summer 1974), 624–25.
Hisami, Hushang. (Review of *Ā-yi bī kulāh*). *Ārash*, 2:2 (Isfand 1346/1368), 107–110.
Ibrahimi, Nadir. "Bāzdīd-i qiṣṣah'hā-yi imrūz," *Payām-i Nuvīn*, 8:8 (Bahman 1345/1967), 82.
Kiyanush, Mahmud. *Barrasī-yi shi'r va nasr-i mu'aṣir dar āsārī as Jalāl al-Aḥmad, Ṣādiq Chūbak, Darvīsh, Akbar Rādī, Ghulāmhusayn Sā'idī, Muḥmmad Riẓā Shafī'ī Kadkanī, Siyāvush Kasrā'ī, Jamāl Mīrṣādiqī*. Tehran, 1353/1974.
Parham, Sirus. (Review of "Qāṣidakhā" and "Shabān-i Farībak").*Rāhnamā-yi Kitāb* (April 1961), 20–22.
Ramon, Nathil. "Profile: Gholam Hoseyn Sa'edi," *Index on Censorship*, 7:1.
Sa'idi, Ghulamhusayn. "The Wedding," Trans. Jerome W. Clinton. 8:1–2 (Winter-Spring, 1975), 2–47.
S.T. (Review of *Bāmhā va zīr-i bāmhā*), *Ārash* (Urdībihisht 1341/1962), 90–92.
Yar Shater, Ehsan. "The Modern Literary Idiom," *Iran Faces the Seventies*, New York, 1971. Pp. 312–14.

KHUSRAW SHAHANI

I. Author's Works:

Ādam-i 'Avazī: majmū'ah-yi dāstān. Tehran, 1349/1970.
Bālā rūdīhā, pā'īn rūdīhā. Tehran, 1351/1972.

Kumidī-yi iftitāḥ. Tehran, 1346/1969.
Kūr-i la'natī. Tehran, 1344/1965.
Vaḥshat ābād. Tehran 1348/1969.

NASIR TAQVA'I

I. Author's Works:

"Āqā Julū," *Ārash,* 2:1 (Tīr 1343/1964), 84–94.
"Chāh," *Ārash*, 2:4 (Summer 1345/1966), 81–84.
"Muhājirat," *Ārash*, 2:2 (Winter 1343/1964), 53–55.
"Panāhgāh," (Khurdad 1342/1963), 58–63.
"Rūz-i bad," *Jung* (Winter 1347/1968), 66–75.
"Tābistān-i hamān sāl," *Ārash* (Winter 1342), 117–120.
Tābistān-i hamān sāl. Tehran, 1348/1969.
"Tanhā'ī," *Ārash* (Winter 1342), 112–116.

II. Translations and Reviews:

Vahdati, Giti. (Review of film "Aramish dar ḥuẓūr-i dīgarān").
   Nigīn, 96 (Urdībihisht 1352/1973), 55–56.

$1.00